For music

McDonald, Graham, 1948-
Song catcher / Graham McDonald.
78203496

ISBN: 1477595880
ISBN 13: 9781477595886
Library of Congress Control Number: 2012910150
CreateSpace, North Charleston, SC

ACKNOWLEDGEMENTS

My thanks go to my wife Coral, the tireless one, for her constant support and belief; to Vicky Wilson for her editing work, interest and encouragement; to Anna Humphries for her proofreading and input.

ABOUT AUTHOR

Graham McDonald has published one earlier novel, *Footprints In The Wind.* He lives with his wife, Coral in a small south coastal town of his native Western Australia.

SONG CATCHER

GRAHAM McDONALD

ONE

Grace drank the last of her coffee, stood up and slowly made her way to the bandstand. The four members of her backing group straggled to their places behind her and, after a brief instrument warm-up, the sleepy tone of a harmonica led her into the Eagles' ballad *Desperado*. Eyes closed and both hands holding onto the mike her husky voice drifted lazily through the classic song until, just as it began winding down on the fading notes of the harmonica, she suddenly stopped. Her eyes flashed open and her body stiffened. For a moment she stared intently ahead of her before her hands fell away from the mike, her legs buckled and she slumped to her knees.

The startled band members offloaded instruments and hurried to her. The drummer knelt beside her and placed a hand on her shoulder. 'You okay, Gracie?'

'I... I don't know Boss. I think I might've just got zapped by the mike.'

'Shouldn' have. There's not enough charge goin' through there to jump-start a li'l ol' mouse,' Boss said, as he waved the back of his hand near the mike stand. 'Cain't feel nothin', he added, before walking over to the mike's amplifier. He switched it off at the plug and began to check it out.

Two of the other band members helped Grace to her feet. She had a frown on her face and after a moment's reflection she turned to their lead guitarist. 'Were you messing around near the end, Chas?'

'Nope... why?'

Grace shook her head in confusion. She turned to another band member. 'Were you on the flute just then, Wayne?'

Wayne had put aside his rhythm guitar to double on keyboard and harmonica for the song. He pointed to the mouth organ resting in a frame on his chest. 'Not unless I was playin' it outta my ass.'

The other musicians smiled but Grace continued to frown. 'You guys didn't see or hear *anything* unusual?'

'Just you takin' a break before the end of a song,' Chas replied.

'Cain't find nothin' wrong heah,' Boss called out. He switched the amplifier back on, walked over to the mike stand and waved the back of his hand next to it again before making a tentative glancing contact. He shrugged his shoulders. 'Nothin'.'

Chas stared at Grace's eyes for a few seconds then said, 'Go home and get some rest, man. We'll finish the set.'

Grace's eyes lingered on his for a moment, affronted by the unspoken accusation. She briefly considered a response but then just nodded. As she turned towards the bar, however, she noticed that the beer advertising sign in the alcove leading to the washrooms was on the blink. So too was the TV that constantly held the bartender's attention. He was busy fiddling with its controls and cursing it when Grace walked over to him.

She stood in the darkened corner of the alcove then looked around the smoke-filled cavern of Jimmy's Place. It couldn't have been the face she thought she saw? Maybe someone of a similar appearance had walked in - unlikely as that was at nearly one o'clock on a snow swept Sunday morning. All she could see now were the same faces of the diehard drinkers she had been looking at for most of the night. She asked anyway.

'Was there a man standing here just now, Ed?'

The bartender kept fiddling with the TV. 'Nope... at this time o' night the bodies range from sittin' down to lyin' down and if any customers are still standin' I ain't doin' mah job properly.'

'Okay, *sitting* at the bar?' Grace responded sourly.

'No one's been to the bar for a while.' He looked at his watch. 'Shouldn't you be singin'?' he asked.

'There won't be any more from me tonight. I'm dog tired. I'm calling a halt.'

'If ya don't finish the last set I'll have to take somethin' off the top o' the pay packet.'

'Yeah... and you too, Ed,' Grace tiredly replied then picked up her coat and walked over to tell the band members she was leaving.

'If ya headin' up to the hospital, Grace, tell Jamie ah'll be in ta see him in the mornin'. Ah've got somethin' fo' him,' Boss said.

Boss Gillespie was a giant of a Texan with a beard down to his chest and a ponytail that hung down the length of his back. As his name suggested, whenever there was trouble about he was usually the one who took charge, pounding away on the drunks that occasionally interrupted their gigs with the same enthusiastic treatment he gave to his drums. When it came to Grace and her son, however, he was a marshmallow.

Grace reached up with one arm, grabbed the big man around the neck and planted an affectionate kiss on his cheek before heading for the door. As she walked past the bar she stared defiantly at the owner and called back to the rest of the band members.

'If we've still got a job here, I'll see you suckers at practice Thursday night.'

Ed smiled as she walked past. "Night, Pocahontas,' he said, watching the shapely form pulling on her coat and gloves before she opened the door to the freezing street. As it closed behind her, the TV and the neon sign flickered on again. 'Make up ya fuckin' mind!' he muttered.

Grace walked a little way down the snow-lined pavement and stopped next to an old, road-scarred Ford Pinto. She opened the door she never needed to lock, climbed in, crossed her fingers and turned on the ignition. The starter groaned, moaned and seemed to die before the engine suddenly burst into life. She clenched her fist in victory and revved the motor mercilessly before letting it settle down into something like an idle. Crunching it into gear she headed towards the town center, the unique music she had heard at Jimmy's still playing in her mind.

Accustomed to Wayne's occasional improvisation, when the sound of the flute had replaced the harmonica fadeout to the song, Grace had continued to sing. But then the tune had begun to change, smoothly evolving from *Desperado's* melody into an unfamiliar one. She had stopped singing and had begun to turn around in curiosity when a buzzing sensation surged from the mike stand, drawing her hands more tightly to it before shooting through her body. The volume of the flute grew swiftly before exploding in an ear-piercing cry which lifted above her, briefly disappeared and then came swooping back in the form of a scintillating guitar riff. Beyond the sizzling run of notes she could hear the powerful voice of a man singing a song from her past and she was suddenly compelled to join him. She sang out, her voice building with emotion until it and the man's were suddenly silenced by an explosion of light behind her. The neon sign above the alcove fizzed, flickered and went out. A familiar face formed in the shadows before quickly melting away again. The guitar riff faded with the image then disappeared into the harmonica's closing notes of *Desperado* and her hands were released from the mike.

As she drove along, Grace pondered the sensation that had come through the mike. In a way, Chas could have been excused for thinking the worst. It felt so familiar, frightening, as though something had released an old demon, a rush of emotions that ended with an overwhelming feeling of sadness.

Her thoughts were suddenly interrupted by the looming appearance of a van stalled on a green light in the middle of the Main Street intersection. She braked, cursed and swerved around the empty vehicle before continuing on, heading toward the north side of town and the Deloraine Hospital.

*

As Grace hit the open road, her thoughts shifted to what the doctor had told her the day before about the ongoing attempt to straighten the congenital deformation of her son's spine.

'He should only need one more operation a few years into his teens, before the growth spurt. After that I don't think much more can be done.'

This was the sixth operation on her twelve-year old son and Grace should have felt pleased that there might only be one more but she could hardly bear the thought of him being opened up again. All she could see and feel was the suffering, her pain rising like the undead out of his, constantly pointing an accusing finger. The operations had helped of course, just as had the several attempts to rectify his severe cleft lip and palate but, along with the scar that slashed across his upper lip, he would always have a twisted gait to mark his physical difference.

Upon approaching the hospital, the usual sense of discomfort and apprehension flooded in and Grace began once more to apply the happy makeup. She parked the car in the almost deserted lot of the hospital then walked quickly to the main entrance.

'Hi, Steve... any escapees tonight?' she called out, as she entered the lobby.

The security officer looked up from the newspaper on his desk and smiled. 'No, Grace. We got 'em all safely strapped in.'

Grace gave a light laugh as she stepped into a waiting elevator and pressed the button for the top floor. Three levels later, the doors slid open before the reception desk of Jamie's ward.

The night nurse raised her eyes from some paperwork.

'Hi, Grace. You're a bit early,' she said, as she glanced at the clock on the wall showing one-thirty am.

'Yeah, I'd had enough. How is he, Christine?'

'He's okay. Ate most of his supper... even watched a bit of TV this evening. He's still sleeping in fits and starts but he's been able to lie on his back for the first time. We should be able to shift him to general in a day or so.'

'My bank account will be so pleased,' Grace sighed.

The nurse didn't see the need to worry the mother about the sudden sweating turn the boy had had about half an hour before. It was during one of her hourly checks that she found him looking feverish but when she took his temperature it was completely normal. She had noted and recorded the time of the incident then checked him soon after to find him okay, awake and listening to music.

'He was awake a little while ago, so you might catch him. I'm gonna make myself a coffee. You too?' she said, as she raised her plump body from her chair.

Grace accepted with a smile and an emphatic nod of the head then walked down the corridor to Jamie's room, slowly opening the door and peeking in.

Jamie had fallen asleep again, a set of earphones leading from a portable CD player resting crookedly on his head. Grace walked over and gently removed them, unsurprised to hear the volume pounding away at near maximum. She switched the player off, put the CD back in its case and placed it on top of one of the two large stacks on the bedside cabinet. *John Lennon Greatest Hits* it read and that came as no surprise either. She figured if ever CD's could be worn out this was going to be one of them.

As far as Jamie was concerned, JL was the man, his fascination with him starting after he heard *Double Fantasy*, the album released just before the musician's assassination. Now one corner of his bedroom was devoted to Lennon, warts and all. It was a shrine filled with books, magazine articles and interview tapes that revealed an angry, complex man; someone reported to have had a mischievous, zany sense of humor but also a capacity to be cruelly sarcastic. But, above all, it was a dedication to the music that softened the hard edge of the man's persona.

Jamie had traced every step of Lennon's musical journey; from before and through his Beatles days to the heartfelt songs of his solo career but one number in particular was a touchstone for him. *Across The Universe* expressed the essence of how music affected him, a cure-all that he played whenever he was down. He also used it on his mother. Whenever she retired to stare blankly from her dark corner of the sofa, he would go up behind her, slip his hands around her neck and whisper in her ear, 'Sing it for us, Mom,' hugging her until she complied. Sometimes it took a little while for Grace to claw her way out of the darkness but in the end it usually worked, the free-rolling melody and carefree tone of the words bringing a sense of freedom to her.

Grace slumped down in a chair next to the bed. Five hours from now she would have to be at her morning job, serving breakfast at the Early Bird Diner. She sighed inwardly at the thought. It was just another of the bits and pieces of employment that she had to do and had to keep, having to pay cash upfront for all of Jamie's treatment because she couldn't find a health fund in the US prepared to cover him.

Her depressing thoughts were dissolved by the welcoming aroma of coffee as Christine entered the room and handed her a large cup of the strong, black variety, received with another smile and a nod.

The nurse quickly checked the drip apparatus that was delivering a mild painkiller through Jamie's arm and then left the room, laying a hand briefly on Grace's shoulder as she went.

'Thanks, Christine,' Grace said quietly then drank her coffee quickly before leaning back in her chair to gaze at her sleeping son. The unfamiliar melody from Jimmy's began drifting through her mind again and in her habitual way she began to softly hum it to Jamie like a comforting lullaby.

It wasn't just Lennon's music that worked for Grace and her son. The love of almost every form of it had helped sustain them through their journey together. From the moment she started to care for him she had filled his world with melody.

It was Classical when he was going to sleep and Rock and Roll when he was alert, punctuated by her soothing, husky renditions of popular ballads and folk songs. There was also the music allowance she started a few years ago, one she could hardly afford but somehow managed to squeeze out of an income constantly drained by the medical bills. He was given ten bucks a week for the express purpose of buying music, and the results of his prospecting CD and tape bargain bins had turned his bedroom into a mini record store.

Apart from Jamie's Lennon collection, the racks that covered the back wall of his room were filled with everything from the Classical masters through to Country and Western. He reveled in every twist and turn that music took, the meaning and rhythm in lyrics as intriguing as the sounds. He saw them as personal messages from close friends and there wasn't a vocal recording in his collection that didn't have his hand-written copy of the lyrics attached. Yet, there was a paradox. While words and music was his universe, in terms of his own output, Jamie was barely able to hit a correct note with voice or instrument. He was not tone deaf but tone dumb, unable to translate what he could clearly hear in his mind, even though he could converse lucidly about all forms of music. Grace figured it was just another punishment but often wondered for whom because her son seemed totally unaware of his shortcomings.

'I'm gonna write a hit for you, Mom,' he had proclaimed one day about six months ago and she had eventually given in to his pleading for the instrument he figured would help him do it, buying a cheap acoustic guitar and a book of basic lessons. He had plenty of tutors in the band and she had helped as much as she could with her own moderate playing ability but after months of practicing his heart out, Jamie hadn't advanced beyond the clumsy playing of basic chords in simple songs. It was even worse when he tried to sing along with the guitar. Although he had mostly overcome the disability of the cleft palate and could talk reasonably well, whenever he raised his voice to hit even the easiest of notes it came out all wrong. Yet, there were parts of the songwriting process Grace was confident he could master. His reading and meticulous transcription of the lyrics had helped him develop a skill for writing rhythmic poetry, some of it advanced for his age.

Grace's humming voice tailed away and, in spite of the caffeine hit she had just taken, her eyes closed in surrender to tiredness. Just as she began to descend into sleep, a voice suddenly pulled her back.

'Sings At Dawn?'

Grace's eyes flashed open at the sound of her Lakota name spoken in her native tongue. She looked at Jamie in puzzlement. The voice had come from his direction yet it couldn't have been him speaking. Even allowing for the distortion that came from the edge of sleep, it was a man's voice and the words were so clear, a world away from Jamie's mumbled and nasally pronunciation of the few Lakota words she had taught him.

Jamie's eyes were wide open too, staring at Grace with a steady and piercing intensity. It brought a sudden recollection of the dead man's stare she had once seen in another's eyes and for one horrifying split-second she thought...

'Jamie!' she cried out, as she jumped from her seat.

Jamie's eyelids drooped and his dark brown eyes softened. 'Hi, Mom,' he said tiredly.

Grace exhaled heavily. She leant down and kissed his forehead with more than usual affection. 'How ya feeling, Hon'?'

'Okay,' he said, but he was frowning slightly.

'I was havin' that dream again, Mom. You know, like in the *Imagine* movie. Where John's sittin' in the white room at the white piano but this time Yoko wasn't there and I couldn't hear any music. He looked like he was writin' somethin' down and then he got up and left the room.'

Grace gave a thin smile. 'I'm not surprised. He probably couldn't concentrate from hearing his voice screaming through those earphones.'

'Mmmm,' Jamie sighed again, staring thoughtfully at the wall for a while, pondering the strong urge he'd had to follow the man of his dreams, before his mother's voice had woken him.

'What was the gig like?' he eventually asked.

''Bout the same as always,' Grace lied. 'Oh, and Boss said he'll be in to see ya *reeal soooon, ya heah*... probably in the morning. He's got something for you but you've got some sleeping to do before you find out what it is, so get back to it, kid.'

'So should you, Mom. You look like crap. Go home... you don't have to babysit me.'

Grace smiled and nodded her head. Jamie had been in hospital for four days now and she had spent the first two nights after the operation trying to sleep in a chair next to his bed. It was to re-assure him whenever he awoke but her late night visits since were as much for her, to ease the loneliness she felt without him at home. She leant over, held his head lightly and gave him another kiss. 'Okay, I'll see ya in the morning.'

'Mmmmm,' Jamie sighed, and then began to drift off to sleep once more.

Grace put on her coat and gloves and walked to the door, but just as she was about to open it she heard a slight noise from behind her; a rustle of sheets followed by the sound of something falling off the bed. She turned around and looked at Jamie. He lay as still as she had left him, eyes closed and breathing deeply. Then she saw a small notebook lying on the floor. It was one of those Jamie wrote his poetry in, always with him no matter where he was. She walked over and picked it up. It was flipped open to a page where there was some verse scrawled and she held it under the bedside lamp to see what he had written. She began to read the words with the expectation that it was another juvenile composition about all the things that pleased or upset his young mind. The first line instantly wiped out her presumption and as she read through the others they began to sing to her.

He is a song catcher
A warrior of the soul
He has come to join the battle
He has come to draw the bow
Music is the arrow
Let him fire it through your mind
And may the heart that is strong catch his songs
and sing them for all that has died

Suddenly, the striking melody from Jimmy's was running through Grace's mind once more, joining the rhythm of the verse as perfectly as a glove sliding over a hand. For the second time that night she stood totally mystified; as good a young poet as Jamie was, the word-thoughts were beyond anything he had written so far. She glanced through the other pages but found nothing more than beginnings to those simple poems; many lines started and several scratched out. She pulled the page from its spiral binding and put it in her coat pocket, walking out of the room as puzzled as when she had left Jimmy's Place. She said a vacant goodnight to

Christine before taking the elevator down, giving a similar farewell to Steve as she walked out into the deep freeze once more.

Powder snow had begun falling and a light wind was tightening the icy grip of the North Dakota winter's night, yet a sense of euphoria warmed Grace from within. In her head the guitar riff was now intersecting the verse, with the sound of her boots keeping time as they crunched upon the thin layer of snow in the parking lot. Her car was generous again and, as she turned on the wipers, their backbeat took up where the boots left off, the converging parts of the song traveling with her out of the parking lot and all the way home.

Two

'Okay, Grace, I'll wake him but you know you'll be talking to a bear this time o' the morning, Chas's wife said, as she walked the phone to their bedroom. 'You feeling okay? Chas said you were suffering a bit last night.'

'I'm fine thanks, Kelly... just tired.'

'You're gonna crash if you don't take some time off from something, woman.'

'Yeah... well I've decided I won't be going into the diner today but somehow I don't think I'll be resting. I want to come over and work on something with the boys.'

'Well, good luck with rounding 'em all up on Sunday. And just remember about calling me if you need any help when Jamie gets home.'

'Thanks, Kelly. I'm taking a week of my leave. It should be enough time for me to get him on his feet.'

'Okay, but the offer stands. Here he is. Chas... *Chas!* It's Grace.'

The bear groaned, rolled slowly over and looked at the radio clock. It showed nearly seven-thirty, about three hours before his usual Sunday morning rising. He groaned again as he held out his hand and took the phone. A couple of snuffling breaths followed before, 'I hope this is important, man.'

'I want you to hear something, Chas.'

Grace put the phone down on the coffee table before her, picked up Jamie's guitar and played the riff she had heard at Jimmy's. All morning she had been wondering whether it was something done by someone else that had been forgotten by her, only to emerge during the strange incident. Chas would know. He had an encyclopedic knowledge of such things.

'Have you heard that before?'

A few seconds passed before, 'Can't say I have. Play it again,' a flickering tone of interest now in his voice.

Grace repeated it.

Half of the bear emerged from his blanket cave and sat up in bed. 'Nope... can't place it. But it's good. Where did it come from?'

'Something happened last night. Can't explain it but it was some kind of a hallucination... and *not* the kind you thought. Maybe it was tiredness that brought it on but that was what I thought I heard you playing at the end of *Desperado*. I've got the chords, too... listen.' She quickly played them through.

Chas glided over the accusation. 'Hang on,' he said as he leant over and grabbed the acoustic guitar always kept by his bed. 'Give us the riff again.'

Grace played and straight after her Chas repeated the riff, note for note at first before his dexterous hands quickly began expanding on it. His effort made Grace feel instantly inadequate but she smiled in appreciation.

Chas did a quick run through on the chords then said, 'All we need now are some o' those things that interrupt the music. You know... them things called words.'

'Got 'em,' Grace quickly replied, as she poured another coffee from the pot on the table next to her. It was her sixth

15

since returning from the hospital, when she had come home dying for sleep but knew that there was little hope of it. She had made a half-hearted attempt, lying in bed for ten minutes while her tiredness battled with the excitement, before giving up and going into the lounge, compelled to stay awake until she could give the lyrics on Jamie's notepaper some completion. The first verse sang of a battle, one that she knew so well, and she carried the idea of music making war on the neglect of culture through two more verses. At the end of each verse she had placed a chorus of *Dream Warrior*, the Lakota song that had rushed out of her at Jimmy's, the final result not a song of what had died but one of impending resurrection.

'Well then, it looks like we got a song,' Chas said as he continued to play, alternating between chords and riff.

Grace scanned the lyrics before her, matching the rhythm of the words with the sound coming through the phone, the genesis of a fine song once again bringing exhilaration. 'I'm not going to work today, Chas. I'm going to the hospital first and then coming over. Can you try and get the others together?'

'Yeah... let's do it. They'll come when they hear this, and if that's not enough, Kelly's doin' a roast beef today. I'll get her to put an extra half a steer in. That'll at least bring Boss a'runnin'.'

Grace hung up then immediately rang the diner, unconcerned about the response she expected to get from the owner and, for once, the loss of pay. After several rings her call was answered by a very loud and agitated voice.

'*Yeah?*'

'Sorry about the short notice, Cal but I can't get in there this morning,' she said calmly, and then took the phone away from her ear.

16

The voice quickly adjusted to the move, bellowing at her from arm's length.

'*Dammit*, Grace... not you, too! Jenny just rang to say she's gonna be an hour late and I've got a Diner here fillin' up with carnivores. I'm runnin' 'round tryin' to flap the fuckin' jacks, fry the steak n' eggs an' serve the fuckin' coffee! Now I'll hafta get Babs in here on a Sunday, and you know what that's gonna do to mah sex life! How's Jamie, anyhow?' finished the owner, a fifty-something former truck driver who often pretended to be a hard case but could never stay that way.

'He's okay thanks, Cal. I'm sorry about this. I've got something I *have* to do today. If you want I'll put in some extra time during the week.'

'Hold it!' The sound of a metal implement flipping food on a sizzling hotplate interrupted the conversation for a moment before Cal replied, 'No need, girl... but you just be careful, ya hear. If I get the freeze-out at home I might just be askin' *you* to hop inta the sack. Then you'll find out what real lerrrvin' is, babeeee!'

Grace snorted with amusement as Cal's singing voice rang off, her body shuddering briefly at the imagery the balding, overweight man had left behind. After hanging up the phone she took a shower, got dressed and had some breakfast before heading to the hospital.

*

'Hey, man, look at you!' Grace said excitedly as she walked into Jamie's room just before nine, surprised to see that Boss had already visited.

Jamie was sitting up with a bright red Chicago Bull's shirt and cap on and a brighter smile across his face. A breakfast tray was set up over his lap with some nibbled food on it and Grace removed it before giving him a careful hug.

'Hi, Mom,' Jamie greeted, and when her hug lingered a little, he added a gentle, 'Okaaaay.'

In response to the rebuff, Grace picked up a cold piece of toast from the tray and munched it defiantly in front of his face.

He smiled slyly. 'That was the bit I just dropped on the floor, right on the spot where they spilt my pee bottle this mornin'.'

Grace fixed him with a dead stare and took another big bite.

Jamie laughed in his honking way. 'You're a whacko.'

'Well, now I know where you get it.'

For a few seconds they exchanged jousting smiles before Jamie spoke again, his voice rising and, as it did whenever he became excited, bringing a lisp with it.

'Boss just left. He's a great guy, isthn't he? He'sth gonna take me to a game in the sthpring. Look he brought me a sthee dee asth well!'

'Uh, huh,' Grace replied, her voice calm, as usual trying to discipline him about the lisp without lecturing. Her measured disinterest, however, was as much for the matchmaking ploy as anything.

She reflected on what Jamie had said as she looked at the album cover of the CD, a collection of Jazz music featuring the drummer, Gene Krupa and she briefly made a silent request to the Greater Spirit that her son would not get interested in playing drums.

He was right. Boss was a great guy but he was unable to settle down to any sort of long-term relationship. She had known him and Chas since the early eighties, when they were all making a fair living out of music, playing and singing on other peoples' recordings, and he hadn't changed one bit since those days. He had never had any trouble finding women, or discarding them, but she wouldn't say anything about that to Jamie. For her it was enough that both of them had him as a friend.

Jamie calmed down. 'He said you were all goin' over to Chas's place today for a jam session. Wish I could go too,' he said, unhappily.

His words suddenly prompted Grace to pull out the piece of notepaper with his verse on it. She handed it to him.

'Where did ya get this from, Hon'?'

Jamie read the words and then looked at Grace confusedly. 'I don't remember writin' this.'

'Well, it's your handwriting and it was in your notebook. Maybe you were just a bit dozy from the painkiller when you wrote it.'

'Mmmmm,' Jamie hummed uncertainly, as he read the words again, a frown on his face. He shook his head. 'Still can't recall thinkin' of anythin' like this. I wonder who the song catcher is. Maybe I was thinkin' of John... but I don't know,' he finished, with a tone of mild frustration.

Grace had been pondering that mystery all through the early morning hours she had been working on the lyrics. They both knew the term 'song catcher' well. Amongst their people it was the title of those who played and sang the music but with the belief that they didn't make the songs; they just caught them as they were sung into the universe by the Great Creator. It was a concept typical of her poetic race and Grace believed in it so strongly that it was one of the few things that she imparted to her son about the Lakota culture, the rest left in a past she didn't want to talk about.

'If you don't know... I don't know. But I've added some more lines and a Lakota chorus. We're gonna put them to some music today. I'll bring the tape of it in tonight.'

'Wow! Yeah, man... can't wait to hear that!'

After spending another hour with Jamie, supervising him as he did the homework she had picked up from his schoolteacher, Grace headed out to Chas's place, a small farm holding he was renting a few miles from town. The other vehicles parked in front of the barn told her everyone had answered the call and as she stepped out of her car she could hear them in full cry. It was obvious they had done a lot of work already and in contrast to her usual approach to practice sessions, she was eager to join in.

There was a large potbelly stove almost glowing red near where the band was playing and Grace stood beside it warming her hands. She listened with growing excitement to the instrumental gestation of the song and watched with pleasure at the increased energy being applied by the band.

Apart from the young, enthusiastic Mitch Monroe, apprentice auto body repairer and son of Deloraine with ambitions that a music career would buy him a ticket out of the town, the experienced members of Blizzard treated most rehearsals as jam sessions. It was how the band had started, playing on the weekend for a bit of relaxation and a few extra bucks before it had gradually turned into a chore. Long ago they had given up any idea of making it big in the industry, although for very different reasons than those of their lead singer.

In the savagely competitive field of popular music, the basic rule for success applied - it wasn't how good you were or what you knew but whom you knew and the way in which you knew them. Chas, for one, had been stung by the rule in a big way. In the mid-eighties, he had poured all his money into producing an album of Rhythm and Blues/ Rock songs after getting an enthusiastic response from a record company to his demo single. After they listened to a tape of the album he was asked to polish it before submitting it again, only to be later told that the sound had become dated in the couple of months he had taken to do the work.

Before he had even begun his career as a recording artist, Chas had been swept away by the tidal wave of the 'new'. Like the Glam-Rock of the mid-seventies, image had become king again, or queen in this case, music technologically castrated, creativity replaced by tail-wagging girl singers with perfect skin and white teeth, singing assembly-line numbers knocked out by pop factories. He heard through the grapevine about the one who had been signed by the recording company virtually at the same time as his rejection. One morning, a few weeks later, he saw the attractive singer at a Los Angeles nightclub, hanging affectionately off the arm of the same record company executive that had been so enthusiastic about his prospects. Although he was sure the foreplay was the same, all record-speak and royalties, it appeared the executive had gotten around to shafting her in a very different way to him.

For Chas, the whole experience had been an advanced course in cynicism and it had also messed up his relationship with his father because he had borrowed money from him to re-mix the album, in a last ditch effort to impress others in the recording industry. His second failure eventually resulted in the family home in Tucson having to be sold, the extra mortgage taken out to pay for Chas's dreams becoming too much to handle. Now his parents lived in a much smaller house in a less desirable part of the city and his father was unable to forgive the dreamer of a son who had put them there.

Chas and his father no longer spoke to each other but his mother still kept in touch and he had sworn to her that he was going to pay back the fifty thousand he had borrowed. He had repaid a small amount but the debt continued to hang over him like a black cloud. He knew he could never repay it all by scraping it from the meager earnings of nothing jobs, the latest of which was piloting a forklift around a warehouse. But as he stood in his barn, with each run-through of the song's skeleton he began to see a way. The dreamer-turned-cynic was becoming a dreamer again.

The band stopped playing and stepped over to the stove where a pot of coffee was bubbling away on top.

'Whaddya think, Gracie?' Chas asked, as he began pouring coffee into everyone's cups. Before Grace could answer he added, 'Let me take a look at those lyrics.'

As she handed them to Chas, Boss handed her a thin wad of folded twenty-dollar notes.

'Ed didn't take nothin' offa the top. Ah tol' him if he did, ah would remove somethin' from the toppa him.'

Grace smiled as she put the money in her pocket. 'Thanks, Boss. Are we still there next week?'

'Oh, yeah... yah know Ed. Lotta noise in a empty can.'

Chas read over the lyrics, his practiced eyes matching the rhythm in the lines with the music they had been playing. 'They fit,' he said, ignoring the political content of the words. He looked at Grace as he handed the sheet of paper to Mitch, who had been leaning over his shoulder trying to read the words. 'Where's it all comin' from, Gracie?'

'From the same place you got yours, I guess. Out there somewhere.'

'Well, I've heard of them comin' this easy for some but they were always a hard grind for me,' Chas replied.

'All I can tell you is that Jamie wrote those first eight lines,' Grace added, still unsure of the words' origination but keen to get him some credit.

'Huh...?'

'Yeah... I found them in his notebook when I went to see him last night, although he didn't remember writing them. Could be all the medication he's been getting. There's been a few things he hasn't remembered lately.'

By now, the multi-talented Wayne Ryder, the quietest member of the group, was reading through the lyrics. He had joined the band six months before, after Boss found him busking in the local shopping mall and invited him along to a jam session. He was on his way to Denver but enjoyed the experience of being part of a group again and decided to hang around for a while, finding a part time job at a car wash to pay for room and board. Like the rest of them he had done the eighties, working with some competent nightclub bands before the old gave way to many kinds of new. Now he was just a wandering minstrel, a native of San Francisco, presently on his third circuit of the USA. Sort of a lesser Woody Guthrie of the Rock and Roll kind, except he had never ridden the rails or written a song that had gone anywhere. Yet, although he could see a chance to be part of something here, as he scanned the words of the Lakota chorus with their English translation next to them, he felt he had to play the devil's advocate.

'It's good but Native Rock's bin 'round for a while now. And there's heaps o' pretty good outfits doin' that stuff. Why would we be seen as anythin' different, except for the fact that, besides Grace, we're all palefaces, and that right there will bring a credibility problem?'

'You said it, man... Native *Rock*,' Chas responded. '*That right there* is all the credibility ya need. We took our rock and roll from the black man and the red ones have taken theirs from ours. Music's music, man, it's always crossin' over, and right now the muse o' this particular music's picked us for the journey back. This number's got somethin' different and ya know it, or ya wouldn't be talkin' about it as though we might just be goin' somewhere with it. I don't know where it's come from but my Strat's bin smokin' since Grace played me that riff this mornin', so let's get on with it!'

The instant Chas said those words there was a yelp followed by a screaming note from his guitar. His dog Jimi, who had been lying near the instrument, hurried towards the people standing by the stove.

'Fuck it, Jimi!' Chas accused, as he turned around, sending the Rhodesian Ridgeback skulking away behind the potbelly. Then, a little puzzled, he added, 'That should be turned off.' He strode over check his Stratocaster, an instrument he had bought only a month before and was now precious with to the point of boring the crap out of everyone. He picked it up from where it was leaning against an amplifier and then checked the amp switch, to find it turned off. He turned it on and hit a string. There was no sound. He flicked the switch off and on again then hit the string once more. This time there came an amplified response. He shook his head. 'Gotta look at that amp wirin',' he muttered, before placing the strap over his shoulder and checking the tuning of the guitar.

The disgraced Jimi emerged from behind the stove and Boss called out to Chas as he patted the dog. 'Take it easy on the hound, man. Y'all gonna name a dawg after Hendrix, y'all gotta expect him to join in once in a whaal.'

The comment brought a laugh from the others but Grace remained straight-faced. She was the only one who had been looking in the direction of the guitar when everyone started at the unexpected sound. She was puzzled by what she had seen. Jimi had jumped to his feet and moved away from the guitar a couple of seconds before it sounded off, the ridge on his back raised higher than usual. As the others headed for their instruments, Jimi moved over to her, his tail wagging limply. She knelt down and took the dog's head in her hands, stroking it tenderly as she stared into his eyes. 'What is it, Jimi?' she posed.

'You'll never get an answer!' Chas called out. 'C'mon, Gracie... let's get this song singin'!'

*

Over the next hour, Grace would become the conductor as the flesh was gradually added to the bones of the song. Everyone was allowed to throw ideas in. Some were adopted and some discarded but free rein was given to Chas on the lead break. She wouldn't sing a note, however, until the instrumentation was in place, most particularly the flute. She then sang only the main verses, away from the mike, honing the lyrics, halting to clip a word, change or add one. When she was satisfied with them she stepped up to the front of the band. 'Okay, *now* we'll get it singing!'

The quiet tone of the flute began seeping out of the silence, gradually growing louder, a slow, measured and muted drumbeat joining it before the rhythm and bass followed. Chas played a subdued role at first, lightly tracking Grace with the melody line as she began singing the first verse, her voice contained, controlled, the rhythm of the words smoothly matching the rocking beat that climbed up with increasing power towards the moment that Grace had been patiently crafting the song for. Everyone knew she had a special voice but when she sang out that first Lakota chorus the effect of it shocked all the musicians into sudden silence.

For a few seconds, Grace stood silent, too, arms by her side, head held high. For one brief moment she felt what she had experienced at Jimmy's, not the release of a demon but a natural rush of exhilaration. Her body relaxed and she turned to the band. Tears were welling in her eyes but there was a broad smile upon her face. 'Well... what are ya waiting for, you guys? Song's not finished yet.'

'Jesus, Grace!' Chas finally uttered.

They began again; no less shocked the second time Grace hit the Lakota chorus but riding professionally through it to be doubly electrified by the sizzling riff that followed. Chas was unable to contain himself and cried out with exhilaration as he played his part. The song streamed with sustained power through two repetitions of verse, chorus and riff, before the melody began to wind down on Chas's fading guitar, the song tailing away to end as it had begun, the dying sound of the flute accentuating the mystery in the Lakota words. Powerful in their simplicity and naturalness, the contrast of the native chorus had lifted the rhythmic lines of the other lyrics and melody to a greater height, soaring upwards on the exploding emotion in Grace's voice.

At the end of the song there was another brief stunned silence, before they looked at each other and broke into a joyous, unified laughter. Chas then added his distinctive vocals to their excitement.

'Jeeesus... yes! Yes, yes, fucking yes! Let's go again!'

Just after they started again, Chas's wife Kelly and their two-year old daughter, Kate entered the barn. Drawn there by the first effort, as the second progressed, Kelly's face beamed with delight; her attractive form moving sensually in time with the song's climbing beat. She grabbed the hands of the small girl clumsily trying to emulate her movement and the two pretty blondes danced joyfully through to the number's end. When it finished, Kelly whooped with exhilaration and clapped her hands madly. 'I don't believe it, you guys! That was just so fantastic!' she yelled at the group of smiling faces.

The band bowed their heads almost as one.

'Your reward will be out of the oven in about half an hour,' Kelly cried out.

An enthusiastic drum roll greeted the news and Kelly laughed but as she turned to go, Kate pulled away from her outstretched hand. 'Me stay!' she loudly declared.

'Chas?' Kelly called out.

Chas nodded back. 'Just don't get too close to that fire, Squeak...and hands over ears!'

Kate frowned deeply and shook her head in agreement before sitting down next to Jimi and obediently placing her hands over her ears.

The band played the song another three times, each effort bringing the improvement that came with knowing where it led. They recorded it on the last performance then broke for lunch. Halfway to the house, however, Chas noticed Kate wasn't with them. He walked back into the barn to find her standing with a pondering finger in her mouth, staring intently at where the band had been playing, Jimi sitting on his haunches beside her, looking in the same direction.

'Squeak! C'mon, man... it's time to eat,' Chas called out.

'Eat - man!' Kate yelled out without turning.

Chas walked over and picked her up. 'Yeah, man. That's right. Let's go.'

As they walked away, Kate twisted in his hold and stared back towards the instruments. 'Eat - man!' she yelled again.

'Dammit, Squeak! And here's me worryin' about *your* hearin',' Chas said, putting her down and ringing his ear

27

before pulling a face and chasing her squealing form out through the doorway.

The euphoria and excited discussion bubbled away all through a long lunch but the feast slowed everyone down. They called it a day soon after, arranging to rehearse the song again on Tuesday night as well as the regular Thursday practice session, and again before their Friday night gig. For once they were looking forward to the weekend performance, intending to try the song out early evening when the place was at its fullest and the drunks weren't.

Grace took the cassette player and tape of the song straight to the hospital, excitedly plugging in Jamie's earphones, for once happily turning the volume up to his level before sitting back to watch his face.

Jamie's eyes were wide open with anticipation, a broad smile joining them soon after the first melodic notes of the flute intro, his hands and feet moving in time with the gradual ascent of the beat. When he heard his mother's powerful voice rising above the melody line he cried out, 'Wow... yeah, Mom, *yeah!*' then listened more intently. As the song tailed away he cried out again, 'It'sth a hit, Mom! You're gonna be a sthtar!'

Lisped or not, the last word touched a nerve but Grace smiled at her son's enthusiasm as he quickly re-wound the tape and played it again. Then, after it had finished, he added something more to the strangeness that had punctuated the previous eighteen hours of her existence. Of late he had shown a rapid, almost spooky improvement in the understanding of song construction but now it suddenly took a giant leap. He began talking to her about the structure of the song like a seasoned musician, making a couple of suggestions that she could see would clearly enhance it and, as she walked out of the room later, one that would change something else.

'Change the band's name to *Warrior*, Mom.' he called out.

Grace was startled by the words that came like a command but as she studied the serious look on Jamie's face she considered the idea. She hadn't even thought about it but a name change seemed right for what could be a new direction for the band. She pondered the word he had chosen. It matched the theme of the song she had titled *Song Catcher* and it seemed logical to apply it to the band's name.

'Mmmm,' she mused. 'But why not *Warriors*, or *The Warriors*?' she offered.

'No. *Warrior* is better,' Jamie emphasized. 'It sounds like the band is one thing... a powerful thing.'

Grace was again taken aback by his forceful manner but she nodded her head slowly and said, 'Yeah... okay. I'll put it to the others.' Then she suddenly snapped out of her pensiveness and pressed her lips to her hand, took the stance of a pitcher on the mound and hurled the kiss.

'Ball one!' Jamie said, as he reached his hand out wide in the act of a catcher going after an errant ball.

'I'll give you ball one, you little shit!' Grace responded. She raced back and gave him the full treatment, planting a sloppy wet kiss on his mouth and each cheek, counting off, 'Strike one! Strike two! Strike threeeee!'

Grace left the room smiling at Jamie's grimacing and wiping but, a couple of steps from the doorway, her pensiveness returned. Now she had to head home to their rented bungalow to do the chores always left to Sunday afternoon but, all the way there and all through the housework that followed, she would ponder the growing mystery around a song and a boy, and what had happened in the barn. When she had sung the Lakota chorus there for the first time the same explosion of energy she felt at Jimmy's had rushed through her once more and, as before, it sounded as though someone were harmonizing with her.

THREE

'Git yo ass movin', Jenny! One special for nine!'

Cal's voice boomed over the clatter of the diner like a PA system and Jenny gave a twisted grin to the woman she was briefly chatting to.

'Gotta go, honey. The whip's a'crackin' again,' she sang out, loud enough for Cal to hear.

'Whooooo... promises, promises babeee. Your place or mine,' came the instant response from the chef, as his hands darted around the hotplate, playing the steaming workbench like a xylophone. His comment sent a chorus of laughter burbling through the diner.

'Grace! Number two!' he called out, as he slapped two plates of the breakfast works on the counter and leant out of the kitchen hatch to leer with great animation as Jenny took her order away.

The shapely waitress obeyed Cal's earlier instruction to the letter, swinging her hips with exaggeration, one hand resting on the left one and the other holding the plate high above her head, before placing it down with a flourish for the man at table number nine.

More chuckling came at the early morning pantomime and a burly truck driver called out as he nodded in the direction of Jenny. 'Hold that order, Cal... I'll have some o' that right there! It'll get mah blood goin' quicker than ham n' eggs!'

'Sho' will, buddy... but in the long run, ham n' eggs be a lot cheaper,' came the immediate response.

Another ripple of laughter passed through the diner and the repartee finally caused the man at table nine to turn his attention from the paper he had been reading. He turned around and looked towards the serving hatch and a puzzled frown formed on his face. When he first entered the diner he had glanced appreciatively at the attractive figure of the woman busily working the other end of the room but now he could see her face more clearly.

Jenny smiled as she placed his bill on the table. 'Don't mind him none, Honey. It's all them cookin' fumes. I think he gets a bit high on 'em.'

'No... it's the waitress there. Her name wouldn't happen to be Grace Howard, would it?' he asked, his eyes following Grace as she collected two plates of food and delivered them to a table at the other end of the room.

'It wouldn't *happen* to be, Honey... it's the one and the very same. Why... you *happen* to know her?'

'A long time ago.'

'A friend?'

'Yeah... a friend,' the man replied, wistfully.

'Ah'll get her to come an' pour your coffee. You got a name?'

'Just tell her it's Mark.'

Jenny bustled off, picked up some dirty plates from another table then detoured to where Grace was taking an order.

'Man over there says he knows you. Name's Mark... said he was a friend o' yours from way back. Ah told him ah'd send you over with his coffee.'

Grace glanced up at the man after Jenny swept past. The name had evoked an instant memory but when she looked at the person glancing back at her she could see little of the Mark she once knew. She quickly turned her attention back to the order, nervous and distracted now. A couple of minutes later, she picked up a pot of coffee and tentatively approached table number nine.

'Hi, Grace,' greeted the man, a warm smile spreading across his face.

'Of all the breakfast joints in all the world...' Grace said nervously.

'I'd say don't give up your day job but I guess that's probably what you'd like to do,' Mark Hammond responded.

'Long time, huh,' Grace said, as she studied her former manager and friend, a man who had once devoted all of his time and energy getting her to the threshold of Rock and Roll stardom before she took the elevator in the other direction. The balding man before her was a far cry from the longhaired young firebrand that had battered down doors for her along the cruel corridors of the music world but the forthrightness was still there.

'What happened, Grace? Where did you get to?'

'This is where I got to,' she said a little sharply, as the pincers of guilt began to close on her. In a diversionary move she added, 'And what happened to you?'

'Life.'

'Grace!' Cal called out from his command post.

For once Grace was pleased to hear her boss's hurry-up. 'Gotta go. Nice to see you again, Mark,' she lied.

'Whoa! After all this time and that's all I get? I'd like to speak some more. When do you get off work?'

'I don't know, Mark. Can't we just let it be?'

She glanced into his eyes and saw the faint accusation there, although he was still smiling pleasantly.

'Look, Mark... I'm sorry I let you down but that part of my life is gone now and I'm not at all comfortable talking about it,' she added, hoping it was enough to escape the net that was closing around her.

'Well, I'm stuck here for a little while and yours is the only face I know in town. I'd just like to have a quiet chat over a coffee... whaddya say?' He stared at her with eyebrows raised in a pleading way.

'Goddamnit, Grace!' came another directive from Cal.

Mark smiled his best smile.

'Okay,' Grace relented. 'I get off at eleven o'clock. I'll meet you at Carlo's coffee house down the street. But I won't be able to stay long. I've got an afternoon job to get to.'

*

Mark stood up as Grace made her way to his table. She had changed from her waitress uniform into tight-fitting jeans and when she took off her heavy coat and shook her long, straight, jet-black hair, he smiled with appreciation.

'You still look in great shape, Gracie. All the bumps in the right places.'

Grace smiled thinly. 'Thanks. That's only because I don't have the time to get outta shape.'

'Hi, Grace. What'll it be?' asked a young waitress.

'The usual thanks, Paula,' she requested with a smile. 'Mark?'

'I'll go with the usual too.'

33

'A regular, huh?' Mark queried, as the girl walked back to the serving counter.

'Yeah. It's my hideaway. I could have free coffee coming outta my ears back at the diner... but it's not the same. Anyway, what brings you to this town?' she quickly asked, determined to keep the focus away from her.

'A van brought me here and it's kept me here since it broke down on Sunday morning. I was heading through from Bismarck on my way to Montana and had just taken off from the set of lights in the middle of town when everything suddenly stopped. Turns out something failed in the computer. A giant pain in the ass I've gotta say, being caught out in the freezing cold at one o'clock in the morning, trying to find someone to tow it off the street before the ghouls came out to strip it. I've got a small business warehousing musical instruments and the van is full of expensive gear. It'd be my neck if it were ripped off. I have to wait here until a part comes in from outta state. There's another red tick for technology. If it had been my old car I probably could have fixed it myself and been away by now.'

Mark pondered something for a few seconds before continuing. 'You know, I've never come this way before. My business always takes me north from Bismarck through Minot and then across the Canadian border before heading back to Seattle through Vancouver. But this time I just felt like going home earlier. It was supposed to be a short cut... makes you wonder a bit, doesn't it?' he finished, with a smile like a policeman that had cornered a fugitive.

It made Grace wonder in more ways than one. The vision of Mark's van stalled in the middle of Main Street flashed across her mind the instant he mentioned it. But just as she had swerved to miss the vehicle then, she avoided

34

mentioning anything about it now. She didn't want to speak of the mystifying sequence of incidents that had started at Jimmy's. She couldn't understand what was going on and doubted anyone else could.

'Thanks, Paula,' Grace said as two cappuccinos arrived, grateful both for the coffee and something to occupy her fidgeting hands, one of which had been nervously fiddling with a bead necklace.

'How long will you be stuck here, Mark?' she asked, almost fearfully, as she emptied a teaspoonful of raw sugar into the chocolate-dusted froth on top of the creamy fluid.

'Till Friday, they tell me. I'll probably hire a vehicle for a few days and see if I can make some sales around the district. I've got nothing else to do.'

Her fears confirmed, Grace felt even more uncomfortable about agreeing to the coffee and chat, wondering how she would be able to avoid him for another four days. Her claustrophobia grew rapidly and she contributed to the next few minutes of trivial conversation in a guarded way.

But that was as long as Mark was able to keep his curiosity at bay. The woman before him was much changed. She was not the same freewheeling individual he had once known, who seemed able to turn in a powerhouse performance on stage with consummate ease. He wanted to know how she had become the quiet, almost serious person she now appeared to be and, besides, he still felt she owed him an explanation.

'Put us both out of our misery, Grace. Just tell me what happened and I'll be on my way. I'll forget you ever hung me out to dry. Why did you run? You know that Galaxy records were drawing up a contract for you to sign after the New York gig. Where did you get to?'

Grace turned and stared out at the street. A haunted look formed in her eyes and her hand moved back to the string of semi-precious stones hanging around her neck. Her fingers began to roll the polished pea-sized pieces again in a vacant, much-practiced way. She knew he deserved an explanation and after several seconds she began to speak, her eyes still staring through the activity outside, her fingers still clinging to the necklace.

'I ran... because I was afraid. I wanted the big time to happen but as it came nearer, I panicked. I knew I couldn't cope with all the attention that was heading my way. I loved singing when I could hide in a group or at recording sessions but no one except Johnny knew how terrified I was about getting up on stage as the front person. I was high on dope at the New York concert. I'd been on it since long before you took me on. The easygoin' gal you knew was propped up by every form of hallucinogenic going round. If I wasn't drinking it or snorting it, I was popping it. Finally I got 'round to injecting it, and that's when Johnny and I hitched a ride on the garbage truck.'

Now that the subject had been broached, Grace began to let it all out. Not even the counselors she was obliged to visit in the three months before she was given care of her child had heard the whole story. Now she was going to tell it all to a man who had been there at the beginning and who had entered her life again like a father confessor, allowing her for the first time to loosen some of the chains she had wound around her.

'Johnny and I went on a long trip after New York. We drove south straight after and ended up renting an old farmhouse in the San Fernando Valley. We didn't see anyone for weeks on end, apart from our dealer, and even he stopped making the trip out there once he realized the money was running low. We must have been there for over six months, although I'm not sure about that. Most of it was a haze. We finally got kicked out for not paying the rent and ended up in a dive in San Francisco... on the Haight Ashbury would you believe. But there weren't no flower power and beads for us, just more of the nightmare.'

The dark vision of what happened in their grubby little apartment formed in Grace's mind and tears began to well at the memory of an overdosed Johnny lying there with that death stare in his eyes. The same intense look in Jamie's had frightened the hell out of her at the hospital two nights ago yet, back then, doped beyond feeling, it had hardly registered. In later dreams, however, Johnny's death mask returned to her in surreal clarity. And those dreams were always followed by waking moments of deep shame, recalling her actions when she realized that the wasted person lying next to her on the dirty mattress, vomit and excreta seeping from his body, was dead. Strung out for nearly two days without a hit, her response was simply to rifle his pockets for the last sachet of heroin he was jealously guarding, after scoring by selling a car radio he had ripped off.

The shame of that action and of where they had both ended up milked the tears from Grace. She pulled a napkin from the table's container to stop the flow.

Mark reached out and held her forearm. 'I'm sorry Grace, let's just forget about it.'

'No, I've gotta talk now,' she said, as she recalled the fresh-faced and excited young kid who had fled Pine Ridge just after her.

Like any of the young ones that had had the opportunity, Grace and Johnny Dark Sky had left the depressing confines of the reservation as soon as it arose. For her it came as an eighteen-year-old when a talent scout had heard her singing in a contest at Deadwood. He had got her work in back-up vocals for a recording studio and subsequently with groups on tour, and she in turn had got Johnny some work as a roadie. They had been friends since childhood but it wasn't until years later, when they had both fallen into the merciless grip of the drug culture, that they became lovers, although more mechanical than heartfelt, just reaching out for the flesh companionship of a like suffering soul. When they had left the reservation, they believed that anything was better than the living death they would suffer there. But they were wrong.

'Johnny died of an overdose and I had his baby a little while later. I didn't even know I was pregnant... that's how far my spaceship had traveled. The dope had messed up my cycles and I didn't even think about it when they disappeared. I wasn't capable of feeling any physical change by that time, except the high of hits and the pain between. The first I knew of having a child was when he arrived. 'Bout the only sensible thing I ever did do during that period was to use clean needles and it was just pure luck that I was at the clinic collecting them when my water broke. I was still half doped when they carted me off to hospital to give birth, and that happened almost as soon as they took me through the front entrance. The doctor calculated that he was about seven weeks premature... and he came with big physical problems.'

Grace stopped there for a brief moment, her fingers now roughly twisting the necklace. The painful imagery of her newborn child lying in a hospital humidifying crib battling withdrawal from his inherited addiction clawed at her and she lashed out at herself again. 'You know, the most terrible thing of all is that even if I had been aware of being pregnant, I was so hooked that it wouldn't have mattered. I know I would have still kept hitting up.'

Grace's face reflected a look – almost of shock – at her admission, before she added another, 'It sickens me to say it but seeing my son suffering the detox from what I gave him was probably the only thing that could've made me climb off the white horse. The simple truth is that, if it wasn't for him being born, I'd be dead now.'

Paula the waitress noticed her favorite customer's distressed state and came over just as Grace took another napkin from the container.

'You okay, Grace?' she asked, resting a comforting hand on her shoulder.

Grace wiped away the tears and her other hand finally let go of the necklace. She looked up and smiled at the young, concerned face. 'Yeah... I'm fine, honey. It's just that this coffee is so damned *good*. Can I have another?'

The girl returned an uncertain smile and went back to the bar.

Grace turned back to Mark. 'So... there it is. In short, I crapped all over everyone's life, including yours. But, hey... guess what? This is the strongest drug I touch now,' she said, pointing to the coffee cup, before adding, 'And I can stand up before a small crowd and sing, but only because I know the drunk bastards take little notice of me.'

For a few moments, Mark searched for some words of comfort, but Grace had just declared that her survival tool was self-inflicted pain and who was he to try and dull its edge? Instead he responded to her revelations with genuine surprise.

'Jesus, Grace... you hid it well. Of all the acts going around I figured you had your shit together more than most.'

'It's the law of the jungle, isn't it? When you're scared you do anything to hide your fear. Don't show your weakness to the predators, that's what most of us learn, don't we? The joke is that I used weakness to cover weakness and showed it to the worst kind of predator.'

'Yeah, well you weren't the only one using back then. The white snuff was taking up a large percentage of my food bill, too. And as far as crapping on others' lives, we've all done a bit of that. I've got an ex-wife and two children back in Seattle who could bear testimony to my bowel movements.'

'Sorry to hear that,' Grace said.

'Don't be. They're not.'

Mark's assessment came dressed with a wide smile and a light chuckle broke through Grace's sniffing.

'That's better. That's the Gracie I knew... enough with the pain.'

Grace kept smiling, 'You... an *instrument* salesman?' she said, now able to look more lastingly into Mark's eyes as she spoke.

'Yeah, sometimes it's as big a joke to me. But it keeps me clothed and pays the alimony. You have to do something when the fun part is over. Anyway, what is this about singing to drunks? Are you still keeping your hand in?'

'Yeah, on the weekends, just to earn a few extra bucks.'

'Mmmm... well, as you would expect with my business, I have to keep my hand in too. I've still got contacts with agents and a couple of small record companies and whenever I do my trips I make a point of going to the local hot spots to listen to the music. I'm still a bit of a prospector. I can't stop looking for that sound. I've steered a few outfits into recording and got a few bucks for the trouble but I can't say I've found anything special. I'm afraid the stuff being done today is gradually leaving me behind.'

'Yeah, us too, we're sticking to standards from the sixties to the eighties. You remember Boss Gillespie and Chas Montgomery. They're the ones who got me back into singing.'

'No kidding? And just how did you three end up in corn-shucking central, anyway?'

'It started with Chas. He married a young North Dakota girl in LA and when Kelly got a yearning to come back and be near her folks, they decided to settle here for a while. They've been renting a small farm for a few years. The lifestyle agreed with them and they've got a little daughter now. Boss came to visit and liked the laid-back change, got a job and stayed too. I ran into him a couple of years ago when Jamie and I were living in Austin and he was passing through to visit his folks out west. He told me that he and Chas had been living here for a while and that there was always plenty of work around town because of the grain mill and the abattoir. When I found that Deloraine had a decent medical center, I decided to join them. I've been here for nearly two years now and we started the band about a year ago, just to jam around a bit. Only been playing gigs for about six months.'

'Mmmmm... what are those two doing for a real living these days?'

'Oh, Chas is driving a forklift and Boss is driving a delivery truck. But they both still know how to play. You never lose that, I guess.'

'Yeah... they were good tradesmen. Have you got a gig this weekend?'

'Mmm...we play most Friday and Saturday nights at a night spot called Jimmy's Place, just out on the edge of town. It's one of those good ol' boys' barns, where you drink as much as you can in the shortest possible time and then give it to the musicians for the rest of the night.'

Grace's next comment pre-empted what Mark was about to suggest.

'Why don't you hang around and come and hear us play on Friday? It would be a change to have a sympathetic ear out there in the haze.'

Grace was now feeling relaxed about the face from the past. As far as she was concerned there was nothing more to hide from him but there was something else besides sociability that had brought the offer. She wanted him to hear the song. Like all artists she needed the approval of someone who knew her craft and despite his 'wheeling and dealing' kind of nature she knew that he was an authority.

'Yeah... I could do that.'

'Okay. Jimmy's is out on the east side. Grover Street... just ask anyone. We start about eight p.m. and go through till two. I've gotta run now. See you Friday night.'

The mood that had been carrying Grace since Saturday night began lifting her again the moment she left the coffee house and, as she put on her apron at Krowenfeldts Drycleaners, she was happily humming the tune of *Song Catcher*.

'You have those fine thighs of yours parted last night, Gracie?' an older woman shouted out from across the room, her comment bringing a burst of laughter from the other females attending the row of steaming and hissing machines.

Grace smiled back in a sly way but the smile reflected a different kind of a secret. The experience at Jimmy's had been like someone applying a jump-starter to her soul, the strange events of the last couple of days bringing a feeling of something building, the chance meeting with Mark somehow connected to it all. She could feel her spirit starting to lift off again, the way it had as a young girl, when she sang with a different voice and for another audience. It was that spirit which had guided her as she had worked to complete Jamie's lyrics a few days before, the freezing early morning turning into a warm summer afternoon, when her grandfather once again took her to the Black Hills. In those graveyard hours of Sunday, she had felt for a brief time the same apprehension on approaching the Sacred Center, the same feeling of being in the presence of her ancestors.

Grace was well named by her mother, Dawn, for - when first holding her child- the cry that came from its mouth sounded more like singing than the squalling protest of a newborn baby. And whenever Sings At Dawn visited the *Paha Sapa* with her grandfather, she would climb to a high place and sing to her ancestors, her voice taking wing and soaring like an eagle across the peaks and the folding flesh of the Grandmother, before its echo drifted back to her on the wind. It was where she felt the strength that was once with her people, and where she watched her grandfather's eyes come alive, only to see them die again during the trip back to Pine Ridge in his old pickup. It was a song he had taught her that she sang out at Jimmy's and his influence that had helped her complete the lyrics she found in Jamie's notebook. But the triumph of completion was tinged with the regret she had felt after seeing his image that night, the memory of him coming as another hit of guilt.

FOUR

Mark Hammond walked into Jimmy's Place at about nine o'clock Friday night. The drinking hole was half-full of people and the resurrected enthusiasm of the group was being reflected in a version of Lou Christie's *Two Faces Have I*. Chas and Wayne were accentuating the falsetto vocals of the sixties hit to comic proportions, trying to get Grace to break up in the lead but she remained in control, her body moving raunchily in time with the beat.

The range of Grace's voice came as a pleasant surprise to Mark, whose initial enthusiasm about coming along had begun to turn into the fear she might be just another version of the world-weary rock singers he had heard in so many watering holes before. A week ago that is what he would have heard but the band's energy had been progressively building ever since the early hours of last Sunday morning. It had taken a giant leap at the Thursday night practice session when Grace first spoke to the others about Mark coming to listen. Chas in particular had been excited to hear about it, although his excitement would bring the first note of dissent to the group. He had long range plans for the song, even if

Grace seemed to be nervous at the prospect of entering the jungle of popular music again. She had tried to put a halter on his rampant enthusiasm by mentioning what they all knew to be a fact.

'One song's not gonna get us anywhere these days... more than anybody you should know that, Chas. You couldn't even make it with a pretty good album.'

Chas brushed the pessimism aside. 'Yeah but none o' those songs were as good as this. If he's still got contacts, he could get us a hearin'. I don't know why you're so reluctant, Gracie. This is a winner. You know it. We all know it. We'll find some more stuff. Maybe we can re-work some o' the numbers off my album. Anyway, why did you invite him along if you don't wanna go further with it?'

The question was too difficult for Grace to answer. Of late, her mind had become like a washing machine, emotions constantly tumbling over one another. She wanted Mark to hear it for the music's sake, yet over the last couple of days she had begun to feel the first faint pangs of the old claustrophobia. Chas was right; the song was a winner, and because of that she now had a real fear that Mark might run with it. The next thing Chas said brought it home with a rush.

'Don't let *your* fears ruin it for us, man. We'd like a chance to drink from the chalice too... and make up our own minds about whether it's poisoned or not.'

His words were not unexpected. She knew he felt resentment about her throwing away her chance at the big time while he had worked his butt off only to have it kicked. She knew that he had never been able to comprehend why she had run. She couldn't quite understand it herself, let alone explain it properly. She had a phobia about something most performing artists would kill for; the adoration of the masses; the screaming for *you*. It was all a drug for those who

45

sought it but poison for a free spirit called Sings At Dawn, who in the end just wanted to go back to the mountains and sing to the sky. But there was also another reason for her reticence, a fear equally as big, although right now she wouldn't speak to anyone of that.

Grace spotted Mark just as she hit one of the highest notes in the *Two Faces* number. Without missing a beat she pointed to a vacant table off to one side of the bandstand.

Mark made his way through the crowd and sat down just as the song began to tail away. A Fleetwood Mac number and a Lovin' Spoonful one followed in rapid succession, before the group stopped for an inordinate length of time to check instruments and have a brief conference.

During the band's silence, Mark gazed vacantly around the room, seeing nothing of interest in the typical mid-west scene until his eyes settled on an attractive brunette standing in a group of girls near the opposite edge of the dance floor. She was wearing the uniform of the location – cowboy hat, jeans and boots, a slung-down lacy top revealing the beginnings of a great bust. Before Mark could complete the full chassis evaluation, the haunting sound of a flute grabbed his attention. He turned his gaze back towards the bandstand just as the other instruments joined with the gentle beginning, the flute's tones gradually disappearing as the drums, the bass and lead guitars began to build an introduction for the vocals. Then Grace's voice sang out - *He is a Song catcher – a warrior of the soul...*

At first, the soft intro of the song had little effect on the distracted, carousing patrons but as Grace began to sing, the impact was instantaneous. From that point the song played the room like a snake charmer, lifting the audience step by step towards the moment when the first native chorus cried out. They couldn't know what the Lakota words meant but when they came they made total contact, the emotion in Grace's voice causing the crowd to explode with cheering and whistling.

The song continued along its plateau of power, before it began to descend again, although no less powerful, to fade out on the same haunting instrument that had introduced it.

For a few seconds there was a kind of collective stunned silence in the room; then the crowd erupted once more into another round of wild cheering and applause. Even Ed behind the bar began clapping, although his appreciation was more for the dollar signs rolling around in his head. Mark did nothing. He just sat there transfixed, not quite believing what he had heard.

'Glad you liked it, folks. That's a number called *Song Catcher*, and we all had a hand in writing it, including my son Jamie,' Grace responded.

A few cries of '*More!*' punctuated the dying applause but the band members were already laying down their instruments for a break.

'Maybe next week,' Grace called back, switching off a tape machine before stepping down from the bandstand.

The group approached the table united in smiles. Chas had the biggest. He almost tripped over a cable in his anxiety to speak with the man standing to greet them.

'Long time, man,' Chas said, as he thrust out his hand.

'Chas... Boss. Thought you two 'd be in rocking chairs by now.'

'Don' know 'bout the chairs, man but as y'all can plainly heah, we're still rockin',' Boss replied, putting a little extra in his handshake for the wisecrack.

Mark grimaced and wrung his hand briefly before offering it with a smile as Chas introduced Mitch and Wayne. He turned to Grace. 'So, *that* is what you wanted me to hear. What can I say that you don't already know? Got any more?'

Grace glanced at Chas just as a waitress delivered their usual tray full of alcohol for the boys and an orange juice for her.

'We're working on some more,' Chas lied, staring back at Grace in a challenging way.

'Like to hear 'em. If they're anywhere near as good, I think I know someone who might listen.'

Chas grabbed the crumb of opportunity before Mark had time to sit back down. 'Maybe ya could take a demo of that one, just as a sample for your someone to hear.'

'It doesn't work that way anymore. Might've thirty years ago but now you need a catalogue of songs almost ready to be burned straight onto a CD.'

A silence descended on the people around the table. No one, including Chas, had really believed that one single was going to do anything for them. But there remained an almost tangible excitement amongst them, Grace included, even though she was finding it hard to get a handle on what was building. A week ago they had been a band going through the motions for a few extra bucks. Now they were talking about recording and, regardless of any reluctance she had shown to Chas, she had begun to search for more songs. All week she had been scribbling down what she could remember of the Lakota ones her grandfather had taught her, trying to construct other lyrics and melodies around them in the same way as *Song Catcher* but so far nothing had worked. She scanned through Jamie's notebook each time she visited him in the hope that more lyrics would again magically appear scrawled across a page but there was nothing. In fact, since that night he hadn't written a word of poetry, a mystery in itself.

Mark sat through the next set of songs hardly registering the performance as the melodic power of *Song Catcher* kept playing in his head. There was no doubt. It had that magic of the instant hit about it, the killer riff, the words, the balance and the most important ingredient of all – it was different. If they could come up with more, there might be some real business here. When the band came back to the table for another break he made a proposition.

'Tell ya what I'll do. If you can give me a few more, I'll take them to the people I know and see if I can get some interest. Here's my card. I've gotta go now. I need some shuteye. I want to be in Helena by lunchtime tomorrow.'

The group nodded at Mark's comment of 'Good luck' as he left but they knew more than that would be needed. New songs were required and regardless of Chas's enthusiasm, right now no one was quite sure where the next one would be coming from.

FIVE

Jamie came home the following Monday afternoon but from the time Grace picked him up at the hospital there was a strange quietness about his manner. He hardly spoke at all on the trip back, dismissing her concerned query with a vague, 'I'm okay.' He was clearly distracted by something, and when she settled him in his bed, the first thing he did was to pick up his guitar and start strumming some of the chords he knew, although this time they weren't accompanied by the usual wailing.

The lack of vocals was a relief to Grace but the sound of the guitar constantly stopping and starting, as though he was searching for something eventually began to work on her nerves. By late afternoon she'd had enough and ordered him to take a rest. He was sound asleep when she looked in on him again just before preparing the evening meal but, as she stood at the kitchen bench a few minutes later, she heard the guitar start up again in the same disjointed way. Her eyes rolled upwards in resignation and her mind switched off as she began peeling vegetables and slicing up some beef for a stir-fry. Halfway through the task, however, her attention was caught again by the lack of tortured sound coming out of Jamie's room.

Grace paused and listened, seriously hoping that she and the guitar were going to be given a rest but, just as she began to believe so, Jamie started up again. Her face twisted into a wry smile upon hearing the first twanging note and she turned her attention back to slicing the meat but then her knife-hand suddenly froze.

The distinctive intro to the very familiar song immediately caught her singer's ear; a single note on a high string, to a higher one, then down again to dance through a combination of repeated notes before quickly settling into the chords, driving the song like a slow train running. Then she heard Jamie's voice take up the vocal, not pronouncing words but singing the melody in the way of the muted choral layer used in parts of the recorded version.

Grace stood transfixed, knife still frozen in place, amazed to be hearing the acoustic backing and lyrical lines of *Across The Universe* drifting note perfect out of her son's room. She listened, ears acutely tuned to the performance, only to be further amazed when halfway through the song its rhythm began to change, seamlessly drifting into the form of another melody, similar to the driving structure of the first but distinctive in its own way. It was a melody she couldn't recall ever hearing and she listened to several bars, fixing it in her mind, before curiosity finally overwhelmed her. She put the knife down and quickly and quietly moved along the hallway to Jamie's room. Just as she approached his partly opened door, the music stopped. She halted, waiting for it to start up again but after a several seconds of silence slowly pushed the door open. When she looked into the room, Jamie was sitting up in his bed, the guitar across his lap, his eyes staring in the same sharp, intense way that had frightened her at the hospital.

'Jamie!' she called out, as she moved quickly across the room.

The loud exclamation startled Jamie and he grabbed the guitar protectively, genuinely fearful that his mother was going to make him wear it.

'Sorry, Mom. I'll put it to sleep now,' he said, as he slipped it under the blankets.

Grace should have laughed but she just peered at him. The stare had gone from his eyes the moment she had spoken. For a few seconds she continued to search for it there, before finally speaking.

'It's okay, Hon. What was that you were just playing?'

'Ohhh, the usual stuff.' Jamie handed her the opened book of sheet music that was on his bedside cabinet.

'Why, pretty damned good, was it?' he asked, smiling cheekily.

Grace smiled too but she didn't answer. It was better than pretty damned good but it held no resemblance to the song on the page before her, a piece called *Russian Nights*, with the stated requirement that the beginner guitarist play it in a moderate waltz tempo. In the hope that she might hear the mystery song again she told Jamie that he could keep practicing until mealtime.

'Great!' he cried out, whipping the guitar from its resting place as she left the room.

A minute later Grace wished he had left it there when the standard racket started up again, this time with wailing vocals added. Now she hurried to get the meal ready and put an end to her suffering but before she served up the food she took the time to hum that mystery melody into a cassette recorder.

Later, Grace took the recorder to bed and played the tape over and over again, her humming rendition of Jamie's melody added to and intersected by some of the Lakota songs she had been writing down in an exercise book over the last few days. She eventually fell asleep with the recorder still playing, but while her body slept, her mind wouldn't rest. It kept swimming through the swirling mixture of words and melodies. On and on the cacophony of disconnected noise and words went. It sounded just like one of Jamie's usual recitals, causing her to toss and turn with frustration, until the tape clicked off and a familiar beep woke her.

Grace's eyes opened with a start and as her mind began to clear she thought she could hear the sound of a muted voice, much like the warbling of their noisy refrigerator but louder. She rolled over and looked into the hallway and saw a glow reflected on the half-opened door to Jamie's bedroom. A keyboard began clacking away furiously and then the sound of the voice came again.

'Dammit, Jamie!' she muttered, as she climbed out of bed. She pulled on her robe and bustled down the hallway, wing-clipping punishments foremost in her mind. Just as she reached his door she heard the muted, mumbling sound of the voice again and then a louder, clearer word emerging from the middle of it. 'Yes!' it sounded out in contained triumph.

'Right!' she muttered.

The glow of the computer screen lit up the room and when Grace opened the door she expected to see a small figure seated before it playing games. Instead, she caught the culprit just as he was climbing back into bed. But there was something oddly robotic about his manner and her desire to rebuke him was replaced by a softer enquiry.

'Jamie?'

There was no reply as Jamie lay down. He seemed oblivious to his mother's presence even though his eyes were open and staring. He pulled the bedclothes over himself and then closed his eyes, his breathing soon coming deep and rhythmic.

Grace was caught between suspicion and concern as she walked over to his bed. She decided to test him, but quietly, not wanting to wake him if she had got it wrong.

'I know you're awake, Jamie, and if you don't open your eyes I'll tie a knot in your willy,' she whispered in his ear.

There was not even the slightest hint of a smile twitching on his lips and now she became more worried. She had occasionally heard him mumbling in his sleep before but had never known him to walk in it. With his back still in its early stages of healing she saw the danger. Quite apart from ignoring the doctor's instructions not to sit up in a chair for a few days, it was all they needed for him to trip over something and end up back in hospital. She turned and walked over to the computer; a secondhand one that the boys in the band had all kicked in for on Jamie's birthday last year. He had been slowly two-finger typing his poetry in it and Grace recently bought a used printer so that he could put his efforts onto paper, although they were being recorded at the rate of only about one a fortnight, kept on hold because of his preference for playing computer games. But this time the screen was showing the blank, dull gray of his poetry file. She scrolled it back to the last text he had typed in, quickly scanning through the words of a piece she had read before. It held nothing new as far as she could see. She scrolled to the end of the last page again where the computer froze, waiting for a command to insert a page break. Then she went through the shutdown procedure on the computer, her mind too tired to puzzle any more.

Grace took another brief look at Jamie then left him to his dreams and went back to bed. She fell quickly asleep but not long before waking in the morning she would have a powerful dream of her own. She was standing on the prairie, alone in a sea of grass that was turning from green to straw, waving gently before her as the north wind whispered of summer's approach. From far away, she heard a sound, something like the rumbling hooves of the large herds of cattle that were rounded up near her home before being trucked away. But she could see no cattle as she looked towards the horizon; just the rolling hills and, upon the top of one, a tiny speck of a shape appearing, slowly making its way down the slope towards her, as if being blown on the wind. She heard a faint whistling sound, again far away, joining with that vague rumbling, echoing tone that occasionally lifted in pitch like the cry of an animal, lending an eerie rhythm to the figure's approach. As it got closer, she suddenly felt a strong sense of familiarity, quickly followed by an all-consuming sense of sadness. Closer and closer it came, until halfway down the slope, just as she began to make out the first indistinct outline of a horse and rider, the dream faded. The rumbling sound became the thunder of a six o'clock goods train, shaking her bed and rattling the walls as it rolled slowly past their back fence, then a voice honked out from down the hallway.

'Breakfast, woman!'

Grace opened her eyes and lay there stunned for a moment, the inexplicable sadness still lingering from the spell of the powerful dream, her eyes moist with tears.

What's goin' on out there in the kitchen?' The voice honked again.

Grace wiped away the tears then got up and slowly dressed. She made her way to Jamie's room, pushed the door open and stood with hands on hips, fixing him with a bemused stare.

A smiling face peered out of the blankets.

'Some hotel... I've been callin' room service for five minutes!'

'I'm sorry, Sir. What would it be that you require for breakfast this morning?'

'Burger, fries and a coke would be nice.'

'So that'll be muesli and toast, followed by a glass of milk and your pills. Comin' right up, Sir.'

At the sound of the groan, Grace turned to go but something caught her eye on the floor near the printer. It was a curled up sheet of paper lying where they sometimes did when the printer spat them out, the hockshop bargain coming without a catching tray. She walked over, picked it up and read the words imprinted on it. Then she looked at Jamie.

'What?' came the response to the accusing stare.

'Have you been up messing 'round with the computer this morning?'

'*No!*' came the affronted reply.

She looked at the sheet of paper again; her eyes running down the set of lyrics, matching their rhythm to the melody she had been humming and listening to for most of the previous evening. The mystery moved on. She was sure that the sheet of paper wasn't there last night. She would have walked right over it. That was puzzling enough but even more puzzling were the words upon it. They conveyed something that, for a brief moment, caused her hands to tremble.

'What is it, Mom?'

Grace sat down on the bed, put her arm around Jamie and handed him the piece of paper.

'This.'

Jamie began to read out aloud, the words sounding as if they were a translation of the dream Grace had woken from just minutes before.

'Out there, the wind is sighing
over the ancestral land
Whispering through a sea of grass
sharing secrets with the sand
It's sings in praise of the prairie
listen, if you can
You'll hear a song of freedom
a ballad of horse and man.'

'Where did they come from, Mom?'

Grace stared at the computer, got up, walked over and turned it on, the sleep-breaking sound of last night beeping through her mind once more.

'Whatcha doin'?'

'Just checking something.' She opened up Jamie's poetry file and shifted it to the end. Once again, a blank page stared back at her. She scrolled back to the last piece of text, with the same result as last night. She went forward to the blank page and lingered there for a few seconds, before hitting the insert-page-break command. The next page came up, and, against all technical logic, there were the lyrics.

Grace pondered the mystery. The used computer had played up before but finding the text was a minor part of the puzzle.

'Well?' Jamie enquired.

'You don't remember writing these?' Grace asked, as she turned around and stared at the innocent face.

'No!'

'You don't remember getting up last night and turning the computer on?'

'Yeah, like I wanna die before I turn thirteen, *motherrr!*'

Grace turned back to the screen and read through the lines once more. It was clear her son had been sleepwalking, and it could only have been his hands that typed the words into the computer. Something beyond reasoning, however, told her to no longer question what was guiding them. Not for the first time this week a voice had spoken to her - one she hadn't heard since leaving Pine Ridge; one that had been effectively stifled by her journey through a wider society, yet seemed only a whisper away - the vision of her grandfather, the creation of *Song Catcher*, Mark turning up in her life again and now the beginning of another song. It almost seemed as if her past was ganging up on her, the incomplete lyrics forcing her to think about their theme and bring completion. It was as if she was being taken on a paper chase into the spirit-dreaming world, being handed gifts with conditions. She decided to accept them now no matter how much fear she held about where they might take her. She switched off the computer and turned to Jamie with a look of determination on her face.

'What's goin' on, Mom?'

She stared at Jamie for a moment. 'We've got something to do today, Hon,' she declared.

*

At the end of that day Grace and her band would have another song to sing, the songwriting collaboration mysteriously begun with *Song Catcher* steadily maturing as the hours went by. The construction of the new number, however, wouldn't come without some difficulty. Once again Grace added two more verses to the lead and used a Lakota song called *Ride the Wind* as the chorus line. Jamie had helped with some of the wording and rhythmic structure of the new verses, but his most valuable input would come after Grace thought they had nailed the song. She had done a fair job of finding some basic chords to the melody and by late afternoon felt her efforts with voice and guitar were sounding good enough to be taped. However, as she began to set up the cassette player for recording, Jamie made a suggestion that would turn everything upside down. He had been quiet for some time as his mother repeatedly sang the song, seemingly unable to take any further part in its creation but, just like he had on *Song catcher*, when his advice came it was as if from an experienced musician.

'Try using the Lakota song as a backing, Mom. Just below the chords, so you can hear it as a continuous faint sound... like the wind blowing.'

After all her hard work, Grace at first felt almost resentful at the advice but once again his words had come with such authority that they forced her to re-think. She saw a problem in executing his idea, however. Who would sing the backing chorus while she played the guitar and sang the lead? Jamie swiftly supplied the answer.

'Strum the chords and sing the chorus into the cassette player, and then play the tape as you sing the lead into my sound system.'

A crooked smile formed on Grace's face. It was something she should have already considered. She had spent enough time in recording studios to know how to provide a backing track. She nodded at her serious little arranger then did what he suggested, strumming and singing several versions until she had one good enough to use behind the lead vocals. Then she recorded the combination onto Jamie's music system and, when they listened to the result, their faces broke into wide smiles. Grace's voice shadowed itself hauntingly in the chorus, sounding like the words of Lakota when calmly spoken, flowing like a gentle wind across the undulating contour of the prairie, whispering through the grass.

'Come here, genius!' Grace grabbed her son and gave him a kiss full on the lips.

Suddenly her collaborator turned into a boy again. He wiped his face with animation. 'If that's all the thanks a genius gets I'm gettin' outta the songwritin' business!'

'Oh... okay then, well what about one of Pedro's pizzas with the works.'

'Now ya talkin'!'

That would be how their day ended. Grace rolled the TV into Jamie's room and they lay on his bed eating pizza while their minds nibbled at the junk food of the small screen. She left his room after he fell asleep, retiring to bed satisfied with what they had achieved that afternoon but troubled about something that lay ahead. She kept thinking about the four lines she had added to the first verse of the new song...

The Lords of the Plains still ride the wind
the people's spirit still remains
And like the wind that keeps on blowing
their time will come again.

Despite their current downtrodden status, the belief in her people's resilience and endurance had been instilled in Grace long ago by her grandfather, in his words and in his being and, as with *Song catcher*, his influence had hovered constantly during the writing of the song she had named *North Wind*.

George Looks Back had brought Grace up from the age of six, after both her parents had died within the space of a year; her mother first, from tuberculosis; her father, Howard Eagle Star, whose Christian name Grace later adopted as a surname, from the plague of hopelessness and despair that affected so many who lived at Pine Ridge. Young, full of life and ambition, before going to the Vietnam War and coming back old, tired and aimless, he had tried to stave off the depression that came from chronic unemployment and poverty with any kind of alcohol or drugs. He was killed late one night on the path to purgatory, namely the unlit road that led to Whiteclay, Nebraska, a town located just outside the border of the reservation that existed almost solely as a liquor outlet for the residents of Pine Ridge. Like a trader's store operating from Fort USA, it supplied the booze that, by law, couldn't be sold inside the reservation. It provided an end to Howard's hell when he lay down to sleep on the road after returning from another drinking binge in the town and a car full of drunks ran over him.

Grace's father was thirty when he died, and her mother twenty-nine, both their premature deaths making a contribution to the pitifully low average life expectancy on Pine Ridge reservation. But her grandfather was one of the few contributing at the other end of the scale. When she had left he was in his mid-sixties and still going strong, although it was to her great shame now that she didn't know if he was still alive.

For several years after leaving the reservation, Grace had kept in regular mail contact with her grandfather, but it had been over thirteen years since she had sent the last letter, the communication petering out as she began the demolition of her life. His replies were always short ones but often contained more wisdom and humor in a page than could be found in a shelf-full of books. She had kept all of them until they too became lost in the blur of her free-falling past. She had hung on to one thing though; the distinctive semi-precious necklace he presented to her the day she left Pine Ridge. It had belonged to her grandmother and held the rustic colors of the earth, its green, brown and ochre tones evenly punctuated by sky-blue turquoise and the sun-colored hues of amber. She only occasionally wore the necklace these days but constantly kept it with her, the stones being worried by her over the years into a highly polished state. They were lying on the bedside table now and, as the guilt crept darkly through the night, she reached out to worry them some more.

Many times over recent years Grace had started to write a letter to Looks Back, only to find that there was nothing but regrets to fill the pages. She couldn't write cheerful lies. He had always had an uncanny knack for finding untruth anyway, either in the face or in the spoken word and she was sure he would find it in the written one. As contradictory as it seemed, it was out of her respect for him that she didn't write. She believed she had let him down and that sense of shame would always drag the pen away until it became pointless to even try. Even if he were still alive he didn't know he had a great grandson and his great grandson didn't know anything of him either. She *had* lied about that. Although no less of a crime, it was easier for her to tell Jamie that she had lived in an orphanage after her parents had died; that they were the last of her family, than to explain why she no longer had contact with the person who had kept her on the straight and narrow up until her late teens. She knew that if she told him about her grandfather, then it would all have to come out; that his mother and father were junkies; that his father hadn't died in a car accident but in a filthy apartment with a needle still stuck in his arm and it was because of her weakness that Jamie had been delivered up to the world as damaged goods.

The specters of her past crowded around her in the darkness, the sleep that usually came quickly after her long and busy days now unable to keep them at bay. She could feel exposure was nigh, and it was all because of the music that had come out of nowhere. The Lakota songs she was using as chorus lines were not her songs; they had been handed down to her grandfather through the generations before, and it was the main reason why she hadn't felt comfortable with the idea of giving Mark Hammond the tape of the first one. Now, the respect that for so long had prevented her from writing to her grandfather was claiming her in a different way. She knew if he were still alive she would have to seek his approval to use the songs commercially, and, although she longed to see him again, she dreaded the consequences of doing so. She knew that she would be stripped bare before the calm penetrating gaze of the man who had always seemed to know what she was going to know. It would be even worse for her if those eyes were now staring from beneath a headstone. The haunting possibility that that was where they were gazing from the other night hadn't escaped her either. But it was no use fighting it any more. It felt like there was a magnet pulling her back.

Six

The next day, Grace rang Chas about an hour after he had finished work. 'I've got another one,' she said soon after he answered, then quickly played him the tape of *North Wind*.

There was silence on the line after the tape ended until Grace broke it with an impatient, '*Well*?'

'That is one beautiful ballad, man. Where did *this* one come from?' Chas responded, once again gliding over the content of the words but pondering the faint familiarity he could hear in the construction of the song.

As with *Song Catcher*, Grace was unable to answer fully, and didn't want to. 'Well, the words came from Jamie again and we got the idea of the melody from his favorite Lennon number *Across The Universe*. I dredged up another Lakota song from my fading memory for the chorus.'

'Aaah... yeah, *Across The Universe*,' Chas concurred. A brief silence followed then he added, 'I'll have a bite to eat then come over.'

'Yeah, and bring Wayne and his flute if you can.'

An hour later Chas arrived with Wayne and flute in tow. They all quickly adjourned to Jamie's room, where

64

they listened to the tape of the song several times before beginning the process of polishing. Two hours later, they felt they had everything in place; Chas applying his clean acoustics, Wayne adding the soft, undulating sound of a flute to Grace's double-tracked vocals and Jamie overseeing it all. Soon after, both men bade him a cheery goodnight and left his room, but as Grace opened the front door to let them out, Chas turned and stared inquiringly at her.

'What?' Grace responded.

'Jamie. He's freakin' me out, man. I know he's always been pretty savvy with music but where's this arrangin' thing comin' from? Some of his ideas are pure genius.'

Grace smiled. 'I've said it before. I don't know where it's coming from. But I'm not dwelling on it anymore. I'm just glad he's got something to hang his hat on.'

Chas conceded with a mildly unsatisfied nod and then said goodnight.

*

Two nights later, *North Wind* was being played at Jimmy's to a much larger crowd than usual. Paired with *Song Catcher*, the songs brought an even more ecstatic response than the latter had a week before. It prompted Boss the treasurer to negotiate a better deal for the band, squeezing Ed at the end of the night for a third more of the dollars for a third less of the hours.

From that night the momentum began picking up for the group now called *Warrior*. Several new songs joined their repertoire over the following weeks, coming not in an unfathomable way but via the increased skill and enthusiasm Grace had acquired for songwriting. After the kick-start of *Song Catcher* and *North Wind* she was off and running, caught up in the all-consuming creativity of seeking out words and sounds. She got together with Chas and they scanned through the tapes of his doomed album, searching for riffs and melodies. She pored over Jamie's poems, the ones that spoke of his love for nature, picking out a verse here, a sentence there, and then building her own words around them. But always, the Lakota songs were used as catching threads, their mystical qualities winding through the melodies and connecting all. After a few weeks, including the first two numbers, they had six very good tracks laid down and several more nearing completion. All were recorded on very basic equipment but their originality drowned out any shortfall in technical quality.

Jamie had gone back to school a week after returning from hospital but he too was so completely caught up in his part of the songwriting process that he could hardly concentrate on studies. Every day after school he would wait impatiently for his mother to collect him, his mind racing with ideas of how each song should be set up. All those many thousands of hours spent listening to all kinds of music seemed to have provided him with an instinctive feel for arranging and it was coming out in a distinctive yet faintly familiar way. The knowledgeable Chas had first sensed it in *North Wind* and now observed it coming through in other songs. One day at rehearsal he mentioned it to Grace.

'Ya know... there's a little somethin' of Jamie's friend in most of these songs, Gracie.'

'Yeah... well it's not surprising. These days he seems to be eating, breathing and sleeping his music. Nearly every night he nods off with one of Mister Lennon's recordings blaring in his ear. He's dreaming of the man so much lately that I'm thinking of setting up a bed for him in his room.'

Something else of Lennon's had also been influencing Jamie for some time. He had developed a habit of mimicking the Liverpudlian's accent, picked up from the many interview tapes and videos he had in his collection of Lennon memorabilia. He was quite good at it, the monotone, nasally harsh edge of the man's speech coming through almost perfectly when he spoke in a low tone.

'Well here's to John Lennon. Long may he whisper in Jamie's ear.'

With that, Chas played a few dancing notes on his guitar, finishing with a full strum of the strings that blasted out inordinately long and caused him to fiddle with the controls on the guitar and then the amplifier, before the sound abruptly halted of its own accord.

'Dammit... gotta get this amp looked at before the next show,' he muttered. 'Can't be my 'Strat', can it baby?' he added, as he took a piece of cloth and stroked the candy-apple red body with all the gentleness of a lover.

'Be careful, man. Any minute now that thing's gonna have a orgasm,' Boss remarked.

'That's her purpose, man! She's a genuine nympho... an' she lerrrrvs to scream.' With that, he hit a wha-whaaing note resembling what he called Kelly's thanksgiving speech. But this time the sound drifted away to end with his controlling fingers, all thought of wiring problems forgotten.

In the few weeks it had taken to create their six songs, spring had also come but it wouldn't thaw the snowballing effect of the group's progress. The crowds at Jimmy's had grown to the point where there were now long queues of people waiting to enter, as each weekend a new original was added to their play-list and each night Ed cashed in, with Boss regularly pushing the keys of his cash register. There was a cover charge now and, as well as a rapidly rising fee for playing, he had demanded that they get fifty percent of it. Ed didn't argue; he simply extended their contract. They were then given a two-hour gig on a Sunday night in the more elevated atmosphere of a local country club, which paid double what they were getting for the three hours at Jimmy's. That was followed soon after by an even higher fee for a mid-week booking at a nightclub in nearby Bismarck and soon the jobs that previously had to be done to survive were being jettisoned. Wayne the nomad was first to offload his torture at the car wash and then Chas parked his forklift for the last time, he hoped, followed by what Boss declared would be his final orange juice delivery. Mitch handed in his mallet at the local auto body repair shop soon after. But the habit of twelve years hung on grimly to Grace. She was earning enough now to at least give up one of her jobs, but there was always the thought of those medical bills, and her knowledge of the fickle music business. She didn't trust it any more than she did back then, nor what her fear of it could do to her. As the crowds had begun to grow, so too had the old sense of claustrophobia, and another problem had stemmed from the sudden new direction - Jamie's lack of concentration at school. The first sign of trouble had come with a call from his teacher.

'He was doing so well before the operation, Grace. But now he seems to spend most of the time staring out the window. One day I even found him in some sort of trance and to be quite honest the look in his eyes scared the hell out of me,' the pleasant, young Helen Morris had said.

Grace put the pressure on Jamie to concentrate at school but it had little effect. A couple of weeks later, the less pleasant head of the school threatened, 'If he keeps heading down this track, we're going to have to sit down and talk about whether it will be worth him going to high school next year.'

Those words frightened Grace. She stepped up the discipline and the amount of time she spent with him on his homework, meeting every complaint with an unwavering glare until Jamie realized there was going to be no alternative but to improve his marks.

Another pressure building on Grace came to a head the last time she spoke with Chas. He had been agitating to send their songs to Mark Hammond after they had completed four, but the grandfather connection was holding Grace back. She had tried to delay things with the suggestion that they complete enough numbers for an album before they sent the songs. But with each new number, Chas's agitation grew. He knew what they had and he wasn't about to repeat the mistake of delaying anything again.

'There's no place for hesitation in this game, Grace. This week's caviar can turn into fish eggs the next. It's all in the marketin', man... the when and the where. And the when is now and the where is here.' Then he added more seriously, 'I've got as big a stake in this as you. Some of those tunes are mine remember, and I wanna hear them floatin' out on those radio waves.'

Grace couldn't argue with any of it but she asked him to wait for just one more week before they got in touch with Mark Hammond.

'Why?' came the irritated response.

'Because I've gotta go back to Pine Ridge. It's to do with the Lakota songs we're using. I'm not sure if my grandfather's still alive but if he is I've got to speak to him before we do this.'

'Damnit, Grace! Don't go tellin' me now that they're sacred songs or somethin' and we're gonna get run over by a fuckin' herd of buffalo if we use 'em!'

'If they were sacred, we wouldn't be using them. They are social songs, about the love of the natural world and my people's place in it. You can't see all of that in the English translation but each word holds a world of feelings within. I know you think lyrics are there just to fill the gaps but whether you understand them or not, these are special. They are bringing the power to the songs we have written. They were handed down to my grandfather and they are very important to both of us.'

The emotion in Grace's voice had been lifting as she spoke, and for a brief moment, Chas was chastened but it wasn't long before he fired away again.

'You mean you've had us workin' our butts off on this stuff knowin' all along you had to get permission to use it? How come ya don't know whether your grandfather is alive or not, anyway?'

'I don't want to talk of that,' she said coldly.

Her response didn't stop the irrepressible one.

'What if he is dead... can we use the songs then?'

Grace reflected briefly before replying, 'I guess so.'

Chas persisted, 'I can't figure this. If he taught them to ya, why do ya have to ask permission? Surely he would be proud to hear the songs on a record?'

'It's not just about asking permission, it's about *fucking* respect!' Grace suddenly shouted.

'Okaay, okaaaay,' Chas said, leaning back with his hands up, surrendering before the twin barrels of Grace's blazing eyes, unaware of the inward direction in which they were pointing.

The next day, Grace too would finally surrender. Although she had indicated uncertainty to Chas she had a growing sense that her grandfather was still alive; that the songs were leading her back to him but, before returning to Pine Ridge for confessional, she would first have to kneel before her son. She made the decision in the morning to do it that night and proceeded to be hounded all day with trepidation at his likely response. At the diner she messed up orders and later mislaid items at the drycleaners, before nearly ruining a pair of trousers she had pressed without first checking the pockets, a stick of gum melting into the lining before the peppermint fragrance told her it was there. The supervisor had smelt it too and bawled her out for her lack of concentration as he snatched the pants away and took them to the resident seamstress for a pocket replacement. 'Ya might be a hot shot singer, Grace but unless ya can press a pair of pants properly you aint worth jack shit to me!'

Grace took the comment in the same distracted way she had been operating all afternoon, her fear tightening its grip as she drove out to pick Jamie up from school. As usual, on the way home he bombarded her with suggestions for songs, before her subdued manner eventually silenced him.

'What's up, Mom?' Jamie later asked, as they sat eating their evening meal, his silent mother excluding him in a way she had never done before.

Grace didn't answer immediately. She sat staring dully at him, her gaze unwavering but her courage wanting. Then she noticed the nervous curling of his fingers, a thing she only ever saw before his operations. The pre-op smile came too, the strange 'It's okay, Mom' kind that seemed to reflect both sadness and defiance.

She reached out to hold his hands but Jamie drew them away then looked down at the table.

Grace stood up. 'Come into the lounge… I've got something to tell you.'

They both sat down on the sofa and Grace put her arm around him and pulled him close. She then started to lever the can open and soon the worms began wriggling out everywhere. She spoke nonstop for nearly half an hour and during it she exposed every shame-filled twist in the downward spiral of her past, sparing herself and her son nothing, giving particular emphasis to her belief that her drug- taking was to blame for his physical problems.

Jamie remained silent during the whole period of the purging, not even responding when Grace's body began to heave with her sobbing. Then, after she had stopped talking he got up and went to his room, no sign of emotion and no goodnight.

A few minutes later, Grace dragged her cross to bed, where she lay awake for a long time, praying to hear some sound of recovery coming from Jamie's room. Even a Rap record would have been Beethoven to her ears. But there was not a note of relief and she felt too fearful to go and investigate. Eventually she nodded off, only to be awakened some time later by a voice, the words cutting through her sleep like a knife.

'Don't worry, Mother... we're goin' to the toppermost of the poppermost.'

In her waking seconds, the nasally, Lennon impersonation sounded deeper in tone, and the use of the word 'Mother' came with affection, not in the gently sarcastic or lecturing manner in which Jamie always used it. She suddenly sensed the presence of someone else in her room and became frightened, before calming at the familiar sensation of a small body climbing into her bed and a thin arm sliding around her.

'Mom, when are we goin' to see my great grandfather?'

Grace rolled over and put her arm around him. Relief had come instantly but it was quickly followed by another flush of the nausea she had been fighting all day.

'I'm gonna ask Boss to take us down there sometime next week. I don't trust that car of ours.'

For a while they lay silent, before Jamie spoke.

'I dreamt John was in my room again tonight, Mom. His voice woke me up.'

'Uh, huh,' Grace answered vacantly, reflecting briefly on the words she had heard before Jamie climbed into her bed. 'We're goin' to the toppermost of the poppermost!' was a unified cry the Beatles used to encourage themselves when things were not going so well in their early days. Jamie had heard Lennon talk about it in the *Imagine* movie and was using it often lately when he was joking around with his Liverpudlian accent. And tonight, Grace had been more than impressed with the rendition, if not a little surprised at how her waking mind had made her son's voice sound like a man's.

'And what did he say, Hon?' she asked in the same vacant manner, her tired eyes now closing.

Jamie giggled and said almost guiltily, 'Ah, just the bit about goin' to the toppermost of the poppermost.'

SEVEN

'So this is what ya get fo' whuppin' the Seventh Cavalry!'

Boss had grown up in almost dirt-poor circumstances but after the drive in to the village of Pine Ridge through a desolate landscape littered with rubbish, wrecks of old cars and dotted with clusters of rundown shacks he began to feel his was a privileged childhood. As they entered the village center, indicated only by a scattering of official buildings and stores, he added, 'Don' even look like no town to me.'

Jamie appraised the scene around him with keener eyes. In the little his mother had said about her birthplace she had painted a picture of a place not to be born and it was as she described. It was the expressions on the peoples' faces that depressed him most. Although his own face was physically disfigured, many of theirs wore the stamp of an unhappiness he had never known.

Grace was no less depressed. For the past couple of weeks the music had filled her mind with elevating thoughts of her people but, as she gazed around at the reality, she too had to fight against the old feelings of hopelessness.

Boss halted by the side of the road to allow a woman and two small, barefoot and undernourished-looking children to cross, the boy and girl with their heads down as they lethargically trailed behind the woman.

Grace watched them pass. She remembered the listless ones, whose one decent meal for the day was often only what the school could provide. The girl looked up at the pickup and another stinging memory suddenly caused Grace to turn away. She looked at the bus station, remembering the last time she was there, leaning out of the bus window to wave goodbye to the old man who had stood expressionless below. His words of farewell were still etched on her brain.

'Good luck, Songbird. Go and see what you can make of the outside world.'

Now she had returned from that world like a child coming home from school at the end of a semester, with mixed emotions and petrified at the thought of having to show her pathetic report card to her grandfather. But she needed him to see it and, courtesy of the phone call she had made to the Pine Ridge Post Office the day before, she knew he would be there to receive it.

'Yeah, old LB's still out there. Comes in once a month to pick up his lease check. Just send what you got care of the Post Office,' the female had said before hanging up.

Even though he had almost cleaned out two roadhouses of food during the drive down, Boss had been grumbling about needing something to eat ever since they had entered the reservation. As they moved up the road, Grace nodded in the direction of a filling station complex called Big Bat's. It looked to be the only modernized building in the village, its frontage brightly advertising everything from clothing to takeaway food. 'You can get something to eat over there, Boss. Nothing for me.'

Boss parked in front then he and Jamie went inside. Whilst waiting for their order to be filled, he watched Grace sitting in the car. Her head was down and she was slunk into the seat as if hiding from something, totally out of character for her usually bustling self.

'What's up with your Mom, Jamie? She ain't been happy since we left.'

Jamie didn't immediately respond. He was looking at a small boy standing with a group of women outside, shocked by the disfigurement of his upper lip. It was just like the girl's who had crossed the road in front of the pickup.

'She's frightened of meetin' her Granpa,' he distractedly replied.

Five minutes later Boss and Jamie returned to the vehicle, working on the demolition of two giant sub sandwiches with the lot.

'Follow the highway, Boss,' Grace said, pointing northwest along Route 18, the only main road through the reservation. 'It's about twenty miles out.'

'You sure you don't want any, Mom? This is one great sub. It's got your pickle in it.' Jamie held the sandwich in front of his mother's face, its mayonnaise-smothered innards spilling out of its sides.

Grace shuddered and pushed his hand away.

Jamie was elated with the refusal and began hungrily devouring the sub again. The food disappeared not very far along the highway and the two satisfied diners began happily conversing but Grace spoke little. The fear that had been rising from the pit of her stomach all morning was now threatening to choke her. She was also thinking of what had happened while waiting in the car outside Big Bats. Her attention had been drawn to a group of women standing in a huddle outside the door. They were talking animatedly but an elderly one on the outer edge of the group, initially with her back to Grace, slowly turned around and smiled serenely at her. The woman's weathered face was framed in a bright yellow flower-patterned scarf and it brought an instant but vague sense of recognition to Grace. She turned away, shrinking further into her seat. After a few seconds there had been no approach by the woman and Grace glanced furtively up to find she had gone.

Boss's booming voice suddenly snapped Grace out of her thoughts.

'Outgoin'!' he declared, as another car passed them at very high speed. He was no tortoise on the road but even his eighty miles an hour was being made to look slow. It had been happening regularly since entering the reservation, being left in the slipstream of nomads now riding a different kind of horsepower, their great floating, burbling beasts pouring exhaust smoke and trailing sparks as they bottomed out on the road surface. Both he and Jamie had been amusing themselves by yelling 'Incomin'!' or 'Outgoin'!' as the vehicles approached or passed, giving scores out of ten for their junkyard condition and the speed and recklessness of the drivers. Grace didn't see the humor. She only saw the regular appearance of crosses by the roadside and the face of a close childhood friend that had her twelve years of existence snuffed out in a back road head-on involving her parent's car and one full of drunken young road warriors – May Rose's parents died also – but the drunks survived.

At the approach of the next incoming vehicle she stared at it as she had done with each one that had passed, searching for people she might know, wondering if any of the somber faces inside were other childhood friends, young smiles wiped away by reservation reality.

Ten minutes later Grace directed Boss to take a turnoff and they headed down a gravel track that shook and rattled the vehicle savagely for three miles, before hitting a rise that led down into the barren gully where George Looks Back's tumbledown trailer home stood.

'Stop here,' Grace instructed as they topped the rise. 'You stay with Boss for a while, Jamie. I want to speak with Granpa first.'

Grace started out, the two hundred yards to the trailer home nowhere near the several miles she walked and hitched barefoot twice a day to and from school, yet now it felt like a hundred miles. Respect and caring for the elderly was a strong part of Lakota society and no matter how much she tried to justify her dereliction of duty, her feet were reminding her that she had abandoned her grandfather, each step that lifted the light dust wanting to retrace itself and flee.

The ramshackle abode in the bottom of the gully was surrounded by what looked like a commercial junkyard, set in the middle of the allotment ceded to her forebears in the Fort Laramie treaty of 1868. The three hundred and twenty acres had since been systematically broken up and distributed amongst the members of following generations, then eventually leased or sold off to white ranchers in the ongoing quest for survival. All that was left was a few acres on the edge of the white-owned cattle ranges.

Halfway down the track, Grace suddenly stopped as the door of the trailer opened and a familiar figure emerged. She watched with sadness and affection as the bent old man picked up a bucket and made his way slowly to a pump situated about thirty yards from the home. A mottled, skinny hound followed him to the water source, where he placed the bucket under the pump outlet and slowly worked the handle. Halfway through the task he stopped and turned around to peer in her direction.

Grace now felt like a hunted animal caught out in the open, Jamie's eyes drilling into her from the back and George's from the front. She continued on down the track. The dog began to bark at her approach and moved towards her but the old man with silver shoulder length hair remained motionless and staring. Her heart was pounding, her mouth gone dry, all the rehearsal of the previous hours, the previous years, all the things she had calmly planned to say now dissolving in her fear, her body threatening to collapse before him. She came closer and closer to the statue-like figure, the proud face of the Oglala elder slowly coming into focus, his eyes gazing as they had always done, into her, questioning her. She stopped a few feet before him and opened her mouth to speak but he beat her to it.

'Welcome back, Songbird. What have you made of your journey?'

Grace burst into tears. It was as though she had never been away, as if she really had just come home from a day at school. She stepped towards him, hugged him tightly and sobbed on his shoulder. 'A mess, Granpa,' she replied.

'Well, don't waste your tears there, girl. Aim 'em for the bucket so that I don't have to pump anymore.' The arms he had put around her briefly gave a tighter hold and then let go. 'Enough. Come inside. Bring the bucket,' he softly commanded.

Like an obedient child, Grace picked up the bucket and followed her grandfather. Neither spoke as they walked towards the trailer but George briefly glanced up at the vehicle that stood upon the rise.

From above, Jamie had been watching the reunion closely and Boss echoed his relief as the two figures disappeared inside the trailer.

'Well, it looks like your Mom don' need to be frightened no more.'

Inside the darkened interior of his home, George took the bucket from Grace and placed it next to an empty one sitting under the drain-hole of a washbasin that was fixed to the wall, complete with gleaming taps but no plumbing.

'As you can see, since you were last here I've had the decorators in to re-do the bathroom but it seems to me they might have forgotten somethin'.' He turned on one of the taps and scratched his head as he spoke, bringing a nervous chuckle from Grace. He then sat down at a small table crowded with bottles and jars, eating utensils and the crumbling remains of a loaf of bread, motioning her to a chair opposite.

'Speak to me, Sings At Dawn.'

Grace lifted her head and looked into the old man's rheumy eyes. Then she spoke, tears ebbing and flowing, fingers constantly running along the small stones hanging around her neck, her sad tale listened to in silence, until she could say and sob no more.

George picked up a jar of black jellybeans from the table, took some out, threw a couple to the hound lying on the floor then held the container out to her. 'Give the necklace a rest, Songbird. Have some of these instead. We find that they help.'

Grace uttered something between a cry and a laugh as she took a couple of the jellybeans and joined the old man and the dog, sucking and chewing.

George didn't speak again until he had slowly savored and swallowed his dose, then his voice again drifted quietly through the dark interior of the trailer, delivering some news unrelated to Grace's confession but almost as upsetting.

'They are buildin' a golf resort in the valley. We only heard about it late last year and they have moved swiftly. They brought the heavy machinery in some weeks ago and have put up walls at the entrance and fences to stop us seein' the damage they do. Some people have been out there to protest but the police drove them away. They tell me some of the younger ones have been protestin' for months through this thing they call the Internet but I'm afraid there is nothin' that can be done. The greenback has spoken. I haven't been out there since spring last year but I want to go one more time.'

'Bastards!' Grace declared. The valley was the one beautiful part of her childhood, a sacred place where two creeks ran into one and where the spirit of her great, great grandfather rested. As a young girl - every year on a certain day- her grandfather would take her to the valley and she would climb to a high place and sing to the spirit of her ancestor, a warrior-poet called Eyes That Cut, who had died there in the aftermath of the Battle of the Little Bighorn. They were his songs that she sang, handed down through the generations of her family, a bloodline of music that had now brought her back to where it had all begun, seemingly for her to begin again. She stared at the floor, deep in thought. She had been waiting for the moment to bring up the subject of the music and, like another piece of paper in the chase, the news of the valley had provided the way.

'Granpa... a few weeks ago I had a vision. I heard a flute playing a song I'd never heard before. I heard the cry of an eagle and it brought *Dream Warrior* back to me. Then I saw you.'

Grace went on to give Looks Back a full description of what had happened at Jimmy's; the day, the time and all that had followed; the lyrics and music coming from Jamie; the meeting with her former manager and her fear of the journey the songs seemed to be taking her on. When she finished, George stared intently at her for a few moments then spoke.

'Sing me this one you have named *Song Catcher*.'

Grace turned to look out the open doorway and then began to sing.

George sat with his eyes to the ground, listening closely to the lyrics and showing no sign of emotion until the first chorus, when Grace's voice rose like an eagle out of the midst of the striking melody. He suddenly looked upwards and began to sing the Lakota words with her, his feet beginning to shuffle lightly on the floor as if in a dance, before falling silent again as Grace moved into the second verse. He remained so until Grace finished the song and then said, 'You have caught a fine song. You must do as it says.' He stood up and went to an old cupboard standing in a corner of the cramped living quarters. He opened a bottom drawer and after rifling through its contents pulled out a worn hard-covered folder hinged with strands of leather thong. He handed it to Grace.

'Take the songs. They are part of your people's blood. Make it flow again.'

Grace nodded solemnly. The folder was an old, respected friend and she opened it with due reverence before briefly leafing through the yellowed pages. There were dozens of songs written down in now faded ink, although some of them were sacred ones she knew she couldn't use. All had once been committed to her child's memory and as soon as she glanced at those she had forgotten, they began to sing to her once more. She closed the folder and hugged it to her chest.

'Thanks, Granpa. I will.'

'Now, bring me my great grandson,' George commanded.

*

While Grace was in the trailer, the restless Jamie took a walk along the top of the rise, where he stopped for a while to stare out on the cattle range. A light wind was blowing and in the quiet away from the car it seemed to whisper through the new grass like a voice. He closed his eyes and softly spoke the lyrics of *North Wind* then abruptly stopped halfway through when he heard another sound far above him. He opened his eyes and looked at the sky but there was nothing to see except a few puffs of white cloud marking the blueness. The faint, high-pitched cry then swept up from the gully and he turned to see his mother waving at him.

Boss drove them down into the gully where Jamie hopped out and entered the trailer without any of his mother's apprehension, excitedly looking forward to seeing his great grandfather, although at first it was hard to make him out in the dark interior.

'Jamie, this is your great grandfather, George Looks Back,' Grace said, watching both of them closely.

'Come here, boy,' George said, beckoning with a finger.

Jamie stepped forward unhesitatingly and when he was within reach, George took his forearm firmly and pulled him in close. He put on the glasses that were hanging around his neck then held Jamie's jaw as he studied the scar across his upper lip, before settling on the eyes that stared back unwaveringly at him. 'Mmph,' he grunted as he nodded his head. He then stood up and held out the jar of jellybeans. 'Take some and come walk with me.'

Jamie helped himself to as many as his small hand could hold, smirking at the disapproving frown on his mother's face before following her and George out the doorway.

As the three emerged from the trailer, Boss got out of the car and Grace introduced him to George.

'Granpa, this is Boss, a friend of mine. He was kind enough to bring us here. He's the drummer man in the group. Boss, this is George Looks Back.'

'Hi y'all, Mister Looks Back,' Boss said, offering his hand.

George lifted his glasses to his eyes, looked up and nodded blank-faced at the big man as he shook his hand. He then moved past him, glancing at the ponytail hanging down Boss's back as he went. 'Be careful 'round here, big fella. That scalp o' yours 'd look mighty good hangin' on a lodge pole.'

Grace chuckled as George walked off, while Jamie gave Boss a playful punch in the belly as he passed.

Grace leant on the front of the pickup and watched closely as the two figures walked slowly along the track, skinny dog in tow; the bent, bow legged old man and her runt of a son with his twisted gait presenting the picture of perfection to her. She could see they were talking as they walked, or at least Jamie was, his face frequently turning up towards George's. Just as they were about to turn a corner and move out of sight, Looks Back's hand reached out to rest briefly on Jamie's shoulder. The gesture momentarily stunned Grace. She had never seen her grandfather show his affection in such a physical way to a relative stranger, blood relation or not.

'So, man... how did it go?' Boss asked.

'Good, fine. Granpa's okay with the songs,' Grace said, with a slight tremble in her voice. 'And there are more in here,' she added, holding up the folder before placing it in her bag.

It was about three-quarters of an hour later that the old man and the boy returned, both expressionless and seemingly content with whatever had passed between them. The three visitors would leave soon after but before they did, Grace handed her grandfather some money.

'I'm making a bit extra with my singing now so I'll be sending more, and we'll be back sometime during school vacation to take you out to the valley.'

George nodded briefly in acceptance then spoke softly as he stared at the boy who was checking out the tattered interior of his thirty-year-old Ford pickup. 'I don't think you have made such a mess, Songbird.'

Grace smiled, hugged him goodbye and then walked quickly to Boss's pickup, calling Jamie as she went.

'What's wrong, Mom?' Jamie asked when he jumped in to the vehicle to see her wiping her eyes.

'Nothing... now.'

George raised a hand and, as he waved goodbye, he recalled the melody that had awoken him very early on that Sunday morning, at exactly the same time as Songbird's vision. He knew it was the same time because he had checked the clock on his bedside table when the melodic sound pulled him from his sleep. Its arms had shown a few minutes to one. The sound was muted but gradually grew louder and shriller then it turned into a familiar cry before slowly fading away.

George had put on his boots and a heavy coat and followed the cry out into the wind and snow, trudging fifty yards up the slope before climbing over the cattle fence and moving out onto the open prairie. After a few more paces he came to a halt, searching the sky. The wind suddenly dropped, the clouds parted and the light of a full moon exploded across the white landscape, causing him to shut his eyes tightly against the sudden glare. It was in that moment he saw the image of his granddaughter. He could hear her singing *Dream Warrior* and a powerful voice shadowing hers, before an explosion of light instantly wiped away her image. A man's briefly flashed in her place. The song *Dream Warrior* changed to a Lakota one he had never heard before and the man's voice grew more powerful until all was suddenly erased by the clouds drawing a curtain across the moon. The wind and snow resumed and sent him hurrying back to his trailer.

*

After the pickup disappeared over the rise, George went inside the trailer and sat down at the table. He took some more thinking pills from the jellybean jar, put one in his mouth and reflected on what he had experienced that Sunday morning. It had seemed to happen in the blink of an eye. He had checked the clock again when he got back into bed to find the second hand still ticking past three minutes to one. There were times since that he wondered if it had all been a dream. Now, Grace's story had confirmed his vision, as had the boy's appearance, the latter making sense of what he had seen in its last moment. He threw a couple of jellybeans to the hound staring expectantly up at him. They chewed at each other for a while then he spoke to the animal in a soft low voice.

'A song catcher has come, old friend.'

*

The atmosphere in the pickup on the drive back to Deloraine was even more subdued than the journey down that morning, although Boss tried to sing and joke the other two out of their distracted moods. Jamie was especially unmoved, unusually silent in the company of his big friend. Grace observed his manner with curiosity, wondering what he and his great grandfather had spoken about. It wouldn't be until after he had showered and gone to bed later that night that she broached the subject.

'Are ya gonna tell me what you and Granpa spoke about?' she asked, as she rubbed some ointment on his back.

There was a brief silence before Jamie spoke.

'I'm still a little mad, Mom... findin' out about my relatives after all this time. I don't know how you could keep it all from me.'

'It's called fear, Jamie,' Grace calmly replied. For now, she had done enough bloodletting. Her grandfather had raised her spirits that morning, and all she wanted to know at the moment was what he had imparted to her son. 'Are you gonna tell me what he said?'

Jamie relented, his petulant manner quickly replaced by the excitement he had been suppressing, his mind buzzing with what he had learnt on the walk that day.

'He didn't say a lot but he told me some fantastic stuff... about my great, great, great grandfather. Anyway, I think that was how many greats there were. Eyes That Cut. What a terrific name!'

Grace hummed in agreement.

'Looks Back told me that Eyes That Cut fought with Crazy Horse. *Can you believe that*, Mom?'

'It's true. But maybe you should call him Great Granpa, or just Granpa.'

'Ah, *crap*, Mom! He told me to call him Looksth Back.'

Grace gave a short tugging rebuke on a small ear.

'Owww!'

'Go on... what did he say?'

'He spoke mostly about music. He said it was a voice that connected us all, to each other and to nature. He said that song catchers were important people... that Eyes That Cut was a great song catcher as well as a great warrior and the Lakota songs we are usin' came from him. He asked if I played an instrument but when I told him I had a guitar he seemed a bit puzzled.'

Wait till he hears you play it, Grace thought.

'For the rest of the time we sat lookin' out on the prairie while he just kept wavin' his hand through the grass, or chewin' on it.'

A reflective silence followed from Jamie, and then, 'He doesn't talk much but he says a lot.'

'Yeah, he does,' Grace concurred, and then added, 'But no one gets to talk much with you around, do they?'

'Guess not,' came Jamie's sleepy reply.

'That's it,' Grace declared, slapping him lightly on the butt as she pulled his T-shirt down. 'Time for sleep... *schooool* tomorrow,' she sang, as she stood up.

'Do I have to go tomorrow, Mom?' Jamie asked hopefully.

'Yes! One day off is more than enough. You've got a math test coming up soon and you're still struggling with that subject.'

'Aaar, stoof the fookin' math testht!' came the sudden declaration in Liverpool- speak.

Grace clipped the back of Jamie's head with a light flick of the hand, 'Don't use that sorta language!' she rebuked, unable to stop herself smiling but quickly straightening her face again as Jamie turned over and stared into her eyes.

There was a brief silence before he made a declaration. 'I just wanna write songs, Mom. I've got so many ideas in my head sometimes I think it's gonna burst, and I'm not gonna let schoolwork drive 'em outta me.'

Grace was startled by the defiance and the intense look in his eyes, taking several seconds before she could attempt to recover her position.

'Education will help you write more songs,' was her limp response.

The phrase sounded like a throwaway line from a schoolteacher and Jamie's deadening gaze confirmed the ineffectiveness of it. Then he changed the subject.

'When are we gonna see Looks Back again?'

'Soon. I promised to take him somewhere during summer vacation. It's a place I want you to see as well. Now go to sleep. You are still going to school tomorrow.'

Jamie sighed unhappily and closed his eyes.

Grace gave him a light peck on the forehead and walked towards the doorway but just as she switched off the light, something made her glance back into his room. The light from the hall was cutting a line across the poster that hung on the wall above Jamie's bed, meeting the darkness of the room just below the penetrating eyes of the very familiar face, granny glasses balanced on a hawk nose. From the half-shadow, John Lennon gazed with the similar piercing intensity she had just seen in her son's eyes and she stared thoughtfully at his face for several seconds before finally making her way to bed. There, she opened the container of the cassette she was going to send to Mark Hammond, took out the cardboard label and next to the songwriters' names of Jamie Howard, Grace Howard and Chas Montgomery she wrote Eyes That Cut. She turned off the bedside lamp to lie staring into the darkness for a long while, thinking about what her grandfather had told her about the valley. Her anger and frustration had been steadily growing on the drive home and now she was almost cringing with pain at the thought of earthmoving machines plowing through her ancestor's resting place, gouging away the flesh of the Grandmother.

EIGHT

The three front-end loaders swung around and came in for another sweep, the roar of their motors echoing through the hills surrounding the small valley and their black diesel breath pluming into the frosty air. In staggered formation they advanced, peeling off the dark soil and pushing it towards a row of pegs at the lower end of the valley, where they raised, upended and emptied their mouths before bouncing away for another approach.

Gary Schroeder watched as the machines came in again, occasionally slapping his arms around his body to keep the circulation going. As head surveyor on the Hidden Valley Golf Course development he was supervising the earthworks on an artificial lake being dug out halfway down the valley. It was where two spring-fed creeks joined together and when the thaw came, they would be a natural feeder for the lake and other water hazards that were to be placed around the course. But it was the present hazard of the creeks that had Gary tramping around in the late winter cold of the Black hills, the early earthworks scheduled to temporarily contain their flow before construction began in the spring.

Powder snow began drifting through the valley and he shivered at its onset. It was almost a metaphor for his life at the moment. A few weeks ago he had been enjoying the sunshine of Southern California, settling there after fifteen years working as a freelance surveyor on large projects all over the world. He had earned big money and saved enough through those years to build a decent investment portfolio, including the purchase of a luxury apartment in Huntington Beach, leased out and paid off while he roamed the planet. Its high rent return and good appreciation had convinced him to invest all of his funds in a similarly managed apartment complex planned for nearby. He bought two apartments off the plan and, although he had to take out a three hundred thousand dollar loan against his apartment to get them, he figured that when the development was finished, the income from it would allow him to sit back and relax for a while. But he wouldn't even get to the chair. A few months into the project's construction, the developer went broke. As it transpired, Gary's and everyone else's money was being used to transfuse another project that was hemorrhaging from cost overruns. The ultimate collapse of that project finally sucked everything into an insolvency black hole. What followed were costly legal proceedings by the investors which he knew would turn into years of the same with no guarantee of recovering anything at the end.

Although shocked by his losses, Gary swiftly adapted to reality. With mortgage payments to meet, his share of the investor groups' legal fees to pay and his contract at a Canadian mine site about to end, he had to find work quickly. He put out feelers amongst his industry contacts and it led him to the Prestige project. After a telephone enquiry and an emailed resume, he took a flight to New York for an interview at their head office. A week later he was told he had the job so he leased out his apartment once more then found one in Rapid City, where Prestige were basing their operations. It had all gone smoothly but, soon after starting work, he had begun to feel uncomfortable about taking the contract on.

As Gary waited for the machines to bring in more soil, he gazed across at one of the reasons for his discomfort. Referred to by him and the other workers as 'Stalag 13', the machinery compound had an intimidating effect, with its ten foot high metal-sheeted fence topped with razor wire and four 'SS guards' housed in transportable accommodation, manning a booth at the gate in shifts around the clock. They were all distant, uncommunicative types who looked like nightclub bouncers and their heavily armed presence had created a climate of unease on site. Whilst he was aware of the sensitive nature of building in the Black Hills and the need for tight security, the amount applied to the compound had puzzled him, considering a substantial fence had already been built around the entire site.

His thoughts drifted back to the job interview and the quizzing he received over the Black Hills ownership issue. At the time, he had truthfully replied that he had no strong feelings on the matter. He was aware of the history of it, how the Lakota had won a sixty year-long legal battle in 1980 to prove ownership of the land taken from them over a hundred years before. They had refused the monetary payment offered and in the twenty years since, the amount, including interest had grown to several hundred million dollars. He had wondered why they just didn't take it and run. He couldn't see any chance of what they considered to be sacred country ever being handed back. Wherever he had worked in the world, progress eventually took priority over such things. He had never felt particularly good about seeing native peoples pushed aside but the fact that he had already taken part in the process elsewhere gave him no moral ground to stand upon regarding the Black Hills. The atmosphere that prevailed on site, however, had begun to tilt his ambivalence, especially after the day he witnessed a group of protestors being brutally forced away from the entrance by the guards, in tandem with some local police. He had just arrived for work and as the protesters filed past his vehicle they had verbally abused him, but it was the utter hatred in their eyes that had most affected him.

Gary turned his face away from the guard gazing fixedly at him from the compound booth then watched as the loaders deposited more soil and swung away again. He leaned down to peer through the lens of the theodolite to check the row of pegs defining the height of the lake's retaining wall. As he turned the instrument from one peg he muttered a curse at something restricting his view of the next one. He ran down to remove the object before the loaders came in for another sweep, expecting it to be just another piece of the tree roots the machines had been constantly kicking up. However, when he pulled the dirt caked object out of the earth, something stopped him from hurling it away. About two foot long and six inches in diameter, it felt much lighter than timber. He brushed some dirt off it to reveal what looked like a bundle of old leather. He studied it for a moment then secretively placed it under his jacket, away from the eyes watching from the booth. He then picked up a piece of tree root that lay near his feet and made a show of throwing it out of the way before walking back to his Chevvy pickup. Using the pretence of retrieving a plan from the cab, he slipped the bundle under the seat.

An hour later he was seated in his vehicle having a cup of coffee, the object resting on his lap. The brittle binding around the bundle had broken into pieces as he attempted to unwind it and now he was examining a large corner of the wrapping that had snapped off when he tested the stiff folds of the material. He was peering with great interest at the faded upper part of a painted figure on the leather when a black Jeep Cherokee pulled up next to him. He quickly shoved the bundle under the seat as the unwelcome form of the site manager climbed out and hurried to the pickup.

Gary's upper lip curled with disdain. Hal Whitman was another part of the job he wasn't enjoying. He had previously checked up on the site manager through the industry grapevine. At just over thirty, nine years younger than him, he was a ruthless go-getter who always managed to bring his contracts in under time. Initially, Gary saw only benefit in the appraisal as it increased his chance of a very generous early completion bonus. He soon learned, however, that the price of it was going to be high. He had worked under some difficult site managers in his time but this one was way up there on the pushy bastard scale.

'Mornin' Schroeder... any coffee left?' the hyperactive man with the designer-mess hairdo asked as he climbed in next to Gary, rubbing his gloved hands energetically. He immediately added, 'You gonna have this finished today? We need to get that clay liner in asap.'

'Cup in there somewhere,' Gary said, lifting his head unenthusiastically towards the glove box. His supply had to last him all day and he hadn't allowed for freeloaders.

Whitman rustled through a pile of papers and other discarded items, found the dirty cup and made a show of wiping it out with a tissue before pouring some of the dark steaming liquid into it from the large thermos on the seat. '*So*, today?' he asked after taking a couple of sips.

'It's getting there.'

Whitman's thinking and speech were always in rapid-fire mode but Gary's laconic reply brought an almost manic response. 'Faster than your attitude I hope! How long has everyone been on a break anyway?' he said as he studied the three stationary machines with the drivers chatting and drinking coffee in one of the cabins.

'Not long.'

'It's been long enough to drink coffee,' Whitman said as he finished his and tossed the cup back into the glove box. 'Get those machines movin'! And where's your survey hand, anyway?'

Gary took a casual sip of his coffee before answering. 'Didn't need him today. No point in both of us freezing our balls off.'

'Yeah, well you make sure he's back here tomorrow. I want you to get on to finishing the layout of the entrance road. And I want you...'

Whitman's cell-phone interrupted any further instructions and getting a broken signal he climbed out of the pickup and ran back to his vehicle. He jumped in, started it with a roar and drove off machismo, wheels spraying mud and phone clamped to his ear as he headed for the top of the valley.

Gary waited until Whitman's vehicle had disappeared over the rise behind him before reaching down and finding the broken corner of the object he had placed under the seat. He had just taken a big risk. At the interview, specific mention had been made to him about any artifacts found on site; no matter how small, they were to be immediately handed in and not spoken about to fellow employees or, more importantly, to outsiders. The ruling had nothing to do with State or Federal laws regarding any archaeological finds. Apart from the finding of human remains no action was required by developers if any artifacts were uncovered during the construction of a privately funded project on private land. It was about the fear that protesters could use the knowledge of any kind of find to stir up public interest and disrupt progress of the project. Underlining the company's paranoia in this regard was a broad clause in every worker's contract allowing for instant dismissal if any employee was considered to have done anything to threaten the project's completion schedule. Just the fact that Gary had not instantly informed anyone of his find would get him the sack. It would be a black mark against his name in the industry but, although he was in no financial position to gamble with his future employment prospects, his natural curiosity took over.

He put the broken corner back under his seat, hit the horn then got out of his car and waved his hand in a circling motion to the men sitting in the pay loader. Work resumed and several hours later the earth formation of the lake was complete. Tomorrow they would begin work placing the clay liner on it from the giant stockpile of material that had been trucked in the previous autumn.

Gary, however, had other things on his mind as he headed back to his Rapid City apartment. That night he checked the Internet and found some instructions on how to soften the rock-hard buckskin wrapping of the bundle. For such old leather items he needed a tray of cold water mixed fifty percent with ethanol to kill the fungi then he had to suspend the bundle above it and cover it all with a plastic tent, leaving humidity to do the job. The next morning, he bought some ethanol and made a tent out of some wire and cling wrap. He then hung the bundle from the top of it, above the tray of fluid, before going to work.

Within a day the process had begun to work and, that evening, Gary started carefully unwrapping the outer casing.

Every night over the next week he slowly unraveled more and, as the interior began to reveal itself, the end of each working day became a race back to his apartment to continue with his amateur archeology. He became obsessed by it, at times forgetting to eat as, bit-by-bit, new sections of what would finally open out into a three-foot diameter pictograph were revealed to him.

It was shortly before one o'clock on a Sunday morning when he carefully flattened out the last fold of the thin buckskin, uncovering another bundle wrapped in faded red cloth. He put it aside and briefly surveyed the complete piece of art. The inside of the buckskin was stained but the drawings in dark outline could be clearly made out, although the colors of red, yellow and blue were faded. They defined the life path of someone he now felt close to, the days slowly revealing a story winding around a circular trail full of figures; of Indians fighting Indians, animals being hunted, people dancing and, towards the end of it, unmistakable blue-coated images carrying swords and rifles facing up to a group of warriors. At the very end, away in the bottom corner there lay a man on his back, with what looked to be the same person rising out of his chest. This figure was painted in a different color to the rest of the pictograph, his image outlined in a rusty, dark brown substance that tended to flake away as the bundle was unrolled. But it was the same image of the warrior prominent in all of the set pieces and on the corner he had initially broken off. This showed his seated figure with what appeared to be knives flying from the eyes and small birds from the mouth.

Gary turned his attention to the red cloth bundle. As he carefully unfolded it, some of the fragile material fell away at his touch and he could see bone underneath. He hesitated but his curiosity soon overcame his apprehensiveness. He tentatively pulled the rest of the material away and was relieved to find, not human remains, but a rolled up bone breastplate. There were other objects wrapped up inside and he eagerly unrolled it, to reveal a ball of pliable leather about as big as two cupped hands, a separate piece of hollowed bone about eight inches long, a small braid of dried grass, a lock of black hair and two eagle feathers. He carefully prized up the top layer of the leather ball and could see an object inside, encrusted with the same brownish flaky material as on the pictograph. It looked like the kind of mummified flesh he had seen in documentaries about Egypt and the ancient remains found in European peat bogs. He quickly covered it up and put it aside then picked up the flute. The smooth, white hollowed bone was closely beaded in colors of red, black and yellow for about an inch at one end, where two small feathers were attached. Five holes of varying diameter were placed about an inch apart down the middle.

Gary wiped the mouth of the small flute with a cloth dabbed in ethanol, rubbed it dry then placed it to his lips and gently blew on it. His tentative breath brought a soft but eerie sound as he alternated his fingers over the holes in the manner of playing a trumpet. He messed around for a couple of minutes searching for tunes then placed it back on the table. He suddenly felt very tired. He had pushed it a little further this evening knowing he was near to revealing the bundle's contents and that he had Sunday off. He looked up at the wall clock to see an hour of it had already passed and he got up from his desk and headed for a shower and bed. All through his ablutions, however, the strange tone of the flute kept playing in his mind. It remained there after he drifted off to sleep and, as he entered the dreaming zone, it began to play a soft and lilting melody sounding as if it was coming from far away.

NINE

The sound of the eagle-bone whistle drifted up through the cottonwood trees in peaceful contrast to the activity in the camp a few hundred yards away, where people shouted, dogs barked, dust swirled and horses whinnied in protest as their owners attempted to lassõ them.

The distinctive sound of the whistle confirmed where Fawn had said her husband would be, down by the river, catching his songs. But Walks Softly couldn't see exactly where his friend was as he fought his way through the thick foliage near the water's edge.

'*Hó-ye-ya!*' he called out loudly.

Eyes That Cut murmured with irritation at the sound of the voice. He had caught a new song and was playing it to some sparrows he had enticed to the ground with a few crumbs of pemmican. They had been pecking around his cross-legged form when the interruption from his friend suddenly sent them flapping away, calling out with alarm.

'Dreaming again?' came Walks Softly's accusation, as he burst through the brush into his friend's hiding place.

Eyes That Cut looked up at the intruder, all dressed and painted for battle, the top half of his face blacked out and the bottom all white. His softened countenance changed back to the sharp-eyed look that gave him his name.

'If I am it must be a bad dream,' he uttered, and then followed with, 'Have you ever thought of changing your name, my friend? It seems to me that, for someone called Walks Softly, you cover the ground like a buffalo with a lance up its fuel-making end.'

'And *you, Tongue* That Cuts?' came the instant response.

Both men remained straight-faced but their eyes twinkled with the exchange.

'Can't you hear the commotion in the camp?' Walks Softly finally asked.

Eyes That Cut had vaguely heard something in the midst of his flute playing but once again the music was in control, holding everything else at bay as he searched for another melody on his modified instrument; the eagle bone whistle they had all laughed at when he had made five holes in it. It created music instead of the unearthly, fear-inspiring sound that warriors used the hollowed out bones for when going into battle. Now, they sat around the fires and listened with pleasure to the song catcher with his instrument of many notes and his fine singing voice. Often other bands would stop by to hear him sing his songs, and after sitting for hours this morning beside the river he had another one to add to his repertoire. All he could think about now was to sing it to Fawn, the keeper of his songs, his doe-eyed wife of the never-ending mind who held everything she heard and saw like the sky held the land.

Walks Softly could see the familiar dazed look on his friend's face and didn't wait for an answer.

'Riders from Crazy Horse's camp came in a little while ago. He is organizing the bands for battle. More thieves are upon the road! I have brought your best pony.'

Eyes That Cut had never really been interested in the way of the warrior and often opted out of the raids on tribal enemies. Stronger motivating factors than tit-for-tat stealing of horses and the gathering of scalps were needed for him to leave the dreaming world of his music. But being led by Crazy Horse was one of them and chasing the white man from his country another. At the sound of the war chief's name he got to his feet and followed Walks Softly to their two ponies. Then, as they had done in almost every activity since childhood, the two men made a competition of the ride to the group of tepees in the distance, entering the camp at a full gallop, charging their way through the milling crowd of people and animals before pulling their mounts up in front of Eyes That Cut's lodge. He slid off his pony's back smiling at his victory by a length before bending down and entering through the open flap of his home.

Inside, Fawn had already laid out his battle gear and when he appeared she began dressing him, while outside, the other warriors called out loudly as they rode past his lodge, criticizing him for his tardiness as they galloped off. Eyes That Cut ignored their intrusion and quietly sang the new song he had named *The Water Talks* to Fawn.

Fawn deftly fitted two eagle feathers to the back of his head and tied the thongs of his breastplate around his neck and the small of his back. She then applied a broad stroke of red ochre across his face, running diagonally from over one eyelid and across both lips to end at his chin. It was her husband's statement that, in battle, beauty could not be seen or music played.

'That is enough,' she declared.

'You have my song, wife?'

Fawn nodded, a thin, nervous smile on her face.

Eyes That Cut picked up his tomahawk, the breech-loading Spencer he had taken from a dead foe at a previous skirmish and a small ammunition bag. He touched his wife's face briefly and smiled in his sad, defiant kind of way before leaving the tepee.

Fawn emerged to watch him go. Her eyes shone with pride as he galloped off after the war party. In peace, Eyes That Cut was as gentle as any man could be, always singing his songs and speaking with nature, but when needed in battle he was as fierce as any in their band. She wasn't smiling, however, as she watched the men galloping away, gesturing and shouting, urging each other on to brave deeds. As they disappeared over a rise she softly sang the words of her husband's new song. Like many others it was in homage to their land and she feared its words would become his epitaph.

'Mother
I sing for you
I fight for you
I die for you'

It was the third time this summer that the band had been called away in defense of their country, continuing almost ten summers of constant interruption to tribal life since the early victories Red Cloud had had against the US army along the Bozeman trail. The Lakota called it the 'Thieves Road', a trail that had opened up their country to the flood of white men looking for land and gold. Red Cloud's successful campaign had forced the government into drawing up the Fort Laramie treaty of 1868, legally ceding the Black Hills to the various bands of the Lakota and Dakota people. However, the document had only served to delay the invasion of the hunting grounds and their sacred *Paha Sapa*. Thanks to an inflated assessment by journalists attached to an army expedition led by Brevet Major General George Armstrong Custer- that 'the hills were filled with gold from the grass roots down', the seekers of the yellow metal were pouring in. Their presence was in total defiance of what had been written in the treaty but so many treaties had been made and broken, and the woman with the eternal mind could see what was up ahead and what was surely being left behind.

Fawn walked back inside their lodge with her ten-year-old son, Runs With Horses and six-year-old daughter, Sky. She took a frame of wood with a piece of buckskin stretched upon it and, with her children watching intently, she began to add some more of Eyes That Cut's story to the pictograph. Skillfully, she sketched the figure of a husband and father riding off to another battle in a war she knew all the warriors of the Lakota could not win.

The fabric of the free and independent society in which Fawn had grown up was fraying at the edges. More and more, her people were settling around the agencies, taking handouts and ceasing to roam the prairies at will. Even her father, White Hand, had become one of the agency people. He had been a fine warrior but he was old now and worn down by the fighting of his youth. He didn't want to starve out there on the prairie where it was getting harder and harder to find game. Like many others he had taken his grant of land handed out in the Fort Laramie treaty and settled with Red Cloud at the agency in northwest Nebraska that bore the Chief's name. For the sake of their two children, White Hand had tried to convince his daughter and her husband to join him but, as reluctant as he was to make war, Eyes That Cut held the same fierce pride and love of freedom that Crazy Horse did and he was prepared to die for it - and for him.

Beloved of his people, Crazy Horse was a fearless but quiet, intelligent man who, when dreaming himself into the real world of the spirit, once saw his horse dancing as if it were wild or crazy. Eyes That Cut had caught a song about his leader's dreaming medicine and courage in battle. He called it *Dream Warrior* but it also reflected his own powerful dreaming where not a horse, but music, danced. It had been doing so since he was a boy; since that first strange dream of a white man dressed in dark clothes, seated in a white lodge. Each time, in this dream, a small woman dressed in white walked through, opening the sides of the lodge and letting the light in, as Fawn would so often do for him. Although he couldn't quite see her face, her long black hair gave him a sense that she was one of his people. The woman would sit with the man before a big, flat, white box where his fingers made strange but peaceful music as they ran along the edge of it. He couldn't see his face either, only the pale fingers that told him he was a white man, or a ghost. One day, he hoped that, when he finally left the shadow world, he could meet this song catcher, whose strange music had led him to make a fine flute and sometimes helped him complete his own songs.

*

The attack on the latest group of intruders ended as few of the later battles would. After a short skirmish that brought no deaths but several wounded on both sides, the superior numbers of the Lakota forced the gold-seekers to head back the way they had come. But it was a tiny victory as all through the summer many more of their number managed to evade the fierce defenders of the Black Hills and enter its heavily wooded environs. Some of the prospectors would be chased out and some killed but, instead of making them comply to the treaty, the politicians in Washington decided to send the army into the northern hunting grounds of the Plains tribes to enforce an ultimatum that they go to the reservations. A great number resisted and about a year later, in the late spring of 1876, the man who had initially inflamed the conflict led one part of a three-pronged expedition into a valley of the Little Bighorn river.

Eyes That Cut was not with the others that dispatched Long Hair and his men in less time than it took to skin a buffalo. He was away visiting some Cheyenne friends when they were attacked by a force under the command of a Major Marcus Reno, the first commander to make the mistake of rattling the hornet's nest - an encampment spreading for almost three miles along the west bank of the river. Reno's surprise thrust was soon turned into a retreat and then a rout but during it, Eyes That Cut received terrible injuries. A soldier, whose horse had been shot from under him, fired at the charging warrior from a kneeling position. The bullet smashed through his upper teeth and lip, just missing the eye when it deflected off his cheekbone. The impact of the slug threw him off his horse and he landed badly, fracturing the lower part of his spine and rendering his legs useless. He was rescued by other warriors but would suffer terribly from his injuries in the days that followed. The native remedies failed to have any effect on the infection that swiftly came to the face wound, his once handsome countenance swelling to ugly proportions and his mouth constantly seeping with pus. It was almost impossible for him to eat and he grew weaker by the day but it was the broken back that took most of him away, having to lie strapped to a travois and be tended to like a helpless baby while his people fled from their victory.

The US army had suffered one of their greatest defeats in all their wars with the Plains tribes but it turned into a greater defeat for the Lakota, who were to be endlessly punished after their brief glory, hounded across the plains and through the mountains by a vengeful government. Straight after the battle, the bands began splitting up and disappearing into the surrounding country. Eyes That Cut, Walks Softly and their families joined a group of about fifty Oglala heading for a place of refuge in a southwest corner of the Black Hills but, one late summer afternoon, just as they neared their destination, the searchers caught up with them.

In the early morning of that day, during another sweating, pain-wracked sleep, Eyes That Cut dreamt once more of the white song catcher but, this time, the woman wasn't there and he couldn't hear any sound coming from the white music box. The man's hands seemed to be doing something else, before he suddenly stood up and walked out of the lodge. Eyes That Cut was drawn to follow. He stopped at the entrance to another white lodge but the man was nowhere to be seen, only a small form lying on what looked like a burial platform covered with white robes. He stepped into the lodge and then all dissolved into whiteness.

*

The Crow scout lay on the ridge, his cold, narrow eyes surveying the group of Lakota moving through the valley below and, after calculating how many warriors were amongst them, he quickly belly-crawled backwards away from their vigilant gaze. He jumped upon the pony he had tied to a tree some fifty yards behind, walked it for a hundred, trotted it for another and then urged it more quickly towards the cavalry troop now slowly winding its way through a gully about a mile to the south. A few minutes later, fifty of the troop were moving out at a full gallop, leaving ten men behind to escort the supply wagons. They topped the rise just as the refugees were approaching the end of the valley and beginning to move up the ridge that separated it from the next one. At the command, the soldiers moved quickly down in single file and lined up a few hundred yards behind their quarry. For a moment they hesitated there, the officer in charge holding his men back, hoping their superior numbers would intimidate and bring surrender rather than a battle against a foe he knew was already defeated.

Captain Henry Carver wasn't at the fiasco on the Little Bighorn but had spent many years fighting the Lakota and other Plains tribes. He had begun his service as a brash Second Lieutenant hell bent on bringing the 'savages' to heel but over the years had gradually developed a respect for their courage in battle and their pride as a people. Now he felt sadness at seeing their world coming to an end and held no joy at being in the vanguard of those chasing them into history. He would wait in the hope that a warrior would separate from the group and ride out with a message of surrender. A few minutes later one would ride out but not in the way he had hoped.

The people heard the soldiers coming well before they saw them appear at the top of the ridge, and by the time the blue column had moved into formation at the bottom, the women, children and elderly, most of them on foot, had separated from the warriors and begun to move up the slope before them. Fawn was at the rear, leading the horse dragging the travois upon which her husband lay but, as she tried to hurry it along, Eyes That Cut called out for her to halt. He then told her to dress him for battle and bring Walks Softly to him.

A few minutes later, adorned with his two eagle feathers, breastplate and the distinctive flash of red running along the edge of his face wound, Eyes That Cut was lifted onto his pony by his friend and another warrior. His trunk had been strapped tightly with a corset of rawhide and, to hold him upright, his feet were lashed together with thongs passed under the pony's belly. He moaned with pain all through the process but, as he took his rifle from Fawn's hand, for a brief moment he fell silent, his hand lingering on hers as he looked into her eyes. Then he nodded at Walks Softly and screamed with pain as the savage blow applied to his pony's hindquarters sent it exploding forward. He passed through the line of his fellow warriors at a full gallop, his body shining with the sweat of fever, his chilling cry holding them momentarily transfixed as he flew away on his suicide run.

The sound of carbine hammers clicking back rattled along the line of soldiers at the sight of the horseman racing towards them but the captain spoke calmly to the lieutenant by his side, telling him to issue an order for them to hold fire. He had seen the 'bravery runs' before. Always they were frightening but mostly they were done as a face-saving act before talking could commence. Yet, as he watched this warrior coming on, he grew puzzled at his appearance. His was not the graceful, fluid motion of the expert horsemen he knew. Instead the rider appeared stiff, clumsy, as though it were a dead man strapped upright to the horse. Then he heard the wailing sound, not the triumphant shouting of a defiant buck but a deep and terrible cry that brought both wonder and fear, before the cry began to change to a melodic chanting.

Many of the soldiers lined up behind their captain were raw recruits just a few days out of Fort Robinson and a few weeks from basic training in the East, some still learning how to control a horse. Brought in for the big roundup, or turkey shoot as they were led to believe, the only 'Indians' they had seen were the so-called tame ones that hung around the fort. When they saw and heard the lone warrior racing towards them, total confusion reigned. This was not the way they figured it would be. They were supposed to be doing the attacking and, as the rider got closer and no command came to fire, the nervous shifting in saddles brought a similar nervousness from the animals underneath. They tossed their heads, whinnied and began to stamp their feet, rapidly escalating the tension.

The savage closed swiftly and his strangely comical motion inspired a drawling comment from one of the veterans. 'This one looks like he's bin chuggin' firewater fer lunch.' His words were followed by him spitting a gob of tobacco juice that kicked up the dust below his horse. A few of his older peers chuckled, while the paradox of what the young soldiers could see only increased their fear and uncertainty. They glanced nervously at the more experienced men, seeking reassurance, but the gaze of the hardened veterans remained fixed stonily on the form that was rapidly closing on them, a rifle raised defiantly in one hand, the other grasping the horse's mane.

The shock that traveled up from every hoof beat of Eyes That Cut's pony met the fractured intersection of his spine and flared out through his body as though his raw nerves were connected to the earth his mount was pounding across. He screamed louder in the attempt to mask the all-consuming pain but all it did was open up the half-healed wound of his mouth, causing blood and pus to run freely. The sound spurred his mount to run faster, increasing the agony that filled his mind like the searing light in the first stages of the Sun Dance. Halfway from his objective that is what he decided to see. He turned his face to the sky. His mind passed through the bright curtain of pain and he sang to Fawn.

In the darkness
I see you
Your light shines as the sun

As he sang the words, he raised his rifle and fired, without aim, without care.

The rifle's report was instantaneously met by another from the group of soldiers and although the panicked shot from the young soldier missed his target by a good six feet, the salvo that immediately followed hit the horse and rider like a hailstorm.

Eyes That Cut's body jerked with the impact of the bullets that made popping sounds as they passed through his primitive corset and breastplate. His head snapped back with one that grazed his skull and his rifle flew from his hand as another tore open his forearm. His other hand fell from the horse's mane. His body slumped and swung about wildly but the thongs lashed around his feet still held him to its back. His violent movement urged the pony to go faster, its battle heart at one with the rider, until a bullet ruptured it and only momentum drove it forward.

The pony's legs began to buckle about twenty yards away from the confusion of troops trying to control their terrified mounts. Ten yards away from them it died but its body continued on, barreling into the milling mess of soldiers and horses with a sickening crash of bone and flesh. Several soldiers were sent flying from their mounts. Horses ran off in terror, one of them limping away with the broken half of a foreleg swinging around freely. The general panic increased when the soldiers saw the other warriors charging towards them, only a hundred yards away now and closing with the same fearless purpose as their predecessor. Unable to form a close defense quickly out of the confused ranks, the order was given to retreat back up the slope of the ridge behind. The men on foot were scooped up as the troop galloped towards the ridge, where they quickly dismounted and scattered amongst the protection of the rocks.

The warriors pressed home their temporary advantage but, after exchanging a few shots at the entrenched troops, they swung away again. They had little ammunition left after the encounter at the Little Bighorn and didn't want to waste it or reveal their position, riding away in a seemingly unconcerned manner as part of the subterfuge.

Walks Softly hadn't ridden on with the others that chased the soldiers up the slope of the ridge. He stopped where Eyes That Cut had fallen, quickly dismounted and cut his mangled body from his pony but, as he did so, he heard a faint moan and saw his friend's now dulled eyes slowly open and stare at him. For a few seconds the two men gazed at each other, until Eyes That Cut nodded weakly and closed his eyes again. Walks Softly then kneeled behind him and, chanting a song, he lifted his friend's head and wrapped an arm around it, embracing him for a brief moment. With a swift and powerful twist he then sent him to the real world.

Tears rolled down Walks Softly's face as he took out his knife, cut away the corset of animal hide and removed the breastplate. He couldn't take his friend's body away, his own tired pony was now hardly able to carry him and he knew the soldiers would soon be chasing them again. Before they did he would retrieve the most important part of a warrior. There was no time for the fire but he made the motion of washing his hands and cleansing his knife in the imaginary smoke of the sweet grass, crying out the brave deeds of his friend whilst doing so. He made three motions with the blade as if about to cut then did so with the fourth, slicing into the chest cavity of Eyes That Cut and removing his heart. He then cut away his friend's breechclout, quickly wrapping the warm organ in it, before cutting off a lock of his hair and placing it in the rolled up chest plate along with the two eagle feathers. He completed his task just as the others returned to him, then jumped upon his pony and rode away, still crying out his admiration for his friend as he went.

Captain Carver watched them go. He knew that their lack of willingness to remain and fight was about more than being outnumbered. He knew that if they had had enough ammunition they would have hung around longer. He would take his time following, knowing it would be easy to track the group and bring them to heel. They would be tired and hungry and the longer that debilitating process was allowed to continue the less resistance there would be. He waited for the supply wagons to arrive and for the stray animals to be rounded up or destroyed and about half an hour later set off again. When they reached the place of Eyes That Cut's demise, the Captain called a brief halt. He looked down at the ugly mess that remained of the warrior and gave a slow almost imperceptible nod of respect. He told two men to wrap him in a blanket and place him in one of the empty wagons they had brought for the expected dead and wounded. He then ordered the column to move out again, following the clear tracks like wolves after a weakened prey.

The warriors came upon the rest of the people in a valley, where two creeks ran into one. When Fawn heard their approach, she didn't look up with those anxious to see whether husbands, brothers or sons had returned. She had already begun to mourn. She had stopped at the top of the slope as the rest of the group hurried away, listening to the sound of her husband's voice drifting to her on the wind and watching as he and his pony pierced the enemy like an arrow. She then turned away and followed the others, bracing herself for what she had been expecting ever since he had been wounded at the big battle. But when Walks Softly caught up to her and gave her all he had retrieved, the strength fell away and she dropped to her knees and wailed. While the others continued on, she took a knife and made several cuts on her arms, unmindful of the warning Walks Softly had given her that the soldiers would soon be upon them again. At that moment she wished he would cut her heart out and place it with her husband's. But as she watched her people scurrying away she saw her two children lagging behind, staring back at her with sad, frightened eyes.

'I will follow soon,' she called out to Walks Softly.

As the others disappeared through the trees above the valley and headed for a canyon on the other side, Fawn used her knife to dig a hole as deep as she could in the path of disturbed ground they left behind. Opening the bundle she had been carrying on her back she took out the pictograph and her chewed stick paintbrush. Dipping it into the blood now streaming down her arms she quickly painted the figure of her man lying on his back with his spirit rising from his chest. She then laid out a piece of red cloth on the pictograph and placed upon it the items Walks Softly had given her, adding a piece of quickly braided dry grass and the special eagle-bone whistle. She rolled everything up in the buckskin story of Eyes That Cut, tied it with a thong and buried it, marking the place with three round stones set in a triangle, each three paces from the hole. She was fearful that her band was about to lose everything but if she survived she would come back for her husband's Spirit Bundle and set him free in the proper way. Until then he could lie in the arms of the Grandmother.

Leaving the valley behind, Fawn walked up the long slope of the hill and entered the wall of pine trees that ringed the base of the granite outcrop rising above the forest. She caught up with the remainder of the group just as they began to enter what they had hoped would be the sanctuary of a hidden cave but now feared might be their grave.

Dusk was falling by the time the soldiers had reached the valley where Fawn had buried the Spirit Bundle, and they would spend the night there next to one of the rippling creeks before moving on early the next morning. As Captain Carver had expected, the tracks of their quarry were easy to follow and when the scout returned to tell him that the group were holed up in a cave only half a mile ahead, he called a halt. This time he would take the initiative in trying to find a peaceable end to the situation and approached them unarmed under a white flag accompanied only by a sergeant who had fluency in Lakota.

Fleet Foot, an aging chief long past his fighting prime came out to meet the two soldiers. He listened quietly to the request for him and his people to surrender, with the promise that no harm would come to them if they did, and then responded in a calm, resigned way. 'I cannot believe your promises. I see that our people have already come to great harm by your presence in our land and that you seek to finally kill us by sending us to the reservation. I ask you to leave this sacred place. But if you choose not to, you must know that even though we are mostly old people and women and children, there is not one who will not fight you if you attack.'

Captain Carver half-expected the answer and with a heavy heart he ordered his men up to within sight of the cave mouth where they could apply crossfire into it. He had his sergeant make a final request that the people inside surrender and received the same defiant answer, followed by a volley of gunfire that wounded one soldier. The soldiers were ordered to reply but the shooting battle didn't last long. After several minutes of intense fire, there would be no more shots fired from the cave and no answer to the third request for surrender. Instead, a haunting, moaning sound drifted from the mouth of the cave, as if the mountain itself were crying. The captain ordered the men to hold fire and then they waited. The sound of suffering continued, building in volume before it gradually ebbed away. A few minutes later the survivors of the barrage began to straggle from the cave.

The next morning, the column set out for Fort Robinson. The dead and wounded were placed in wagons, the others trailing behind on tired ponies or walking beside them, with cavalry outriders as their guards. Walks Softly, his wife and six-year-old daughter were three of the nine who had died but Fawn and her two children had come through physically unscathed, only to be delivered up to a bleak future. Eyes That Cut was buried along with the other dead at the Red Cloud Agency near Fort Robinson. Fawn then joined her father and the others struggling to become farmers, their free, roaming life replaced with three hundred and twenty acres of prairie along with seeds and the agricultural implements to plant them.

The planting of those seeds would bring little result from the marginal soil but others sown long before were now beginning to produce their desired crop. From the moment the government started talking about buying land from the Lakota and Dakota people, the fragmenting process of promises and handouts began, slowly splitting the people into the progressive and traditional camps that would bring growing internal conflict. The murder of Crazy Horse, held by a former warrior-turned-agency policeman while a soldier bayoneted him to death, was just part of the bitter harvest to come. The greatest war leader of the Lakota was now dead, and so too, according to the US Government, was the Black Hills issue, when an unwritten 'sell or starve' clause was invoked not long after the so-called massacre on the Little Bighorn.

There was a requirement in the 1868 treaty that the signatures of three quarters of all adult males in the tribes were needed before any changes could be made to it; this requirement was fulfilled by threatening those living on the reservation that their rations would be cut off if they didn't sign the forced bill of sale for the hills. As far as the other half of the warriors who had been in the north with Sitting Bull and Crazy Horse were concerned, they were simply dismissed as hostiles and excluded from any further negotiations.

The sacred country had been stolen but Fawn would go back to a special part of it a year after Eyes That Cut's death, when a decision was made to re-locate the Red Cloud Agency north to South Dakota, later to be known as the Pine Ridge reservation. Although now a long journey from her husband's grave near Fort Robinson, she was closer to his spirit's resting place in the valley. However, upon her return to it she couldn't find any sign of the marker, just a ring of stones nearby circling a campfire the soldiers had built on that day over a year before. Without the markers to help her she would spend most of the day digging holes near where she figured the Spirit Bundle to be before finally giving up, accepting that it was where the Greater Spirit wanted Eyes That Cut's spirit to rest. But every year of her remaining thirty-three, on the anniversary of her husband's death she would return, bringing her children, grand children and great grand children to the place where his spirit resided. There they could feel the beauty and power of the land and be reminded of who they were, the trips becoming like a school excursion to a cathedral, the songs of Eyes That Cut their hymns.

Fawn died in 1910, in a small wooden shack on a tiny corner of the Great Plains her people once ruled. She had been born a child of the wild prairie but had lived long enough to see it tamed and the relentless white tide wash the color out of the tribes. Yet the woman of the never-ending mind held the songs of her husband in her heart and before she died she would have a scribe record them for those that followed. They sang to her of the sun, the wind, the sky and the earth, and in her dying moments they would set the child of the prairie free again, sending her racing, long black hair flying out behind, through the sweet clover, the yellow cornflowers and wild rose. Down along the river and through the cottonwood trees she ran, entering the real world with joy, the music of a special flute sounding much clearer and sweeter than ever before.

TEN

The faint tone of the flute drifted out of the other disconnected pieces of music and singing that had constantly interrupted Gary's sleep, its waking sound coming like the finishing touch to a mad symphony. During the night he had gone on a strange, visionless journey through a dreaming wonderland peppered with bits of rock music, jazz, folk, classical and even snippets of blues numbers from the repertoire of his old band. What had stood out of the musical kaleidoscope more than most, however, was the combination that he had heard just before he woke. It was a mixture of a woman singing indiscernible lyrics, a falsetto voice singing an Indian lament and the sizzling notes of an electric guitar, all finally dissolving in the finishing notes of the flute.

He got out of bed, dressed and headed to the kitchen to make a cup of coffee. He stood at the kitchen bench drinking it, his brain itching. The sound of the flute continued to haunt him but now it was playing a distinctive, melodic tune. He went to the living room, grabbed his acoustic guitar from where it had been leaning in a corner and sat down on the sofa to trace the melody from his dream. He figured he must have heard it someplace before but he just couldn't place it.

After half an hour, Gary put the guitar away and went to his desk. He picked up the flute, studied it for a moment then blew on it again, briefly filling the room with its eerie sound before placing it back in the red bundle with the other items. He took away the paper weights that he had been using to keep the pictograph flattened out and it immediately curled back to near its former shape. He placed the red cloth bundle back inside it then wrapped it in several sheets of newspaper and hid it behind some books on top of a wall unit. He then turned on his computer.

Ever since Gary had started work on the bundle, he had been intending to find out about its significance but the all-engaging task of opening it had taken precedence. Now that the contents had been revealed, he decided to spend his Sunday off trawling through the Internet searching websites relating to the Plains tribes and their rituals. His search continued over the following days and during them he would learn a lot about their culture and the sorry circumstances in which they now existed, but it wasn't until later in the week that he found the information he was looking for. As well as time spent on the Internet, after work he had been spending a couple of hours in the Rapid City public library, going through the Native American shelves. Finally he came across a book written at the end of the nineteenth century, recording the customs and songs of the Teton Sioux branch of the Lakota nation. The object he had found was a most sacred thing. Made after the death of a loved one, the Spirit Bundle was a holding place for the soul of a dead person until a suitable period of mourning had passed and then, in accordance with ritual procedures, a relative or appointed member of the tribe would open the bundle and set the spirit free. This was done during a final ceremony and feast, when the personal items wrapped within the bundle were handed out to chosen people.

The suitable period of mourning, which could be up to a year, had long since elapsed for the bundle that Gary had in his possession; through circumstance he had become both the master of ceremony and the lone recipient of its contents and he was not at all comfortable with it.

Apart from the indefinable kind he felt in music, Gary had no spiritual inclinations. His ultimate career reflected his practical nature, suitably filled with the accurate levels, angles, degrees and minutes of the surveyor. However, over the next couple of weeks, his mind began to expand. He continued to explore the websites and, after joining the public library, brought home armfuls of books dealing with the Lakota culture. It became as intriguing as his quest to unwrap the bundle. He began to see a poetic symmetry in their spiritual beliefs and rituals, including a strong connection to music. Through his reading, he would enter a mysterious world of dream catching and vision seeking; full of people that revered nature and believed strongly in the interconnection of all life - natural and supernatural. And regularly punctuating the information he found on spirituality were the words *Paha Sapa*, or Black Hills, a place that was the center of the Lakota spiritual world, the fight for which had been going on since the first Europeans had entered its mountainous precinct. During his investigations, he also came across a website protesting about the Hidden Valley project. Its tone was not abusive. It was more a plea for people to understand the strength of feeling that the Lakota had towards their sacred place.

The words of the protest message made Gary feel even guiltier about invading the sacredness of the Spirit Bundle and he was nervous about doing what he knew he must do next. His action of unwrapping the bundle had qualified him as a clumsy white man, unknowing and uncaring of Lakota culture and, no matter how good his intentions were of returning it to its people, that's how he would be seen. He couldn't imagine any Native American being pleased about him carrying the sacred object around like a lost dog. What could he say? 'Excuse me... Is anyone looking for an ancestor's spirit? We've just dug one up.' Of course, there was the easy way, leaving it somewhere with an anonymous note attached; but that wasn't his way. First, he would have to resign and that would add to his dilemma. He had never had trouble finding work in the industry but when it became known that he had handed over the bundle, and the Native American activists would make sure that it was, he would be blackballed as a trouble maker. He would have to find some other form of employment. But what could he do? Apart from a string of lowly jobs after leaving college, when he spent several years trying to make it in the music world, all he had ever known was surveying. Insecurity at the thought of not being able to service his bank loan weighed heavily on him, but not as heavily as the Spirit Bundle on his conscience. The sooner he moved, the sooner he could work on resolving his employment problem.

It was a Sunday, a day when the site was completely shut down after a week of continuous twelve hour shifts, day and night. At first, Gary had thought these shutdowns were a little strange for a company hell bent on sticking to its completion schedules but eventually he saw that productivity was unaffected - probably it was improved by having the rest day. But the strict condition that no one could visit the site on that day unless prior arrangements were made still mystified him. Whitman had mentioned to Gary that he was going to be out on site that Sunday, checking the holding capacity of the lake. He typed up his resignation and headed out there to present it. It didn't matter to him now that he would be breaking the rules.

A contradictory mixture of relief and discomfort traveled with him all the way to the site but, as he approached the entrance, these feelings were replaced with curiosity. A long, empty flatbed truck was about to be let out through the gates. It was the kind of vehicle that transported earthmoving machinery but it didn't belong to the South Dakota firm that always brought the machines from the rail head at Rapid City. This one had Californian plates.

After the truck came through, Gary was about to drive in but was startled to see the electronically operated gates close before him. The guard came out of his cubicle, stepped through the personnel gate and walked up to Gary's vehicle.

As they always did, both men nodded unsmilingly at each other.

'Today's a shutdown. No one's allowed in unless they're on my list,' the guard stated sharply.

'Is Whitman here?'

The guard hesitated for a moment before giving a quick nod.

'I want to see him. Can you get him up here?'

'I'll see.'

The guard went back to his cubicle and made a call then came out to tell Gary that Whitman was on his way.

Whitman arrived much sooner than Gary had expected. He got out of his vehicle and quickly stepped through the personnel gate.

Gary stared as Whitman approached, noting the aggressiveness in his body language. He wound down the window. Whitman spoke before he could say anything.

'What are you doing here, Schroeder? You know the rule about prior arrangement!'

Gary glanced at the envelope on the seat. He was even more eager to hand it over now but his curiosity about the truck and the extra edginess he perceived in Whitman's manner instantly put his business on hold.

'Didn't have much on today and I was interested in how the lake was handling that inflow. I figured if you were here I could take a look.'

'I've checked a couple of times today. It's nearly full and holding. Go back to town.'

Gary nodded, paused and then posed a needling question. 'Another machine come in?'

Whitman gave him a dead stare for a moment then said, 'From another site.' He turned and walked quickly back to the gate.

Gary backed into the car park then drove off towards the highway. He looked into the rear vision mirror to see Whitman hurrying to his car and then speeding up the road towards the site. His curiosity increased on the drive out and when he hit the highway tee junction he turned right instead of left and headed south a couple of miles then west on a dirt track until he came to the boundary fence of the project. A vehicle entrance gate had been placed there to allow for access to a future radio, phone and TV tower site and Gary had been given the keys a week before to allow him to survey the area.

He unlocked the gate and drove in, heading towards the top of the ridge that overlooked the golf course. He parked his pickup a couple of hundred yards from the top and walked the rest of the way. He carried a pair of binoculars he kept in his vehicle and when he reached the top of the ridge he steadied them against a tree trunk and peered down at the machinery compound, now darkened by afternoon shadows. Whitman's Jeep was parked outside and he could see the top half of a very large pay loader parked just inside the compound. Next to it he could see the white roof of a van. Occasionally, a trail of orange sparks came from near the rear end of the pay loader and the sound of steel being cut echoed through the valley.

After several minutes, the cutting tool went silent and soon the blue flash of a welder lit up the compound. About half an hour later, it stopped and a plume of black smoke rose out of the pay loader's vertical exhaust pipe as it was moved to a far corner of the compound and then parked. Soon after, the compound gates opened and the white van reversed out. Gary focused on the license plate then took the glasses away from his eyes, a deep frown on his face. He noted the distinctive Statue of Liberty icon in the middle and wondered what a van from New York could be doing on site. There had been a few visits from the big wigs in the New York head office but they always flew to Rapid City then hired vehicles. Whitman emerged from the compound straight after the van, closed the gates quickly and spoke briefly with the driver before the vehicle headed up the hill towards the main entrance.

Gary returned to his vehicle and, after exiting the site, drove slowly out towards the highway. Another question nagged at him as he went. He wondered why an extra pay loader was needed. The earthmoving machines had been going day and night since the project began and the bulk of their work had been done. He picked up the envelope from his seat and slipped it into the glove box. He had decided to do some research of a different kind.

That night, Gary visited the company's website. He had previously studied it before writing his job application and had been impressed then by its meteoric rise. As well as in North America, they had won several big contracts in other countries, a factor that had encouraged him to apply for the Black Hills position in the hope it would lead to more work overseas. Initially, he found nothing more on the website than he already knew, the 'About Us' section trumpeting their success in always completing difficult projects on time and in mostly remote locations. However, it was in a section listing those projects that he found some curious information.

The thing Whitman had said about the pay loader coming from another site had intrigued Gary. At the moment the only other project he knew about in North America was one in Canada. How did the machine come to be shipped from way south in California? He also knew that the only project south was the construction of an oil pipeline project in Ecuador - but why would the company bring one machine from such a distant location? They could be leased anywhere in the US.

It wasn't until after he had closely studied the location and duration of all the company's projects and pinpointed everything on a world map that he saw a pattern. At all times, there were projects in North America running concurrently with those overseas, and the overseas projects were located only in certain regions of South East Asia and South America, all of them in or bordering countries that were known to harbor illicit drug producers.

ELEVEN

'Hello, Grace speaking.'

'Grace... It's Mark.'

Mark's voice had a serious tone to it and Grace responded apprehensively.

'Yes, Mark.'

'I got the tape today.'

A few seconds of silence followed.

'This is great stuff, Grace. If you can get an album together it could be huge.' he said, his words still coming in a subdued, serious way.

'Well don't sound so happy about it!' Grace blurted out.

Mark had been listening to the tape constantly for over two hours and had been floored by the new songs. During that time the seed of an idea that had first come to him on his drive back from Deloraine had germinated and grown. He was bubbling with excitement about it but something was containing his enthusiasm. He continued to speak in a matter-of-fact way.

'I don't want to take this to a record company. This music is something special and I'm prepared to put my money where my mouth is. If you can get enough songs together for an album and if you all agree, I'd like to produce and promote it. If I sell my business, I'll have enough to finance the proper recording of the songs and cover the cost of the CD manufacture and marketing. You'll have total creative control of the whole thing. It'll be out on the streets in a fraction of the time it would take a record company, assuming they take it. And I've got plenty of distribution outlets. I can use my contacts at the music stores I've been selling stuff to for years. There's a couple of hundred of those and I know I could get the record into a lot of them. This won't be about selling CD's from the trunk of a car after a performance. It will be as professional as my experience can make it and I'm as confident of doing it properly as I am of your music.' He hesitated there for a moment then added, 'But I need to know something, Grace.'

'Yes?'

'I feel this music's going to put you up before big crowds again. You'll have to face up to that if you want to promote it. And eventually the termites will start chomping on you, digging up the past. You know what they are like. They usually find everything and, if they don't, they'll manufacture something. Will you be able to handle it? Would you run again?'

Grace didn't immediately answer. With the completion of each song she had felt the pressure building and what Mark had just said brought it all in with a rush; all the memories of the claustrophobia that came with expectation, the hands reaching out for all of her and the anxiety attacks which had choked her voice - until the drugs set it free again. But it wasn't just about her this time. Regardless of her fear, she realized that she had no other option than to go where the songs were taking them all. And she had become tougher of late, purging fears as great as the one she knew she would have to face again.

'I can't say I don't have the same fear but I've got a son now. The songs are more important to him than anything else. I want the music to be a success for him... and for my people.'

The steadfastness of Grace's words released Mark's excitement.

'Right! Run it by the others and call me when there's a decision. By the way, who is Eyes That Cut?'

'He's my great, great grandfather. He created the Lakota songs we're using as chorus lines.'

'And Jamie Howard... isn't he your son?'

'Yes.'

'Didn't you say he was twelve-years-old?'

'In the body... between the ears I believe he may just be a hundred. He's written some of the lyrics and he's turned into a damn fine song arranger.'

There was a brief silence as Mark digested that unlikely thought and then his excitement spilled out again. 'Jesus, Grace, what great marketing value... a twelve-year-old kid arranging songs with choruses created by his ancestor!'

Grace sat by the phone for a while after Mark rang off. She couldn't agree for the others but in her mind everything was falling into place. She had hurt him once and whatever proposal he came up with, she would support. He was part of the thing that was approaching, just like the rider of her dreams, who was, night by night, closing on her - still unrecognizable and still bringing that overwhelming sense of sadness and puzzlement. She had tried to analyze the dream, thinking that maybe the rider was her fear, but it felt much more than that.

Grace got up from her chair and headed to the living room. She and Jamie had been on a song search when Mark had called and the translated and typed out copies of Lakota songs from her grandfather's folder lay scattered about the living room floor. There was no 'if' about them writing enough songs for an album. Since mailing the tape there were four more completed and another one about to be born. Like all good songwriters, mother and son were working to a formula now. They were using some of the melodies off Chas's failed album, adding Lakota verses then building lyrics around them, with Jamie working out ways of elaborating the melody with the instruments they had in the band and, of late, some they didn't.

'That was Mark,' Grace said as she sat down on the sofa. 'He's got a proposition. He wants to produce the album.'

'Good,' Jamie said. 'We don't need any record company to stuff up the songs. I want you to sing this one,' he immediately added, holding up a piece of paper.

Grace's mouth twisted in bemusement at Jamie's dismissive response. 'We need to get everyone together to discuss this,' she asserted.

'Yeah, *okay*,' Jamie replied with slight irritation, impatiently waving the sheet of paper at her.

Grace shook her head in resignation and took the piece of paper. At the top was the title *The Mountains, I* and below it were just thirteen words in English printed next to the Lakota ones.

They read: *The mountains, I*
   the rivers, I
   the trees
   the Grass
   the Earth, I

She softly sang the lyrics in Lakota, and then the English version.

'Yeah. That's gonna work,' Jamie declared, and then got up and headed to his bedroom.

'Hang on! What about helping me tidy this up?'

The only reply was the beginning of George Harrison's *Within Without You* coming from Jamie's bedroom, the sound of a sitar floating from the hi fi like a cobra rising from a snake charmer's basket, swaying in time with the throaty sound of a tabla drum.

Grace sighed and began gathering the scattered song sheets. She had confidence about the songs but was dismayed by Jamie's blind optimism. Their success seemed a done deal to him, although he was constantly trying to improve them. Lately, he had been listening to cultural music from all over the world, searching for sounds; Arabic music with its sensuous mystique; Celtic ballads sung by female voices that drifted out of his room like soft mists and Latin American rhythms of fire and passion. But there was one sound Jamie had been totally captivated by.

Late one night, when listening to Radical Radio, a Chicago station that played non-mainstream music, Jamie had heard a song called *Sunset Dreaming* by an Australian Aboriginal band called Yothu Yindi. He was so impressed by it he emailed the station's DJ Ray Cicconi about the group and was given the name of the US distributor of the album *Tribal Song*. A week later he had the CD but at the expense of almost three weeks' music rations. He listened to it over and over for days, or more specifically, to one particular instrument.

Jamie loved the ghostly bass tones and high-pitched yelping sounds of the didgeridoo and was further impressed to find out they were all achieved through a piece of hollowed tree branch, the tones varied only by the breathing skill of the user. Grace was less enthusiastic. The sound of the didgeridoo brought something vaguely familiar to her ears, faintly troubling her mind.

Jamie had found many other sounds through Ray the DJ, with whom he had gradually developed a friendship, sometimes getting an email about the music he was going to play that night. That was how Jamie was introduced to the throat singing of the Inuit late one evening and he had woken Grace up to play what he had taped, excited about the connection he heard to the falsetto and vibrato in her voice when she sang the Lakota choruses of their music.

Grace observed with fascination Jamie's constant searching for improvement in their music. His arranging skills were improving by the day, leaping at times, leaving the original versions of the songs floundering in the wake of his driven creativity. She had been dragged along in his slipstream, reluctantly at first, considering the work that had already gone into the songs but, when she showed reluctance, he assured her in his enthusiastic way.

'I don't wanna change the songs, Mom. I just wanna make 'em better.'

He explained what he wanted to do, gradually becoming frenetic about his ideas, more changes being added as he joyfully discovered something else during his explanation. The essence of his idea was that the songs should carry a mixture of sounds from other cultures but with Lakota choruses paramount and connecting them all.

'It's what Looks Back told me, Mom. He said music connected everyone, no matter where they were in the universe. He said it's one language that speaks to us all and we can make our voice stronger, Mom. It won't take much to do it. All we have to do is find the right instruments and voices.'

His eyes glowing with enthusiasm, Jamie played the tape of the original six songs, interrupting them when he considered this or that musical instrument or vocal should be introduced.

As she listened, Grace's reluctance gradually turned into wonder. Jamie was methodically pulling the songs apart and re-constructing them, showing her how added parts could fly like the Lakota choruses, hovering in the territory of their cultures just long enough to add richness to the songs before returning to the Rock and Roll at the heart of them all. Cultural crossovers were as old as music itself and the concept of fusion and 'world music' was not new but by the time Jamie had finished his demonstration, Grace was as excited about the multicultural blending of sounds as he. Still, there would remain the logistics of finding the musicians and vocals he was enlisting for each song and, as she listened to *Within Without You* being played for the third time, she knew a sitar was about to be added to the list.

She placed the dozens of sheets of paper back into their folder, grateful again that Looks Back had given her the tattered old book from which she had copied the songs and that a woman called Fawn had the wisdom to not trust them to the memory of oral history. If not for any other reason, she would like to see her great, great grandmother's devotion rewarded by the songs' exposure to a wider audience than just the small gatherings of people that they were once sung to. She wanted to do it for her grandfather too, the man who had taught her the songs and much else and who appeared to have had the same paternal influence on her son.

Grace thought about the promise she had made to take Looks Back to the valley. Although she was fearful of what they would both see of the place they held so dear to their hearts, it had become imperative for her to do so.

TWELVE

The decision to go with Mark's offer came after a brief meeting of the group the night after his phone call, although there was really nothing to decide. It was about guaranteed action against only the possibility of being recorded. No matter how good the music, Chas, Boss and Grace knew that when it came to financial investment, the executive decisions of recording companies could be a long time in coming.

Grace rang Mark that night. 'Congratulations. You are now the manager of a geriatric rock group.'

'Yeah, well the Stones are still rolling and others, too. But most importantly the young ones are listening!' Mark responded with undisguised enthusiasm.

'I've had someone chasing my business for a while but I won't be waiting until I've sold it. I'm going to move on getting this set up straight away but, before I start organizing the recording side, I need to know when you'll have enough songs for the album.'

'We're almost there. I can send another tape if you want.'

'No, that's okay, but I want you to do a few other things. Step up the number of gigs you are playing and keep a sprinkling of your originals amongst the material. Let everyone you come across know that you're heading to the recording studio, and if you get any opportunities for interviews, take them, no matter how small the coverage. Plug the songs at every opportunity until I can take over the PR. I'll be in touch soon.'

*

In the days that followed, Jamie and Grace completed two more songs – *The Mountains I* and *Buffalo Run.* They now had the minimum twelve songs needed for an album but the biggest thrill for Jamie was the opportunity *Warrior* had been given for some exposure in the media.

Word of mouth about the group's unique sound had been rapidly spreading through the district and a local television station had picked up on the story, inviting Grace and Jamie in for a five-minute interview during an afternoon teen show called *What's New?* It was to be the first airplay for one of their songs and Jamie insisted it be *Buffalo Run*, the one he had written the words to at school the week before. That day he was supposed to be learning something about rice production in China, instead he was away with his great grandfather chewing sweet grass and listening to the wind blowing across the cattle range that was once a prairie. He was thinking of what Looks Back had told him, about how he imagined the sound of buffalo running by whenever the cattle were being rounded up, the lyrics to *Buffalo Run* coming effortlessly, the lines rolling like a thundering herd over the plains. Later they were to be intersected by Grace's voice, carrying the verses from an Eyes That Cut song called *Buffalo Moon* and striking at Jamie's words like the hunters that once followed the animals. The band had worked hard for several days to get a decent version on tape for the show.

Jamie took to the interview like a pro. After a few bars introducing the song, he answered most of the questions, with a subdued Grace giving back-up information, although the questions asked by the young female presenter of the show didn't go much beyond the 'gee whiz 'and 'wow' variety. The interview wasn't long enough to give any deep insight into the unlikely songwriting partnership but the girl did finish the segment with a prophetic statement.

'Let's hear it for Grace, Jamie and *Warrior*... the next big thing in music!'

The audience didn't need prompting. As the song cut in again they whistled and clapped as the two guests left the studio. The station's switchboard mirrored their enthusiasm, lighting up with callers eager to find out where they could get the music even before the segment had finished.

The next day, Jamie went to school a star. At the lockers, girls that hardly ever spoke to him now hovered near as he sorted his books for class, crowding around him and plying him with questions.

Jamie's celebrity greeted him in the classroom too, where his teacher started the lesson with the words, 'It seems we have a famous song writer in our midst. Well, there'll be no autograph hunting while class is on.' Then, near the end of the lesson, she pointedly walked up the aisle to his desk and, placing her diary down before him, asked in a loud voice, 'Do you think you might be able to sign this for me?'

The whole class broke out in laughter and Helen Morris felt happy for the boy she had watched with interest and concern ever since he had entered her class at the beginning of the year. She had seen the dreamers before but this one had a strange stillness about him, of late seeming to spend the entire class period in some other place, as much as she tried to bring him back. She had spoken to his mother about his lack of concentration but it hadn't had any effect on his dreamy behavior, although she noted his homework and his exam marks had improved sufficiently to save him from having to repeat a year. Yet, early last week, her interest in him had suddenly jumped to another level when she had looked up from her desk to see that intense gaze of his once more staring fixedly at the blank blackboard. She had leaned over into his line of sight and signaled him to get back to the reading assignment but he just kept staring in that same trance-like manner. It worried her and she got up and walked towards his desk. His eyes were still fixed firmly ahead as she approached but, when she stopped beside him, his head suddenly dropped. Satisfied that he had gone back to reading his textbook, she was about to walk away when she saw him flip open the small notebook he always had on his desk and begin to write something in it. She stood and watched with acute interest as his pen smoothly transcribed the words of a lyrical poem, running in an undulating, rolling rhythm through two verses of eight lines each, its style polished and mature.

'Where did you get that from, Jamie?' she asked.

'Huh?' Jamie responded, looking up with surprise to see his teacher leaning down and peering at something written on his notebook. He quickly scanned through the lyrics. It had happened again and he had no explanation for it. But it was his writing and it was the theme that had dreamed him out of the classroom. He answered truthfully.

'Ah... I don't know Ma'am. They just pop out sometimes.'

'It's *yours*?'

'Ah... yes, Ma'am.'

Helen stared at it for a moment, still a little doubtful about its origin.

'It's really good, Jamie. But for now I'd like you to go back to the lesson. It'll be question time soon.'

Helen wouldn't ask him any questions on geography and the ones she did fire out to the class in general were asked vacantly, the answers not really listened to as the words of the poem kept drifting through her mind. They would do so for days after, until they surfaced in another form yesterday, when she came home from work and turned on the TV to hear the early news. What she got instead was the end of *What's New?*, a program of inane teenage speak and matching music that usually irritated the hell out of her. But this time she was stopped short of changing the channel when the music leading into the Jukebox segment came rolling and rumbling to her ears in the form of a great Rock and Roll number. It was the thundering drum introduction that grabbed her attention before the familiar words sang out from a powerful female voice, and then, as the song faded away, she was amazed to see Jamie and his mother seated on the interview couch. She sat down on her own sofa with a wide and fascinated smile on her face, eyes glued to the screen, and when the interview finished she shouted out, '*Yes, Jamie!*'

Helen continued to smile all through her evening meal and again, afterwards, when she was marking papers for a math test and came across Jamie's mediocre effort. She had worried about the future of the physically and racially disadvantaged little boy; the one who kept mostly to himself at school seeming not to have any friends at all, always to be found during recesses and sports periods with those earphones on, reading books or scribbling things down. He was never going to scale the academic heights but maybe he was destined for other things, she thought, as she hummed the melody of *Buffalo Run.*

Thirteen

The bandwagon's speed picked up during the week following Mark's phone call to Grace. He reached an agreement on the sale of his instrument business, registered his new one and organized the drawing up of contracts for the group. He then did a quick tour of some of his customers in and around Seattle informing them of the impending change and sounding them out as distribution points for the sale of the CD. As he had predicted, all who heard the tape readily agreed to give the future album a trial. Meanwhile, back in Deloraine the group was doing as he requested. They stepped up performing, adding two more gigs a week to the four they were already playing, while the twelve original songs soon became seventeen, most of them worthy of going onto the album.

The group had settled into their style now, the distinct lyric and melody hooks, guitar riffs and licks fitting perfectly in place with the Lakota songs to form the rich patterns of a musical kaleidoscope. And with the addition of the new songs, they had more scope to balance the rockin' and the rollin'. A softer touch was needed in places and two of the originals were dropped in favor of a couple of new compositions, one of them an instrumental number that Wayne, Mitch and Boss had been secretly working on for weeks, ambiguously titled *Sweet Grass*. It was the direct English translation of one of the Lakota songs, with Mitch's bass guitar interpreting the native chanting and Wayne's flute carrying the melody line, Boss's steady, muted drumbeat representing the earth that the song sprouted from. The peaceful track had a similar feel to Fleetwood Macs' classic, *Albatross*, yet it almost certainly reflected a flight pattern of another kind, inspired mostly by Wayne's fondness for a dried form of vegetable matter. The song's name provided a bit of discussion but the piece instantly went in, so too did a solo contribution from Grace; a song that needed only her voice as an instrument. Its Lakota title *She Comes To Me* was changed to *Come to me* and the lyrics and physicality Grace added turned it into a steaming love song, sexuality dripping from every line. When she first sang it to the others, it brought a loud comment from Chas.

'Jesus, Grace... I think maybe it's time ya got back into the workforce!'

Spirit Rising was the title Grace insisted on for the album and during another week of almost constant emails and faxes between manager and performers, the starting date for its recording was set for two weeks later. Contracts were agreed upon and drawn up, ready for signing when the group reached Seattle. Mark had registered his enterprise under the name Aktrix Records, a play on Grace's remark about their geriatric rock band. It included a managing agency for musicians as well as a producer, manufacturer, wholesaler and retailer of records, with a song-publishing arm attached. He had seen enough of the industry to know that all the bases had to be covered to protect his investment, but even though he was taking all the financial risk, the royalties for the group would be generous. Because of the smaller overheads in his one-man approach to making and marketing the CD, the group would be getting nearly double the normal percentage of income from record sales. Those responsible for writing the songs would get even more, plus seventy percent of all income from the publishing of their compositions. Jamie was included in all the legal documentation and given a major share in any songwriting royalties because of the arranging skills he had brought to the music.

Those arranging skills would become increasingly evident to Mark in the period leading up to the recording date. Although he hadn't met Jamie, they soon became friends via the telephone and emails. Much of their conversation revolved around Jamie's requests for musicians of all kinds, explaining in detail which songs they needed each one for.

Mark had made a list which grew into a file; the search for what Jamie was requesting adding an extra burden to the days that no longer held enough hours. But the kid seemed to know exactly what he was doing and he hunted out everything enthusiastically. With his contacts he soon managed to find the musicians required, exotic ones included. He even found someone playing a didgeridoo in Vancouver when he took the purchaser of his instrument business there to introduce him to some of his customers. The young white Australian with dreadlocks was sitting on a sidewalk in Chinatown playing for coins when Mark gave him his proposition – two hundred bucks for a day's work. 'No worries, mate... I'll be there,' was his laid-back reply. Mark hoped there wouldn't be as he looked into the slightly glazed eyes of the youth with no contact address or cell phone. The other request he thought would be difficult to meet was for throat singers. This was also quickly solved when he found out that two Inuit from Alaska were visiting the Seattle Conservatory of Music, displaying their skills for students studying techniques of vocal harmony. The young women were happy to lend their voices to the album when the cultural theme of it was explained.

Everything was falling into place for Mark. He felt exhilarated and caught up in the music's momentum, as though nothing was going to halt it. Even the most important part of the equation, the sound engineer, had been provided before he organized the studio. He had been taking coffee alfresco in uptown Seattle when a disheveled individual emerged from the passing throng, glanced briefly at him then kept walking.

It had taken Mark a moment or two to register Marty Donnewitz's face but then he hurried after him. When he caught up with him, he soon found that the man hadn't changed since he last saw him in the eighties. The small, nerdy-looking individual still dressed like a clothesbasket and his manner hadn't improved; he was the same gruff individual that had once held all his recording artists in a grip of fear. He responded to Mark's cheerful greeting with just a nod and a grunt, but it didn't stop Mark. He quickly broached the matter of the album, determined to get him to listen to the tape even if it meant frog-marching him to the car. After a rapid-fire description of *Warrior's* music he was relieved when another nod and a grunt came.

'So, what have you been doing with your life,' Mark asked as they headed to his car.

'Nothin' worth talkin' about,' Donnewitz sourly replied and the rest of the walk passed in silence.

Sullen temperament or not, Donnewitz was responsible for producing some of the best albums of the eighties. He knew a special sound when he heard it and, after listening to Grace singing just one of the songs on the tape he nodded approval. 'I'll do it, but don't get a studio set up with all that digital shit. I want it wired up the old way.'

Mark was ecstatic about the instant agreement, although he couldn't get a number or address for organizing the timeline for recording, just the promise that he would be rung within a fortnight. He felt insecure about that but knew, although Donnewitz spoke very little, he was a man of his word. A few days later he found a studio suitable for the hands-on control that Donnewitz demanded.

*

With the list of requests filled, everything was in place for the band's move to Seattle and Jamie was in a constant state of excitement at the prospect. He was hardly able to wait the ten sleeps before they were to leave, restlessly wandering the house and badgering his mother about going sooner. Then, early one morning, a week before they were to go, his focus shifted completely.

The dream that had been visiting Grace on and off for weeks came again that morning; the horse and rider once more moving down the slope of the ridge and through the waving grass of the prairie at a slow walk, once more bringing the feeling of deep sadness. This time, however, they moved beyond the misty curtain of the previous dreams, their indistinct outline sharpening, the usual low rumbling soundtrack receding, replaced by the shuffling, kicking sound of hooves. The images kept approaching her until the horse stopped a few paces away and the rider slid off its back.

The warrior's body was clearly defined, a young man in his physical prime, slim, smooth muscled and dressed in the Lakota way for war with two eagle feathers poking up from the back of his head. Yet his face was hidden, shaded in darkness, and he held something in his hand that Grace couldn't make out. It looked like it was an unusually long quiver of arrows. Then a light suddenly appeared behind him and turned all of him into a shadow.

'Mom?'

Grace squinted at the glare of the hall light. 'Jamie?'

'I wanna go visit Looks Back.'

Grace looked at the clock. It showed just past four o'clock. 'What... whaddya mean?'

'I wanna go visit Looks Back... *now!*'

Grace sat up in bed. 'C'm here, Hon.'

Jamie moved over and sat down next to her.

'What's this all about? I thought we had agreed to go down there after the recording session. You're the one who's been breaking his neck to get to Seattle early. Now you wanna go somewhere else. There's less than a week left and we've still got some rehearsing to do. There's that interview we have to do with the local paper. And I haven't even started on packing for the trip yet. I just don't see how we can manage it.'

Jamie became agitated and stood up next to the bed. 'I *havth* to go, Mom!' he yelled at her.

'Okay... okay,' Grace said calmly as she pulled him back to the bed and put an arm around him.

'What's happened, Hon?'

'I had a dream. Looks Back was in it. He called my name.'

'That's it?'

'Just about,' Jamie said solemnly.

Grace knew by the tone she wouldn't be getting any more. She ran through the logistics. It would have to be a two-day trip this time if they were going to go out to the valley as well and the sooner it was done the better.

'Okay, let's start getting our things together,' she said as she pushed Jamie off the bed and climbed out of it. 'I'll hire a car and we'll leave as soon as we can this morning. And this one's going down on the bill. It's gotta be worth a couple of weeks of washing *and* drying the dishes.'

'Thanks, Mom.'

Grace held his head briefly as he gave her a light hug, still wondering what was going on in it - what part of her dreams were his dreams.

FOURTEEN

It was late morning when Looks Back heard the car coming over the ridge. He watched impassively as it made its way down towards where he was seated under the hole-ridden canvas lean-to of his trailer. Rarely did he have visitors or visit anyone these days, having outlived most of his friends and relatives. He had also outlived his curiosity about people, any intrusion upon his solitude greeted with varying degrees of disinterest. Today was different, however. Although his fading eyesight couldn't yet make out the people in the Toyota compact, even before it had rolled to a halt, he stood up with purpose, stepped out into the spring sunshine and walked towards the vehicle.

To Grace, it looked like her grandfather was waiting to be picked up. Jamie was sure it was so.

'Hi, Granpa,' Grace said to the unsmiling man, as she and Jamie stepped out of the car.

Looks Back nodded and then looked down at Jamie.

Jamie said nothing. He just stared into Looks Back's eyes.

'Well, Jamie?' Grace enquired.

'Hi, Looks Back... we've come to take you to the valley,' Jamie finally said.

'Yes,' Looks Back said. He shuffled past them and climbed into the back of the car.

It took about an hour and a half to drive out to the valley and little was said during the journey, most of the conversation coming from Jamie, until he was silenced by his first clear sighting of the Black Hills and the sound of Looks Back and his mother quietly greeting them in Lakota.

From twenty miles away the rock formation covered with pine trees rose out of the flatlands like the dark fortress it once was, a spiritual beacon to the first Lakota that had set eyes upon it, and still so to those who believed it was the center of the earth.

Grace swung off Highway 18 then drove the last few miles on a new road built for the golf resort project, its coming advertised by a giant billboard at the turnoff. Grace figured that the best place to get a view of the valley would be from a point a few miles south of the main entrance. It was at the end of a rough track they had often used in the past, although she was concerned about whether the compact would be able to handle it and whether Looks Back could still manage the hike in from where it ended. First, however, she wanted to see what they had done at the gateway to the valley.

A grand entrance loomed before them, an eight-foot high designer wall, stretching a hundred yards either side of a pair of arched and ornate wrought iron gates. Running out from each end of the wall were security fences that snaked their way back into the hills like a couple of razor-backed serpents. They could see nothing of the valley from the gates, just the gray tarmac that carried on straight and flat for a quarter of a mile before it began to rise and then disappear over a hill, from behind which came the constant drone of building activity.

Grace drove the car into a graveled parking bay and the three of them gazed through the gates at the two burly security guards staring back at them, bug-eyed shades and guns on hips accentuating their belligerent body language.

'Progress has come. Now there is a good road for the thieves to drive in on,' came the softly spoken comment from the back seat. 'Unless you brought a bazooka with you, I don't think we'll be goin' through there.'

There was never any thought or hope that they would get through the entrance but Grace wanted to see it, to be affronted by it. She kept staring at the two men behind the gates, hatred in her eyes.

The two guards stepped through the personnel access gate and then swaggered over towards the car. When they reached it one of them leant down and knocked on Grace's window. She pressed the button and let the window drop a few inches without looking up.

'This is private property. Unless you're here on business, you'll have to leave.'

Grace turned slowly around and looked defiantly up at the man. 'This side ain't private property and, in the unlikely event that you can read, you'd find the history books say that *that* side ain't either. Legally, it still belongs to our people, no matter how many beads have been offered for it!'

The man stared at Grace coldly then put his hand threateningly on the handle of his revolver. 'Take it to your politician, babe. Now move your ass or we'll move it for you!'

As he spoke, a Chevy pickup stopped at a boom gate on the other side of the wall and the other guard quickly walked back to let it through, having a brief conversation with the driver before opening the gates. The sandy-haired man driving the vehicle stared intently at Grace as he drove past, their eyes meeting for just a moment.

'Move it *now*!'

Grace turned around to see the man now had a gun in his hand. She felt a wise tap on her shoulder from the back seat and, after a few seconds of staring defiantly into the man's eyes, she started the car and tramped on the accelerator, sending the vehicle spinning in a circle around him, spitting gravel and dust as she accelerated away.

'Okay, let's go south!' Grace said, as she slammed the car through the gears, her temper rising with each shift.

*

A few weeks had passed since the mystifying incident in the machinery compound and Gary had visited the tower site every Sunday since in the hope of seeing more abnormal activity. Nothing else had happened except that the pay loader, delivered from California and left standing idle in the corner of the compound for two weeks, suddenly disappeared one Sunday night, trucked out under the cover of darkness. It only added to his suspicions but he had no proof and, even if more did turn up, he couldn't gain entry to that fortress to check it out. He couldn't question anyone on site either for fear it would get back to Whitman. If he was right and Prestige suspected him of knowing something, he wouldn't just be sacked. In the end he decided to blow the whistle anonymously and from afar. He would resign, inform the Drug Enforcement Administration of his suspicions and let them do the investigating.

Gary's decision to finally hand in his resignation had come one morning on site as if it were ordained for that day.

Whitman was in his office in Rapid City so he decided to take it straight there but, when he was driving out through the gate, something that had been pushed to the back of his mind came back into focus.

'Just some fuckin' redskins, probably protestin' again' was what the gate man had told him when he enquired about what was going on outside the entrance. But they didn't look like the protestors of a couple of months before; glum figures huddled together, lifting up their protest signs and staring at him darkly, hurling abuse as he drove into the project. These looked more like sightseers. As he drove past, he was struck by the woman's face, not just her attractiveness but a presence that he couldn't quite define. He had to speak with her. He stopped his vehicle before the tee junction, got out and waited. Soon the small car was speeding towards him and he stepped out onto the road and waved it down.

'Damnit! What now?' Grace moaned.

'Maybe he wants to trade some o' them beads for the car,' Looks Back said. His comment was followed by a rustle of paper in a pocket and then the sucking sound of a jellybean on the tongue.

The two seated in front burst into laughter as the car slowed down and rolled to a halt adjacent to the pickup. They were still smiling when Gary walked across to them.

'Hi,' he said when the driver's window was wound down, a little surprised by the amused faces.

Grace's smile faded and she nodded curtly.

Gary saw the apprehension in her eyes. 'Don't worry. I'm not part of security. I just wanted to talk to you about something.'

'About what?'

Gary had been certain of what he wanted to say but now he didn't quite know how to start and there was an inordinately long silence before his answer came. 'I... I'm not sure how to put this.'

Grace stared at him for a moment then declared, 'Well, mister, if you ain't sure, we the hell ain't either. Now if you don't mind, we've got somewhere to go.'

She put the car in gear and made to move off when a tap on the shoulder came again.

'Hear what he has to say,' Looks Back said. He wound his window down and held out a paper bag to Gary. 'Have a jellybean... it'll help loosen your tongue.'

Gary smiled and took the offering. 'We'll have to get off the project road. Follow me.'

Grace stared with suspicion for a few seconds more. 'Okay,' she finally said, then tailed Gary's pickup out onto the highway, heading a couple of miles south before pulling up behind him in a rest area.

Gary got out of his car and walked over to Grace's. 'Let's take a seat over there,' he said, indicating towards a concrete table and bench seats located under a small tree. The three got out of their car and followed him.

It appeared that the jellybean had worked. As soon as they sat down, Gary spoke.

'This is hard for me. I am head surveyor of the Hidden Valley project and I know that will make you hate me. What I'm about to say will probably make you despise me.'

The others sat silently as Gary spoke haltingly about what he had found poking out of the earth on that freezing winter morning. He called it a Spirit Bundle and began to describe what was in it when Looks Back broke in.

'How do you know what it is?'

'I've been studying the culture of your people ever since I found it.'

'How do you know who our people are?'

'I don't. I just assumed that you are Lakota; the same as the others that have come out here.'

A short silence followed, before Looks Back spoke again.

'It is the Spirit Bundle of my great grandfather... Eyes That Cut.'

The calm statement shocked Gary. He began to nod his head slowly as the pictograph formed in his mind. Now he knew the name of the figure with the knives flying out of his eyes but he was left speechless by this meeting with his direct descendent. Just as with the decision to resign that morning, he felt that strings were being pulled from some other place; that he was not in control.

Silence reigned while everyone waited for the old man to say more but Looks Back just kept his gaze fixed ahead, over the highway and towards the Black Hills.

Gary finally found his voice. 'I'm not proud of what's going on in the valley but, apart from giving you the Spirit Bundle back, with my sincere apologies for opening it, there's not much more I can offer.'

'Why do you continue to work there?' Grace inquired pointedly. Her fears that the bundle would be unearthed during the project had been realized and, although relieved that it had been found, she was seething.

Gary pondered her question for several seconds, his eyes firmly fixed on her cold stare. He felt like saying that it seemed he had been waiting for her. He suddenly stood up. 'Just wait here for a second,' he said and walked quickly to his pickup and took the envelope from his glove box. He opened it as he walked back then handed the resignation letter to Grace.

'I wrote that out not long after finding out about the bundle's significance but something else delayed it. I can't tell you about it at the moment. It's just a suspicion I have that there is some illegal activity going on with the development company. Believe it or not, I was just heading into the Rapid City office to hand it in.'

Grace briefly skipped through the letter, noting the date. She handed it back with a quick nod. She didn't really need to see it. She had been pondering the connection since Gary first mentioned the Spirit Bundle. Just like the interconnection of the music she had been working on their meeting had come like a finishing piece to a spiritual jigsaw puzzle. She could now see where she was heading and was elated by the thought. There was still a veneer of anger, however. 'Apologies don't mean spit unless actions follow, and there is something you can do. You can help us to get a look at what's been going on in the valley. We know we can't get in through the main gate but your vehicle would be better able to take us in another way.'

'Which way is that?'

Grace explained how to get there.

'There's a fence through there too,' Gary said guiltily. 'It runs around the entire perimeter of the project, but I can get you in. There are access gates not far from that point and I've got the keys.'

Grace stood up. 'Let's go.'

They climbed back into the vehicles and, with Gary leading the way, headed a little further south then turned onto the dirt track that led to the boundary fence of the site. After traveling a mile, the roughness of the track began to test the compact. A heavy thump on its underbody finally convinced Grace to stop and park it in a small gully. They all then squeezed into the cab of the pickup and silently carried on. The track had taken them in a wide circular sweep through the foothills and about a mile after they had left the compact, they came across the fence line and the gate. Gary jumped out and unlocked it, drove through then quickly closed and locked it again. From there it was nearly all upwards, over one small hill and then a steeper one, before Gary finally halted the pickup just below the crest of an even larger hill, its jagged conifer-spiked horizon framed by the roundness of the gray peaks that rose majestically beyond.

Gary pointed upwards. 'If you walk over there you'll get a good view of the valley. I'll stay here just in case someone happens along. Just keep low if you hear me hit the horn.'

Grace and Looks Back resented being told to hide on their own land and they didn't need to be told where to get a good view of the valley either. They knew this place like the back of their hands. Although two generations apart, as children they had both hiked through much of it and memorized its stories, especially the one about the Spirit Bundle and where it rested. But nothing was said to the stranger who had brought them there.

Grace, Looks Back and Jamie got out and walked the remaining hundred yards to the top of the hill and then another fifty or so through the trees on the other side before they could get their good view of the valley.

About a half a mile away down the sweeping slope, the dark soil of newly planted fairways swirled around the valley floor in stark contrast to the rich green of the late spring grass that skirted the tree line. At the bottom end, a large lake sparkled in the sun with several smaller ones shining from designated points in the golf course design. At the top of the valley, the concrete foundations of buildings glared back, with tiny figures moving over and around them, busy laying the first courses of brickwork and erecting scaffolding.

For the two people who could only remember a pristine valley, the scene of its destruction inspired different emotions; Grace's simmering anger went on to the boil, while Looks Back chanted softly, the sound of his voice coming like a tone of surrender.

For Jamie, the sound of Looks Back's singing instantly brought back the memory of his dream and, just as in that dream, when the singing faded away, he heard his name spoken. He turned towards Looks Back and saw again the dream's crushing vision of tears rolling down an old man's cheeks.

'This is what you must see to understand,' Looks Back said, his voice unwavering, his gaze remaining fixed on the valley.

Jamie turned to the front again. His body trembled with the onset of his own rare tears and then an arm was placed around his shoulders.

Grace held her son tightly. The unusual sight of him crying drove her towards tears as well, although not of sadness. She had once stood on such a high place, singing out to her ancestor's presence. Now she wanted to scream out obscenities at those below. Instead, she turned away.

'I've seen enough!' she said.

The three made their way over the rise and back towards the pickup, Grace's body language screaming out as she strode briskly ahead of the other two.

'Don't be too hard on the stranger, Songbird. He is connected to the way ahead. He showed courage to speak with us,' Looks Back called out.

The wisdom fell on deaf ears as Grace steamed towards the man standing next to his pickup.

Gary watched with some alarm as the woman strode purposefully towards him, her eyes like arrows, her mood like a hatchet. He backed away nervously as she got closer, about to raise his arms in self defense as she strode right up to him but, instead of the expected blows, he was hit first with words, the fire in her brown eyes burning into his cool blue.

'You were right, man... I do despise you! You and your fucking kind! You can't leave our places be! You would take everything that belongs to us, even the spirits of the ancestors!' she yelled. Her last words came screaming out in Lakota, the emphatic chopping sounds of the vowels giving infinitely more effect to the universal message of 'fuck you all!'

The mixture of despair and hatred in the woman's voice gutted Gary. He had expected to be abused for his part in disinterring the bundle but he hated being hated by the fine looking woman before him. From the moment he first saw her, he had been struck by the calm native beauty of her face and now, in a perverse way, he found even more beauty in the fiery look that she leveled upon him.

Grace's emotions finally condensed into tears and, in frustration, she raised both hands to pound on Gary's chest. But he was quicker than her and he reached out his arms and held her to him, tightly embracing her as she struggled to get free, her body convulsing with sobbing. He kept holding on, even as she cried out angrily for him to let go. Tenderly, he put a hand behind her head and pulled her face to his shoulder, until her hands slowly dropped to her sides and her body went limp. He let her cry there for several seconds then let go.

Grace stood with her head hanging for a few seconds, emotions spent. Then, slowly, she raised her eyes and glanced up into those of the man before her, the look lingering for a moment before she turned and walked to the passenger door of the pickup.

Looks Back was already sitting in the vehicle from where he had watched the scene, seemingly unaffected. The stranger *was* connected and, with that little glance his granddaughter had just given him, he saw the way ahead opening up for both of them.

Jamie was more affected. At first he was as angry with the man as his mother and was about to tear into him as she struggled to get free of his hold but, when he saw the comforting way he pulled her to him and her submission, he turned away as if embarrassed. A slight smile then formed on his face.

After everyone climbed back in the cab, Gary drove down the hill, but when he got out to unlock the gate, Jamie followed and offered to close it for him. After they drove on again, the small boy continued the thawing process.

'My name's Jamie Howard... what's yours?'

'Gary... Gary Schroeder.'

Jamie continued, 'This is my great grandfather, George Looks Back, and my mom, Grace.'

Gary turned towards the other two passengers and nodded without saying anything. It was hardly the time for any 'pleased to meet ya's', and he was still in a slight state of shock at the woman's performance. Although he had read a great deal lately about the sacredness with which the Lakota held the Black Hills, he hadn't truly understood the depth of emotion involved until it had gotten up close and personal. What he had seen in the woman's eyes had made him run the gauntlet of his own emotions, her pain highlighting his feelings of shame, guilt and inadequacy. But then, with that last little glance, his desire to see her again overruled everything else.

'The Spirit Bundle is in my apartment in Rapid City. I'm going there now. You can come with me if you like or

I can get it to you tomorrow. Just tell me where,' Gary said to Grace as they arrived at the spot where the hire car had been left.

Grace didn't answer immediately. She too remained a little stunned by her behavior. What she knew was going to be a distasteful experience had exploded on her, the years since she had last seen the valley sent, like shrapnel, flying away. It was as though she had just attended the funeral of a dearly beloved, her memories of the valley reading like a eulogy over its deceased form and now, like an undertaker, a stranger was asking her what she wanted done with some of its remains.

'It must be done now,' Looks Back answered for her.

The three transferred to the compact and followed the Chevy along the route to Rapid City. About an hour later they entered its outer precincts and a few minutes later followed Gary up the stairs from the small parking lot behind his apartment building.

'Sorry about the mess but I left here without doing my housework,' Gary said limply, as he opened the door and waved his visitors through.

'What mess?' Jamie enquired, flashing a smile at his serious-faced mother.

Gary went straight to the wall unit, leant up, took the Spirit Bundle from behind the stack of books and handed it to Grace.

'I'll get you something better to carry it in,' he said and walked quickly to the bathroom.

Grace placed the bundle on the desk next to the wall unit and pulled back the newspaper wrapping slightly to reveal what was inside.

Jamie looked on with silent curiosity but an audible sigh came from Looks Back as he sighted the bundle.

Gary came back with a towel and handed it to Grace. He then watched uneasily as she laid it out on the desk and placed the bundle in it.

After carefully rolling it up in the towel, Grace handed it to Looks Back, holding it out on her two upturned hands in a ceremonial way. He uttered an acceptance in Lakota before walking to the door, opening it and heading towards the stairs.

Grace turned to Gary. 'I ask you not to say anything to anybody about unearthing the Spirit Bundle. Also, I will eventually need you to bear witness to finding it but I can't say just when at the moment. And this other thing you mentioned - your suspicions about the company, can you hold off on that? I don't want them to be alerted to anything until I move on the bundle.'

'Yeah, I can do that,' Gary immediately replied, impressed by her purposeful manner. He still hadn't sorted out in his mind what he was going to do regarding his suspicions. They had instantly taken second place anyway to the pleasing thought he would still have contact with this interesting woman. He leant down to the desk and wrote something on a piece of note paper. 'Here's my cell phone number.' He made as if to hand it to Grace then pulled it away as she went to take it. 'I'll show you mine if you show me yours,' he said with a gentle, mischievous kind of a smile.

In spite of her somber mood, a faint smile crossed Grace's face. She leant down and scribbled her number on the notepad then took the piece of paper from Gary's hand. 'We'll go now. I'll be in touch.'

When they reached the door Jamie smiled and offered Gary his hand.

'See ya, Gary.'

'See ya, Jamie,' Gary responded with a smile. 'See ya, Grace' he added.

Grace nodded before she and Jamie headed across the landing but, halfway to the stairs, she told Jamie to go on ahead. She turned and walked back to Gary.

'Can you tell me just when you opened the bundle?' she asked.

'Well, it took me over a week to do it but I finally opened it early one Sunday morning, a couple of months ago. Hang on and I'll check the calendar.' He walked quickly to his desk and flipped the pages of the calendar, tracking the weeks back according to the work duties he had jotted down on the previous Saturdays. 'Yeah, it was Sunday, 26th of March,' he called out then walked back to the door. 'Why do you ask?'

'I needed to know,' Grace stated, before walking away again.

Gary also needed to know something.

'What will you do about Prestige?'

Grace stopped and turned around. Her face was calm but there was a piercing, steely look in her eyes. 'I'm going to sink that development,' she said then walked quickly down the stairs.

Gary closed the door then went to a side window and watched as Grace walked to her car, got in and drove out. The power of her declaration had stunned him. She appeared to be on a mission and, against all improbability, he believed she could succeed. He wanted to know how she intended to go about it. And there was something else he wanted to know. He wondered where the father of her boy was. Did she have a man? It was hard to imagine an attractive woman like that being without one. He hadn't even found out where she was living. He walked over to where his guitar lay on the sofa, sat down and began to vacantly play the chords of a blues song. Before long he was tinkering with that other tune, the one that always seemed to intrude on his playing now. After a while he put the guitar down and went to his computer. He pulled up his correspondence file and changed the date on his resignation letter to the current day then printed it off and put it in an envelope. With it in hand he left his apartment and began walking the few blocks to Prestige's office, unmindful of the person keeping pace with him a little farther back on the opposite side of the road.

FIFTEEN

A reflective silence settled on the three in the car as Grace drove south but as they moved along the highway her mind was slipping into overdrive. The path she had been led along for months was now clearly defined and what Jamie would say a few minutes into the drive was simply accepted as part of it.

'Looks Back wants me to stay with him for a couple of days, Mom.'

Grace just nodded. It was clear whilst she had been away talking to the surveyor that her son and her grandfather had also been speaking about something important. Jamie was about the right age now. Another step towards his manhood was about to be taken and, although a feeling of sadness came with the thought, instead of arguing about the difficulties it would present to their schedule she simply began re-calculating it.

'Okay, I'll pick you up in two days,' she finally said.

'That will be enough,' was Looks Back's final comment before going to sleep for the rest of the journey.

It was late afternoon when Grace pulled into the parking lot of the Sioux Nation Supermarket in Pine Ridge, with a mission in mind. Looks Back had been chewing on his black jellybeans for most of the day, only nibbling a small part of the tuna salad sandwich she had bought for him on their way to Rapid City. Amusing at first, his sugary intake had become a worry to her. Due to poor nutrition, diabetes was at almost epidemic proportions on the reservation, about half of the adult population being affected by it some way. A lack of regular supplies of fresh fruit and vegetables was part of the problem but the regular diet of government-issue generic rations packed with fat, carbohydrates, salt and sugar, was the major factor. Eaten only because they were 'free', the ultimate price was amputated limbs, damaged eyesight and the many other health problems associated with diabetes and Grace saw Looks Back's candy eating habit as a dangerous addition. His calm reply when she voiced her concern on the drive back was, 'I have taken the tests and nothin's shown up so far. I think that maybe the beans are magic bullets as well as thinkin' food.' She was relieved to hear he was taking the tests but magic bullets or not she had decided to at least make him a decent meal before leaving.

The three of them got out of the car and headed towards the long, low-slung red concrete block building that housed the supermarket, weaving their way through a crowded parking lot that doubled for a marketplace. Amongst the buying and selling activity, Grace noticed a scene once so familiar to her, a small group of men and women huddled near a car, glancing nervously around before exchanging money for something from a man on the passenger side, then hurrying or staggering away. One of the men looked their way and stared for a moment before leaving the huddle and heading towards them. She knew about the doper's instinct for strangers, too. Hitting them up for a few bucks was always more successful, even if the lies told were never believed. A sense of panic overtook her. She didn't want to hear the lies nor see the reflection in his eyes. She didn't want to help pay for his journey to hell either but she knew she wouldn't be able to refuse. Jamie was dawdling along in front of her and she pushed him to go faster.

'Take it easy, Mom... I'm not a freakin' shopping trolley!'

'C'mon, let's get this over with and get outta here!' Grace almost yelled, as she finally rushed past him and into the building.

Once inside the supermarket, Looks Back left Grace at the vegetable section and headed purposefully towards another aisle.

'Gotta pick up some ammunition,' the old man said, as he shuffled away.

Jamie quickly followed, the option of perusing fruit and vegetables coming a distant last to virtually everything else in his life.

They all met up again at the checkout, where four large packets of Simply Black jellybeans and one of Jamie's favorites, Puffee marshmallows, joined the queue of items Grace was placing on the counter – three very large t-bone steaks, a dozen eggs, a couple of large bottles of orange juice and the best fruit and vegetables she could find amidst the meager selection. She smiled crookedly and shook her head when she saw the confectionary.

As Jamie stood waiting for his mother to pay for the groceries, he gazed absent-mindedly at the others lined up at the checkouts, skipping across the faces until his gaze settled on a small girl, about four years old, shyly holding onto the leg of a woman. The child's face bore the same mark as his but, just like those he had seen on his previous trip to

Pine Ridge, more savagely so, half her top lip non-existent, her upper teeth twisted at angles. She was staring at him, so he smiled at her. She instinctively smiled back but her face just grew uglier and with a habitual reflex, she quickly covered her mouth and turned away. Jamie looked away also, disturbed once more.

Grace exited the supermarket as she had entered; head down and hurrying towards the car, where she almost threw the groceries on the back seat. She had it reversed out of its bay by the time Looks Back and Jamie arrived but, just as they climbed in, a knock came on the driver's window. Grace pushed the window button, eyes averted from the man standing at the door as she quickly fished through her bag.

'Hey, sister... could you spare a few bucks for...'

Grace handed him a five-dollar note before he could finish, pressing the window up and driving off almost in the same movement, only briefly glancing in the rear-vision mirror at the hopeless looking figure moving back towards his peer group.

'Ya coulda given him a chance to say thanks, Mom,' Jamie protested.

'I wasn't doing him any favors,' came the terse reply.

Several seconds of silence passed before Jamie spoke again. 'I'm just glad his coat sleeve wasn't caught in the window. Coulda been a noisy trip back to the trailer'.

A smile slowly formed on Looks Back's face and a few seconds later, Grace suddenly burst out laughing.

Soon after, they were back on the main road but, about three miles out of town, Looks Back asked Grace to stop by at a lone house, sitting on a rise about half a mile off the highway. She drove in through the same sort of wrecker's yard that surrounded Looks Back's trailer, except that here there were six skinny dogs loudly proclaiming their territory.

An old man was sitting on the veranda of the small timber house, the shade of a large black hat hiding his features, with only his shoulder length silver hair indicating where his face should be. But Grace knew who he was.

'Wait here,' Looks Back said.

The two in the car watched as Looks Back walked slowly towards the house, kicked a couple of the threatening dogs away then stepped up onto the porch and shook hands with the seated man. Grace stared intently. It seemed to her that the shaman had been around forever. He was old when she was a little girl, always held in awe and a certain amount of fear by her and the other children. She remembered how they used to whisper to each other about the spells he cast over the boys and how they didn't behave the same after being taken to him. But as she grew older, she learned about the Vision Quest, the rite of passage for young teenage boys and now she knew that he was soon going to apply his medicine to her child.

'Who is he, Mom?'

'He is a medicine man. His name is William Dream Seeker.'

'What does he do?'

'What has Looks Back told you about these days ahead, Hon?'

'Nothin' much. He just said there are some things I have to learn.'

'Well, Dream Seeker is a teacher... in the traditional way. Granpa is asking him about teaching you.'

Jamie didn't say anything more; he just nodded his head slowly, concentrating as he stared into the dark shadow beneath the hat. He couldn't be sure but he felt the eyes of the medicine man were upon him.

After a few minutes conversation, Looks Back returned to the car. He said nothing about the meeting and no questions were asked as they headed off towards his place.

That evening, Grace cooked her decent meal on a primitive barbecue outside the entrance to the trailer. The three then ate it inside at a table meant for one, where Looks Back did as he was told and ate all his vegetables as well as the giant steak, the bone of which he was chewing on for ten minutes after the meal, before finally throwing it to his drooling hound.

After washing the dishes the three sat outside and, under the light of a paraffin lamp, looked through an old biscuit tin full of aged photographs, the faded images of Jamie's relations being introduced to him one by one. Grace identified most of the people in the photos while Looks Back commented on their place in family history, although he said nothing when they came across one of his wife, Naomi. After Grace told Jamie who it was, the old man picked up the photo, stared briefly at the image then placed it in his pocket.

Looks Back's response to the photo of his wife said many things to Grace and, when she later came to one particular faded black and white portrait, her stunned silence sent an unspoken message to him.

Of course, how could she have forgotten? She knew the elderly woman looking back at her from the photograph but she still turned it over to read the faded ink on the back. *Fawn, Pine Ridge, 1904* it said. She turned it back and looked at the grand matriarch with the floral scarf wrapped tightly around her face and was tempted to add *Big Bat's, Pine Ridge, 2000* to the inscription on the back.

'Who is that, Mom?'

'It is Fawn... your great, great, great grandmother... Eyes That Cut's wife,' Grace said haltingly.

'Yeah?' Jamie responded excitedly He took the photograph and studied the image of Fawn closely, her head held high,

166

her soulful eyes still showing through the deterioration of the photograph.

Looks Back eyed Grace with curiosity as he spoke to Jamie. 'You keep the photo. Take them all when you go. They are of your family. They must be handed on.'

'Yeah? Thanksth!'

Looks Back continued to stare at Grace, drawing her eyes to his like a magnet. She turned and looked at him for just a moment then shifted her gaze back to the photo Jamie was still studying. 'Yes, Hon... they *are* your family. They are part of you, and they are with you,' she said, adding a certain emphasis to the last few words. Jamie looked up and responded with a confirming, almost knowing kind of a smile. A few seconds later she spoke again, broaching the subject that seemed to be at the center of all the connections in her life lately, 'What will you do with the Spirit Bundle, Granpa?'

Looks Back had been thinking about that question for most of the day, the fact that it had already been opened, and by an outsider, was going to prevent him from carrying out the full ceremony but some of it would have to be performed.

'A Spirit Keeper has already been chosen. He has opened the bundle and the spirit has flown but I will follow what is left of our custom. I will keep the bundle for a while before distributing the items in it. Then all that will remain is to bury our ancestor's heart again in the *Paha Sapa*. But right now it is time for me to sleep.'

Grace wouldn't push it any further. She badly needed the physical proof of the bundle for the journey on which she was about to embark but she couldn't ask for it yet.

With Looks Back's last words they all retired to bed, Grace and Jamie bunking down on the floor near the door of the trailer, rolling out their sleeping bags on a blanket in the space cleared for them. The two guests lay quietly for a while, listening to the light snoring of the old man who had gone to sleep the instant he pulled a blanket over him. Then a small voice whispered through the darkness.

'Are you awake, Mom?'

'Mmm.'

'What will the medicine man teach me?'

'He will teach you what to do in the Vision Quest. He will be your guide.'

'What's a Vision Quest?'

'It's the first step to becoming a man... to help you see the way ahead. All of it will be explained to you,' Grace replied, wondering just how much of the quest her son had already been on and how many guides he already had.

Jamie changed the subject. 'What happened to Looks Back's wife, Mom?'

A brief silence followed before Grace replied in a whisper, 'Grandma Naomi died before I was born, from leukemia, just a few years after the war. Granpa doesn't like to talk about it. It saddens him. They were very much in love and he had a hard time afterwards bringing up a daughter on his own, only to see her die too. Then he had to look after me, and, well, you've already learned about how I let him down. All in all, he hasn't had much luck with the females in his life.'

'But you came back, Mom.'

'Yeah,' Grace sighed. 'Now go to sleep.'

A long silence passed, before Jamie spoke again. 'Mom, why are there so many kids here with cleft palates?'

He was answered with what sounded like the heavy breath of a sleeper.

SIXTEEN

A hammering sound woke Grace and Jamie early the next morning and they sat up and peered groggily out through the open doorway. Looks Back was standing about twenty yards from the trailer, pounding a tall wooden stake into the ground and, after a few more blows, he stopped, tested its rigidity and then began to tie something to it.

'What's he doin', Mom?'

'He's fixing the bundle to a spirit post. It's part of the old tradition to keep it in such a place until it is ready to be opened.'

'When will that be?'

'When Granpa decides. It could be anytime. He will know.'

'Is Eyes That Cut's heart really in the bundle, Mom?'

'Yes,' she replied, and then climbed out of her sleeping bag. She walked over and picked up the empty bucket next to the sink. 'Can you go to the pump and fill the bucket, Hon? I'm gonna wash and then make some breakfast before I go.'

'Mornin', Looks Back,' Jamie said as he passed the old man now making his way back to the trailer.

'Seems to be,' came the quiet reply.

169

Jamie stared at the bundle lashed to the post. It was wrapped in some pale buckskin now and the top of the post had a red face painted on it, giving it an almost lifelike presence that kept him at a respectful distance as he walked to and from the pump.

After Grace washed herself in the privacy of the trailer, she dressed in her traveling clothes and then took the carton of eggs out of Looks Back's small gas-powered fridge. She began breaking them, intending to make an omelet.

'No food for us, Songbird. We must begin the fast now,' said Looks Back.

Of course, the first step of the purification, Grace recalled. She placed the egg yolks in a bowl and put them back in the fridge, feeling uncomfortable about eating now. Instead she boiled up some water and made herself coffee.

Jamie was already hungry and concerned about just how long it would be before he would be eating again. The next comment from his mother indicated that it wouldn't be anytime soon.

'Make sure you drink plenty of water during the day, Jamie. I will leave you the bottles we brought with us.'

Grace knew that she was excess to requirements now and gathered her things quickly before heading to the car. She handed Jamie the remaining four quart bottles of water they had brought with them, piling them up log style in his arms.

'I'll see ya in two days, kid. I've decided we won't head for home when I come back. I'm gonna ask Boss to bring me down and then we will go straight to Seattle.'

Grace pecked her reluctant charge on the cheek then took his face in her hands and stared into his eyes. 'Do everything you are told to do, Jamie.' She then gave the same seemingly thankless kiss on the cheek to her grandfather before waving goodbye. She watched them through the rear vision mirror until she hit the top of the ridge, when their backs turned on her and they headed for the trailer. A few minutes later, a battered Ford pickup passed her on its way to Looks Back's place. Driving it was a solidly built young man who smiled widely and waved as the vehicles passed each other. Seated next to him was the medicine man, William Dream Seeker, staring ahead as blank-faced as ever. Grace watched unsmilingly in the rear vision mirror as they carried on, heading towards their men's business.

*

It was nearing dusk, the warmth of the late spring day rapidly fading into the early evening chill of the high country and Jamie was finally alone, in a manner of speaking. A couple of miles away in the valley, where he had taken the purification, were Looks Back and the medicine man's grandson, Jesse Bright Face, the constantly smiling young man who had helped prepare and tend the fire for the sweat lodge. They had brought him to this part of the Black Hills as the final part of his Vision Quest. Although he knew he had to be there, as darkness fell the fear that came with it began to clutch at him and he wasn't so sure of his quest anymore. He hadn't eaten a thing all day and right now he felt as if he could kill for one of Looks Back's jellybeans. He shivered with the cold and climbed into his sleeping bag, perched on a ledge in a rocky outcrop that Jesse had directed him to in the afternoon when he was left to walk the last mile alone. 'Stay there until the morning, little brother' he had said and Jamie could only agree. Where else would he be able to go in the dark, except on his Vision Quest.

The night closed in and with it came the first sounds of its wildlife. He heard a coyote howling and another answering, then another and another until the whole valley seemed to be filled with their sound. He began to imagine them talking about him - 'There's a small boy in our valley, not much of a feed but he would be a good starter, hee hee, hee, ha, ha, ha, owoooooo.' Maybe they weren't coyotes. Maybe they were wolves! Then he thought about grizzlies and cougars, even though he had been told that there were none in the hills anymore. But how did they know that for sure? The country had still looked pretty wild to him when he tramped through it earlier, following a stream that occasionally threw up the splash of feeding trout and where he later saw a couple of pronghorn antelope drinking; if there was that sort of food supply around, why not the carnivores to eat it?

'Remain alert. Seek to find the connection in everything, the father sky, the mother earth, the wind, the stars, even your fear.' The words that Looks Back translated from Dream Seeker drifted through Jamie's mind. It was the last thing the frail old man had said before being driven back to the comfort of his home in Pine Ridge and it was the one thing Jamie had totally understood. He had always looked at things that way, as if everything in nature had a soul, a connection to another world - even a grain of sand. Suddenly, he heard one of those souls rustling through some bushes not far from him and he turned his pen light on and shone it towards the sound. He could see nothing, so he took a swig from his water bottle and began to wade into the center of his fear. Then he called out for some help.

'I'm sthcaaared, John!' he cried out.

There was a brief silence, then 'Don't start with all that little boy shite! Yer out 'ere to become a man so get on with it! And stop listhpin', the singsong Liverpudlian accent murmured across the ledge.

'Ya mean become a meal, dontcha? It's alright for you. You're out there somewhere playin' your guitar, writin' songs and havin' a good ol' time. I haven't even got proper balls yet and there's a good chance they'll be gone by mornin'!'

'Look out! Ther's a fookin' great furry grizzly standin' behind yer!' came the reply, quickly followed by, 'Just jokin', man. It's only a fookin' cougar.'

Jamie honked out loud at the conversation and, when he stopped laughing, he found that the howling had too. The night suddenly became very still. He relaxed a little and, as he stared up into the black, diamond-specked mirror of the universe, the events of the day began to be reflected in it.

Just after his mother had left that morning he had met the medicine man, a creepy, dark-skinned person whose hand felt like leather when he shook it. William Dream Seeker was totally blind and that made Jamie feel even more spooked about sensing those dead, milky eyes upon him the day before. The old man spoke only in Lakota and then not much at all but everything that he said was listened to carefully by Looks Back and translated. Yet the shaman's grandson was a total opposite. He was the happiest soul Jamie had ever met, always laughing and joking and reassuring him that the day would be a good one. But after they had arrived at the sweat lodge site in a southern part of the Black Hills, Jesse had become silent and serious too as he built the fire that would burn for hours, heating the rocks to be placed in a shallow pit in the center of the lodge. Jamie had sat with Looks Back and Dream Seeker during this time, listening to the explanation of the ritual; about how important it was to have the right location, the right kind of wood and the herbs of sage, sweet grass, cedar and, most importantly, tobacco, which was used as an offering to the Great Mystery Power. Occasionally, Dream Seeker would call out an instruction in Lakota to his grandson and Jesse would respond with a word or two of acknowledgement and a respectful nod as he continued with the preparation.

Finally, it was time to enter the tarpaulin and blanket-covered lodge, stripped naked and crawling backwards through the small entry, a very uncomfortable moment for Jamie.

'It is like going back into your mother's belly,' Looks Back had said but all Jamie registered at first was the embarrassment of being naked with the two old men, trying to cover himself and not look at their shriveled bodies and pendulous extremities, although his eyes would linger a little on the scars he saw upon Looks Back's chest. As he entered the lodge he felt overwhelmed by the heat and claustrophobia of its dark, humid interior. It was so hot that he felt like scrambling straight back out but he fought hard against the desire. As the sweat began to purge the physical toxins from his body, just as Looks Back had said, the mind's impurities were expelled as well. It all began to feel entirely normal and, while he was kneeling in what had transformed into an almost welcoming environment and listened to the shaman and his grandfather's constant prayer singing, something began to work on him.

Jamie had learned early in the process that four was the big number in Lakota spiritual beliefs – the four winds, the four elements and the four directions, the hoops that joined everything to the center, with four rounds of prayers to be made inside the lodge, one to each of those directions. He didn't know how long the prayers lasted because, in the darkness, all time felt as though it were suspended, but after each round, Looks Back's would take his hand and he would move with both old men to the next direction, during which time Jesse would open the entrance and add more heated rocks to the pit with a pitchfork. Looks Back would splash some water on them before proceeding and it was during the second round of prayers, as the steam rose with the two men's voices, that the big effect of the ceremony took hold of Jamie. Slowly, the measured rhythm of the singing began to soothe him into a kind of semi-hypnotic state and he began to feel as if he were shrinking back into himself; going back to a beginning; to a center. Later, when he finally emerged from the lodge, he felt as if he were exploding out from that center again, billowing into life. Everything became new and fresh and, as he had walked to the point where he was now, he felt more connected than ever to all around him, as alert as he could possibly be.

A hoot owl suddenly called through the silence and tested Jamie's now razor-sharp alertness. He took another nervous swig of his water bottle and listened to the fluid making its way through him, his stomach finally gurgling as if in disappointment at its arrival. He kept his eyes on the slowly changing pattern of the sky. 'Let yourself float free and the vision will come,' Looks back had told him. But his mind was not ready to stop thinking just yet. He had learned something else earlier in the day when he and Looks Back had sat together for a couple of hours after the sweat, waiting for Jesse to return from Pine Ridge. It was then that he again asked a question that had been bugging him since he had seen the girl at the supermarket.

'Looks Back, why are there so many children here with my problem... my mouth?'

A long silence passed before an answer came. 'Some think that the mother's blood has been poisoned... that all the drilling for minerals in the Black Hills has tainted the water. Some say uranium has been released into the underground streams. Others say it isn't so but more children seem to be born these days with the problem you speak of.'

The universe slowly turned on its axis as Jamie thought long and hard about Looks Backs words, thinking too about the time his mother had sobbed her heart out to him and about what he had seen at the valley. After a while, he began to hear her singing the Eyes That Cut song, *The Water Talks* and pondered on the English translation she had given him. Like jigsaw pieces, the words began to connect with the other thoughts floating through his mind. He pulled his notebook and pen out of a top pocket, turned on his torch and wrote the title of the old song at the head of a new one.

Jamie dropped quickly into the zone, the lines coming in a certain, measured way and without a scratch-out. He applied the translated verses of the Lakota song before each new one, noting that the native words were to be sung exactly in tune and time with the notes in a guitar riff, voice and instrument inseparable. He couldn't hear the riff yet but he knew it had to be done with a slide; the sound mellow, with the tone of muted power his mother sometimes used, like emotions straining on a leash ready to explode, a far away kind of sound. A lazy blues beat was playing through his head as he wrote, underlying all the new lyrics, with a few bars of it separating them from the old. And there was an exotic instrument too working its way into the piece. When he had finished writing, he stared at his work for a while and then read the words out loud, as if speaking to all that surrounded him, starting with the first set of Lakota lyrics, followed by the English ones.

'Mother
I hear your voice
It is sweet and clear
It flows through me

'They say now that the mother's dying
That the needles have tainted her blood
And you can hear her voice a'crying
From the trickle and the flood
She's sending a message to the people
But they listen now in fear

Torn mouths are doing her talking
And poison is all they hear

'Mother
I touch your flesh
It is warm
It is mine

'They say now that the mother's screaming
That the blades are gouging her flesh
That her dead are raised from sleeping
And soon there'll be no place left to rest
No valley for spirits to wander
For the fear of hearing fore
Where the sound of water talking
Just means a poorer score

'Mother
I sing for you
I fight for you
I die for you

'They say now that the mother's pleading
Don't let her cry in vain
She sees the lie of progress
And she's trying to explain
The connection's being broken
The water talks of this
But the last words have not been spoken
We can change them if we wish

Jamie had repeated the last line of the first two English verses several times, gradually fading them into the instrument break he could hear. At the last verse his voice gradually grew louder until he was shouting the last line and then he abruptly stopped, closed his notebook and gradually drifted off to sleep. By the time he opened his eyes again the sun was beating down. He stretched and turned onto his side but was suddenly startled to see a pair of brown feet standing not far from his face. He looked up quickly and saw a boy about the same age as he, long black hair to his shoulders and naked to the waist.

'Dreaming again?' the boy asked.

Jamie peered at him for several seconds before speaking, 'You're not supposed to be here. I'm on a Vision Quest.'

The boy smiled, turned and began to walk away. 'Ho-i-yé!' he called out, motioning Jamie to follow as he made his way down from the ledge.

Jamie climbed out of his sleeping bag and followed, his body feeling strangely but wonderfully free as he raced like a gazelle with the boy to the creek about a hundred yards away. When they got to the stream the boy lay down on the edge of it and let his hand hang under the water. 'Hu-yá!' he cried out after a short while, lifting his arm out of the water and hurling a fish onto the bank. He motioned to Jamie to try it.

Jamie lay down and placed his arm in the water and after a while he felt a tickle on his hand then the cold form of a fish settle in it. He grabbed it and threw it out with an equally triumphant cry. The boy nodded with appreciation and repeated the procedure two more times then, after quickly braiding some grass into a cord, he passed it through the gills of the fish and hung them in the water. Then he jumped in and went for a swim. Jamie joined him and they frolicked together in the way of boys who had known each other for a long time, splashing, laughing and wrestling.

'What's your name?' Jamie suddenly asked the boy.

The boy answered in Lakota.

'What does that mean in English?'

The boy didn't reply; he just splashed Jamie one more time and climbed out of the water then began to run off.

Jamie followed happily, until the boy suddenly stopped and put his hand up to him. Ahead of them was a Pronghorn antelope browsing through a grove of trees and his friend crouched low and crept stealthily up on it, making a motion of firing an arrow before it ran off. They moved on, following the tracks of other small animals until the heat drove them back to the creek. They swam again until they were cool then lay down in the warm sun and went to sleep. Only a brief time seemed to pass before Jamie heard the sound of another voice.

'Gotta go, man. Gotta work on the album.'

The Liverpool accent roused Jamie out of sleep. He opened his eyes. He was back on the ledge, the rising sun rapidly heating up the rocky outcrop. He looked around but could see no sign of the boy. He crawled out of the stifling sleeping bag and sat up, saddened that the dream had ended. Then he heard a voice calling from nearby.

'Where are you, little brother?'

Jamie stood up and waved. 'I'm here, Jesse!' He rolled up his sleeping bag and made his way down the rocky slope.

Jesse greeted him with a thumb clasp handshake. 'Glad to see the grizzlies didn't get ya.'

Jamie smiled but didn't reply. His mind was still fixed on the vision of the longhaired, brown-skinned boy dressed in a buckskin breechclout and he was trying hard to recall his Lakota name. He pondered on it until they reached the stream, where he stopped to stare at the water. Then it suddenly came to him. He tried to get his mouth around the vowels, mouthing it quietly and clumsily several times but just loud enough for Jesse to hear.

'What is it, little brother?'

Jamie made two more tentative attempts to pronounce the name to the puzzled man before him but it still didn't come out properly. He became frustrated and then angrily yelled it out.

Jesse leaned back. 'Whoa, cool it, man!'

'What do those words mean in English, Jesse?'

'Say them again, slowly.'

Jamie sighed. He concentrated hard and mouthed the words as best as he could.

'Sounds like 'walks softly'. Why?'

'I had a dream last night. There was a boy in it and that was his name.'

'You don't have to tell anyone about what happened last night, man. But if you have a need to talk maybe it is Looks Back you should speak to.'

Jamie nodded and they set off again, both quiet for a while, until a conversation about basketball started up and a good-natured argument was carried on between the Bull's fan and the Phoenix Sun's follower most of the way back to camp. A hundred yards away from their destination they could smell the bacon and eggs that Looks Back had begun cooking and they picked up the pace.

Looks Back didn't acknowledge Jamie when he first walked in, he just kept on cooking but, when he had finished and handed him a plate of food, he stared intently into his great grandson's shining eyes and smiled the slightest smile. He then filled his and Jesse's plate and they all sat back and ravenously broke the fast, demolishing the half-scrambled eggs, fry bread and charcoal crisp bacon in quick time.

Half an hour after they had eaten, they left the simple camp that had been set up about two hundred yards from the sweat lodge and, as they drove by its now skeletal willow frame, Jamie stared a little sadly. It had only been a day in his life but he felt strongly that he was leaving something behind and the thought of it brought back the memory of the dream. How real it had felt, just as real as the ones he had had of John Lennon, and how wonderful it had felt to be physically set free, running wild with his friend, before it was abruptly ended in that crazy way. But the end of it reminded him of what was now ahead. He thought of the album and felt a thrill run through him as he remembered the lyrics he had written last night, his mind already working on how to arrange the music before the pickup hit the highway back to Pine Ridge. Jesse unknowingly helped too, when he turned on the car radio and Jamie heard Kili, the Lakota owned and operated station that broadcast to the Pine Ridge, Cheyenne River and Rosebud reservations.

Interspersed with the DJ's Lakota and English radio-speak was rock music of all the varieties you would hear on any station anywhere but with a regular infusion of Native American music, folk and rock. The tribal rock wasn't unlike the stuff Jamie had heard before but the rhythmic beat of stamping feet and the tambourine-like rattle of ankle bells in one of the traditional folk numbers gave him another idea for *The Water Talks*. He pulled out his notebook and started making notes next to the lyrics. His scribbling brought Jesse's attention.

'What ya doin' there, man?'

'I'm writin' a song.'

'Uh huh.'

'He is a song catcher,' came Looks Back's sudden declaration.

'Yeah... you told me it was so,' the big man said.

Jamie smiled with pleasure at his declared status, and then quickly added, 'My Mom's a song catcher too. She's a singer with a band and we're all goin' up to Seattle tomorrow to make an album. And one of the songs is called *Song Catcher*.

'Yeah, I've heard all about your Mom and *Warrior*. Some of our people have been to the gigs. What's the album gonna be called?'

'*Spirit Rising*. It's sorta rock 'n roll but in a different way. We're gonna be usin' Eyes That Cut's songs in all of the tracks. He's my great, great, great grandfather and he fought with Crazy Horse.'

'Yeah, I know that too. Tell you what, little brother. I've got contacts at Kili radio. You send me a copy of your album and I'll get you some airplay... deal?'

'Deal!' Jamie confirmed with a slap on Jesse's upturned palm, and then wrote down his mailing address.

An hour later, he sadly waved goodbye to Bright Face and then spent the next hour hauling buckets of water from the well to be warmed up for Looks Back's weekly wash, in what he called the missionary pot. He sat watching from the step of the trailer as the old man undressed and stepped into the iron bath, set up over a small fire. He was no longer embarrassed by his nakedness but as curious about part of it as he had been in the sweat lodge.

'What are those scars, Looks Back?'

'They are from the Sun Dance,' Looks Back replied, eyes closed as he luxuriated in the steaming water. 'From when I was a young man... when the ceremony was banned by the authorities.'

'Why was it banned?'

'They couldn't stand the sight of us Injuns hangin' round the joint with bones stuck through our chests. Maybe it looked too much like nails through the hands. They figured we were savages and banned everythin' back then. They tried to make us all into whites. It started in the schools when they tried to stop us speakin' our language and if you were caught they beat the crap out of you. But me and my friends always used it when we were alone together. We felt that if we lost our language we would lose our souls. And when we grew old enough, we sneaked away and performed the Sun Dance and other rituals. That's the only way we could hang onto our culture back then, sneakin' 'round, hidin' it, singin' our songs quietly. Not everyone held on though and a lot has been lost but you have some of the songs now and I am glad they will be heard again. I hope by many.'

'How did you put up with the pain of the Sun Dance?'

'I don't really remember the pain. There is a time when you pass through the bright light and leave it behind. When you stare at the sun for long enough, answers come and you are shown the way.'

There was a long silence as Looks Back soaped his hair and face and then used a can to scoop up clean water out of a bucket next to the bath and wash it off.

'Can I do the Sun Dance?'

Looks Back kept slowly and methodically rinsing his hair then, after a while, he put the can back in the bucket and looked intently at Jamie.

'You have already done yours. Your mother tells me that you have passed through the bright light many times. The scars are upon your back and you have been shown your way. You are a song catcher and that is your man's name.'

After the almost casual conferring of Jamie's Lakota name, Looks Back then raised himself out of the bath. 'It's your turn. I don't want your mother thinkin' I couldn't keep you clean.'

Jamie looked at the scum floating on the water and couldn't see how that was going to help. He picked up an empty bucket and scooped it off then hauled some more water from the well to dilute the gray soapy contents of the bath. Then he spent another half-hour lying in it with his cooling wet t-shirt over his head, thinking about his man's name and his man's path.

'Do ya wanna hear the words of a song I caught last night, Looks Back?'

The old man was now sitting clean and freshly clothed under his ragged tarpaulin lean-to, his eyes closed as if asleep. 'Yes,' he replied, without opening them.

Jamie dried his hands on the towel, hanging on an old hat-rack, standing at the head of the bath. Then he reached for his jeans and took his notebook out of a pocket. He glanced at the spirit post, loudly and respectfully announcing the original title, *The Water Talks*, and that Eyes That Cut's song would be used as the chorus between the verses. Then he began to recite the words.

Eyes still closed, Looks Back began to gently sing the old song after Jamie had read out his new words, and when he had finished, he said, 'Yes, it will be a good song.'

Jamie put the notebook away and the t-shirt back on his head, before speaking through it.

'I had a dream last night. There was a boy in it... a Lakota boy. He told me his name. I can't pronounce it properly but Jesse said it sounded like 'Walks Softly'. We went fishing together and tracked animals. It was a great dream. I felt as if he was a good friend. What does it mean?'

Looks back's eyes slowly opened and he stared at Jamie. He deliberated for a while before answering. Another connection had been made but at the moment he wouldn't speak of it to the boy. Finally he said, 'All dreams have meanings. In the end they come. For now, maybe it's enough for you to know he is your friend.'

'Mmmm,' Jamie concurred after several seconds of consideration and then climbed out of the bath. It was getting on towards evening and, even after their lunchtime pile of sandwiches made out of the large steak that Grace couldn't finish two nights before, the hole left by fasting was still crying out to be filled.

'What's for dinner? I'm starvin'.'

'Me too,' Looks Back replied with uncharacteristic enthusiasm. He got up from his seat to walk inside. 'Let's see what we can rustle up.'

Half an hour later they sat down to the omelet that Grace had begun the morning she left, their joint effort more like scrambled eggs with vegetables and was consumed quickly before being washed down with some cold orange juice. After the meal they played several games of checkers, all of which Looks Back won. He was ruthless and chortling in the dispatching of his younger foe, who found it difficult to master the simple forward thinking logic of the game after years of computer challenges that required a lightning response. During this humbling experience however, Jamie would learn a little more about his great grandfather's life. He heard how he had spent a major part of his younger years as a cowboy, punching cattle on other people's land, until the smaller properties were bought up by white interests and the horses mostly gave way to mechanized roundups. His glib declaration of, 'We Injuns made good cowboys... yippee yio!' brought a loud burst of laughter from Jamie. He also learnt that Looks Back had lived virtually all his life on the reservation, the only extended period he had spent away being when he served in Europe during the Second World War. 'The Lakota are warriors and we're always lookin' for a battle. They wanted warriors so lots of us went. But some didn't come back.' He showed Jamie a wound in his calf caused by a German bullet and then went to a drawer and pulled out his service medals, describing to Jamie what each one was for, then pinning the last one to his shirt. 'And this is the one I got for beatin' everyone at checkers', he said with a smile.

Finally, Looks Back declared an end to the checkerboard slaughter and retired to bed, while Jamie went to his spot on the floor and lay down next to the dog. In the darkness his questions continued and, in the hour that followed, he would learn everything of what Looks Back knew of Eyes That Cut's end, retreating into a contemplative silence when the old man decided to speak of the information he had held back that afternoon.

'Walks Softly was the warrior that cut out his heart,' he said quietly, his words slicing through the darkness like the knife that had performed the ritual act.

There was no immediate response from Jamie and Looks Back would listen to the boy thinking for several minutes before one came.

'Why are you called Looks Back?'

Looks Back smiled at the unquestioning acceptance of what he had said and then attempted to answer the unconnected question.

'Ever since I was young I've been lookin' back for our culture, in the language, the customs and the music. We traditionals are always bein' criticized for that but I figure we're more progressive than the so-called progressives. Sometimes you gotta go back before you can go forward. A tree's gotta have roots.'

Silence once again greeted Looks Back and he listened until he heard the deep breathing indicating his guest had gone to sleep. He soon followed but, just as he was slipping away, a muted voice spoke to him through the darkness. 'Maybe your new name should be Looks Back Looks Forward,' it said.

Looks Back opened his eyes and listened. It sounded to him like Jamie was still sleeping but he smiled and uttered 'Hmmph,' to the teasing suggestion spoken in the funny accent the boy sometimes used.

SEVENTEEN

Grace continued her own kind of Vision Quest the day after driving back from Pine Ridge, when a reporter from the Northern Plains Courier came to her house hoping to interview her and Jamie about the music. Instead, the young woman got Grace and Chas and the first declaration of the political message the lead singer of *Warrior* was determined to deliver. Most of the interview had been comprised of pop clichéd questions that revolved entirely around their unique sound until Grace decided to shine a light on the words instead, deftly turning one of her answers on the music into a general statement about where most of Native America found itself today. She said that the old songs used as choruses sang about her peoples' spiritual connection to nature and the modern lyrics reflected the pressure on it today. She added that the richness of the Lakota and other cultures were being worn away by poverty and neglect, finally throwing back a cliché of her own, saying that they were being trampled on by the stampeding greed of capitalism and it would leave all humanity spiritually bankrupt in the end.

Numerous others over the years had expressed Grace's beliefs more forcefully and eloquently and it was only a small local paper to which she was expressing her message, but it was a match to the fuse of what she now saw as the real purpose of their music. The match, however, had also lit Chas's fuse and he let fly as soon as the pensive young reporter walked out the door, his words coming like a verbal version of his Stratocastor in full cry.

'Are you fuckin' crazy? Why didn't ya tell me you were gonna pull a stunt like that? Do ya know what you've just gone and done, bringin' politics into it? We haven't even made the record yet and you've called time-out to the vast majority of the US population! They're gonna think we're a bunch of fuckin' lefties! Are you still on that fucked up trip of yours? Do you still not wanna succeed? Just remember there's others involved. People have quit jobs. Mark's put everythin' on the line to payroll us. How's he gonna react when he hears about this?'

Grace stared blankly as the closet capitalist burst out from behind the doors. When he had finished she calmly said, 'If you could ever stop jerking off that guitar o' yours long enough to read the lyrics properly you would find most of what I just told her is already in them and the moment the record is reviewed, it will come out anyway.'

'Don't insult me, Grace. I know what's in the fuckin' lyrics. I also know that most people don't really listen to the words in songs, but if you keep this up they will and they'll vote with their wallets. The record will sink!'

Grace stared fixedly at Chas for a few seconds then said, 'You underestimate the young.' That was where she left it. This was no time for mentioning what she intended to do with the J card of the record, where, along with the song list and lyrics she planned to add an obituary for her ancestral songwriting partner that would hopefully further the progress of the one being written for the Hidden Valley Golf Resort.

Chas left unhappily, burning over the idea that lyrics might end up dominating the music. That was for his guitar to do and, later that day, he tried to prove it, when they had their second last rehearsal before the trip to Seattle, his riffs and licks just a little more angry, elaborate and drawn out than usual. All it did was irritate everyone. There were complaints about him losing the balance and wasting valuable practice time. When Grace finally turned to glare at him, he relented but not before running his left hand up and down the stem in a suggestive way. It brought a chuckle from Grace and settled the dust of dissent, for a while.

Another practice session followed the next day, ending mid-afternoon when they began packing the equipment van that the others were going to drive to Seattle, while Boss and Grace did their long side trip to Pine Ridge. They would all meet up in the northern city a few days later.

*

Grace looked at Jamie closely as she got out of the pickup. He appeared to be the same happy kid she had left there two days before, greeting her and Boss with his usual enthusiasm. Just before they left, however, he wandered off towards the spirit post and stood before it for a while, staring intently. Then, as they left, she heard Looks Back farewell him with his Lakota name. It was about a mile up the track when she asked.

'So you are Song Catcher now?'

'Yeah, Looks Back said so, and I've got a new song, Mom. It's a blues number. The words go with the Lakota one called *The Water Talks*.'

Jamie whipped out his notebook and handed it to her.

Grace read the lyrics carefully and instantly knew what the first English verse was saying. Beneath the protest message there lay a deeply personal one, addressed to her, a thinly-veiled accusation of what at times she had accused herself - of playing the martyr to her drug habits when the cause of Jamie's problems could also have been the water she had drunk for the first eighteen years of her life. Jamie was using his song to tell her to stop the self-flagellation. She read through the last two verses then handed the notebook back. It seemed that her son had learned a lot in the last three days.

'They're real good lyrics, Hon,' she said.

'It's gotta go on the album, Mom,' came the eerie certainty again.

'Mmmm... maybe we can work on it as we go,' Grace replied thoughtfully, already considering the song's inclusion. She intended to hold fire on getting wider publicity about the valley project until all the bullets were loaded and Jamie's banner-waving number had just slid smoothly into the clip.

Work on it they did, with Grace supplying vocals, Jamie the ideas and Boss the backbeat, the young arranger holding the steering wheel as the drummer belted out his contributions on the dashboard. They still had to find the guitar riff needed for the Lakota verses but, by the time they had reached Montana the next day, an 'a cappella' version of the rest of the song was in the pocket-sized tape recorder that Grace now constantly carried with her.

Another sleep at a budget motel and a long day's drive later they entered the outskirts of Seattle. It was dark by then and the city was living up to its rainy reputation, a heavy downpour making identification of street signs difficult and causing the trio to get lost twice before eventually finding Mark's place, located in a comfortable middle-class suburb.

Boss parked the pickup in the driveway of the stylish bungalow, nosing up behind the van that had arrived there earlier that afternoon. The three raced to the front door, only to meet Mark on his way out.

'Glad to finally see ya but I've gotta run. Late for a dinner date with the CD people. If you hurry inside you might get some of what's left of yours. The contracts are there too. You've got tomorrow morning to check them. We'll do the signing session in the afternoon and then it'll be into the studio the day after. I've hired it for three weeks and it's booked out after that so there's a deadline. I've lined up all the other musicians input for the second week and Donnewitz rang yesterday to say he will be coming over tomorrow to meet you.' He looked at his watch. 'That's it for now. The others know where everything is. You can sort out the bedrooms between yourselves.' He held up a hand in farewell as he raced to his car.

"Bout time,' Chas declared as the three entered the living room. 'We were just about to start on your rations.'

There were half-empty pizza cartons, beer cans and sheets of paper strewn across the very large coffee table in the middle of the room, the band members lounging on sofas around it. Mitch and Wayne raised their hands in greeting and Jamie did the rounds of hand slapping re-acquaintance with the three as if he hadn't seen them for a very long time then swiftly grabbed a large piece of pizza.

The travelers were weary and the night fizzled out not long after the food was polished off, the allocation of sleeping quarters quickly decided. There were four bedrooms between the six of them. Boss was given one on his own because of his chronic snoring, Mitch and Wayne shared another, while Chas whispered to Grace that, considering he had to be away from his wife Kelly for so long, maybe they could bed down together. Instead, he ended up with a bottom bunk in the room set up for the occasional visits from Mark's two boys, Jamie claiming the top one.

When they awoke in the morning, they were greeted by a clear blue sky and a note from their manager telling of more business appointments and that he wouldn't be back until mid-afternoon. The rest of the morning was spent how Mark had suggested it should be, checking the original contracts, copies of which had already been faxed to them a week before. By lunchtime they were all agreed on the conditions and ready to sign. After lunch however, there was disagreement on another matter.

'Jesus, Grace! I thought we had all that in place. Why do ya wanna go an' disrupt the flow? Can't it go on the next one?' Chas moaned at the news that Grace wanted to replace one of the songs with the one she, Jamie and Boss had worked on whilst driving across three states.

Expecting this reaction, Grace had waited till Jamie went into the back garden to play with Mark's English sheep dog before bringing the subject up. After quietening Chas down briefly by saying that it was important to her and Jamie that the song go in, she played the tape and this time the guitarist listened to the words with more interest than usual.

'I knew it! More protestin'! More fuckin' politics!' he moaned and then tried to draw the others into the fray. 'Do ya know what our singer is tryin' to do with the album? She's tryin' to turn it into a fuckin' policy statement on the rights of Native Americans! Pretty soon we're all gonna be standin' on street corners wearin' badges and handin' out flyers and here I was thinkin' we were a Rock 'n Roll band headin' for the bigtime!'

The others absorbed Chas's outburst in the usual deadpan way, before Mitch offered some calm words.

'It's good blues, man. We could do plenty with it.'

Wayne nodded in agreement and Boss added, 'The numbers have it, man. Save ya energy... y'all gonna need it from tomorrow.'

Chas simmered in silence for a little while before suddenly bursting out again, 'And which one are ya gonna take out?'

A brief discussion followed before an agreement was reached, although again by everyone but Chas. *The Water Talks* was a blues number so a blues had to go, and that was a song called *Lightning,* a reworking of one of Chas's old songs and carrying what he believed to be some of his best work on the album. The dropping of the song and the songwriting royalties that would have gone with it started him up again just as Mark came home. He immediately turned to their manager to plead his case.

Mark sat down and listened with fingers tapping out an impatient tune on his kneecaps and, when Chas had finished he answered forcefully. 'I thought that politics was what the album was all about or did I miss something?'

Grace smiled just a little as Mark continued.

'All albums need an edge. The fact that this one is political will give it greater cutting power. Any publicity is good publicity, man, as long as it gets the right people enjoying the music and the wrong ones upset by it. That's the first law of Rock 'n Roll or are you getting too old to remember that? As for the lifting out of any songs, put them on the next album. Now get your act together, Donnewitz will be here shortly and I don't want him getting the impression that there is any trouble, for this is one guy who isn't going to put up with band politics, egos, or petulance'.

Mark stared fixedly at Chas as he spoke and the guitarist pulled his petulance in like a damaged fishing net, needing repair but still usable.

About half an hour later, Donnewitz arrived. The slightly built and intense individual quickly let all of them know who was going to be the boss in the studio, his nervous eyes darting across the floor as he laid down the law about promptness and efficiency. The only time they settled on anyone else's for more than the briefest moment was when he looked intensely at Jamie's. Twenty minutes later, with the preliminary plans in place, he left the house without a goodbye.

What had been said was nothing Grace, Chas or Boss didn't already know, the three pro's having spent almost as much time in recording studios as Donnewitz. That fact caused another outburst from the lead guitarist.

'What the fuck was that?' Chas cried. 'Did anyone see someone come in just now? Talk about musicians' egos. He didn't even say a fuckin' thing about the music!'

A ripple of laughter passed through the lounge before Mark interceded.

'He wouldn't be doing the album if he didn't think you've got something special. Anyway, as far as he's concerned the music's not finished yet. Just humor him. He's difficult but he'll get the job done.'

Chas took this quietly enough and would remain that way during the signing of contracts and the celebratory meal that followed at a Chinese restaurant. But he would go to bed still unhappy over the removal of his song from the album and he merely grunted when Jamie said goodnight, almost resentful of the small boy on the upper bunk for being the cause of his loss.

It was blues music that followed Chas into sleep and, in the very early morning, it played a part in his waking. Not unusually of late he had been dreaming he was on stage playing his guitar but, this time, it wasn't responding to his touch. The sound he could hear was muffled and muted, as if it was coming from a faulty amplifier or the lead wasn't plugged in. He moved over to the amplifier and pressed his ear against it, trying to catch the faint riff, when he felt the stage begin to move under his feet. Soon the large stack of amplifiers was shaking and swaying ominously. He tried to run but fell over. He struggled to get up but the guitar lead wrapped around his ankles like a snake, holding him fast and, all the while, the sound boxes were rapidly growing in number, spiraling upwards and taking on the dimensions of a waving skyscraper. They began to fall from the top level and he frantically tried to crawl away, clawing with terror at the hard shaking surface of the stage until it began to soften and turn into a bed. He was awake now but could still feel the double bunk trembling and hear the faint music playing. He stared with confusion upwards into the darkness.

'What the fuck's goin on up there, man?' he called out.

The shaking suddenly stopped but the guitar playing continued. Then a familiar accented voice came from above, 'Just playin' some o' *yer blues*, man.'

Chas flicked on the light that was clamped to the bunk and immediately noticed something in the corner of the room. The case that protected his Stratocastor was open and the guitar missing. He leaned over the edge of the bunk and looked up. Just as he did the muffled playing stopped.

Jamie was sitting on the edge of his bunk with the guitar across his lap, his hands frozen in the act of playing.

'What tha fuck are ya doin', man? You know not to mess around with my Strat!'

Jamie's head dropped slowly and he stared at Chas.

'Jesus!' Chas uttered, as he drew back from the piercing gaze.

'Huh?' Jamie replied. He squinted and put a hand up to shade his face from the glare of the light. 'What's up?'

Chas stared confusedly at the now sleepy-eyed boy. The kid often joked around in Lennon's voice but it had seemed more real coming from his sleep. The boy's guitar playing had suddenly improved too, the muted riff with the distinctive bluesy construction now firmly caught in his musician's head.

Jamie began to nod off in the upright position and Chas quickly climbed out of bed to take the guitar from his hands.

'Go back to sleep, man,' he said and gently pushed Jamie down into the bed then pulled his blankets over him. He put the guitar back in its case and climbed back into his bunk again, flicked off the light, rolled over and closed his eyes. But as he lay there, he was unable to sleep, his mind refusing to empty of the sound that had come from his unplugged guitar.

'Fuck this!' he hissed as he climbed out of bed. He took his acoustic guitar out of its case and another small item from a bag then walked through to the kitchen where a wall clock told him it was just after four-thirty. He muttered another curse at the thought of being up so early then brewed up a pot of coffee and took everything into the living room. He sat down before the ever-present cassette recorder and, after a few slurps of caffeine, he switched it on then began softly picking at the strings, the glass slide on the ring finger of his left hand swiftly resurrecting the muted soundtrack of his dream.

The riff came quickly, easily and, half an hour later, a habitual early riser was drawn to its sound, wandering into the room with an empty cup in her hand.

'Sounds good,' Grace said as she poured herself some coffee.

Chas switched the recorder off. 'Yeah? Well you can thank your son's nocturnal habits for it and, somehow, I get the strange sensation it's gonna slot right into this new song,' he said, with a nod of his head towards the piece of paper that Grace had left lying on the coffee table last night, the words and Jamie's notes for *The Water Talks* neatly transcribed for the others to read. The disgruntled Chas hadn't bothered with it last night but reached over now to study the words. He snorted when he saw the instruction regarding slide guitar at the bottom of the page.

'Figures,' he declared and then explained what had gotten him out of bed about six hours before his usual rising time, dream and all, ending with, 'I swear to ya, man, the sound I heard comin' from my guitar was like a pro was playin' it.'

Grace got up and walked to the large front window and stood quietly for a few moments, watching the early morning light bringing the leafy street to life. She then spoke without turning around. 'Jamie's been moving around a bit at night lately.'

'Maybe I should strap him into his bunk,' Chas quipped as he switched the recorder on again before running through the riff once more, elaborating on it.

Grace began to softly sing the Lakota words of *The Water Talks*, matching them with the notes of the guitar the way Jamie had excitedly emphasized to her on the road to Seattle. "You know. With that kinda burning... sexy sound you get in ya voice." She smiled with satisfaction at the seamless combination of guitar and voice. 'We're gonna make a great album, Chas.'

Chas flicked the recorder off again. 'Yeah, I know... and it all seems to be comin' so easily. The songs, the record deal, and one of the best soundman ya could find. Makes me think that maybe we're gettin' some help from somewhere,' he said, staring now at the back of Grace's head.

Grace responded with a slow nodding of her head.

Chas looked back at the lyrics of *The Water Talks* and more notes ran from his guitar as he cast his eyes over them. After a while he spoke again. 'I get the general idea of this song but there are things in it that mystify me a little. Torn mouths... blades gougin' flesh. Just what do they mean exactly?'

Grace left her place at the window and sat down on one of the sofas. On the trip to Seattle she had spoken to Boss about the Hidden Valley project and what had been dug up there but asked him to keep quiet about it until she could pick the right moment to tell the others, particularly the explosive Chas. Now it had arrived and, with the explanation she gave to him, she also mentioned what she wanted to put on the J card relating to Eyes That Cut.

'Ya shoulda told me all this earlier, Grace. Would've saved a bit of drama. You know how I feel about ol' ETC. He's part of the band,' Chas's replied in a hurt kind of way.

Soon after, the others began filtering into the room and Chas immediately gave them a colorfully punctuated version of Grace's story, finishing with 'Let's go and kick some ass! Let's get the fat men squealin'! I've got the axe, Boss's got the drums... let's go to war!' He then strode out of the room to get dressed and ready for the first studio session.

The others didn't need their manic lead guitarist to stir them up. They were all hanging out for the recording sessions. After a quick breakfast, they packed their instruments in their van and half an hour later it was being emptied at the studio on the other side of the city.

Marty Donnewitz was already there. He hardly acknowledged their greetings as he fiddled with the soundboards and checked leads and switches. It was the type of studio that he had demanded, one that still had the sort of equipment he was accustomed to using before he left the scene and computers and digitalization took over much of the recording game. It had a quality twenty-four track recording system, mixing console, monitor speakers and microphones. Besides good songs and capable musicians he knew he didn't need anything else to make a good album.

'Home sweet home,' Chas declared as he walked into the main studio and then quickly set up behind one of the mikes.

Boss walked straight past him carrying a bass drum, placed it in an isolation booth and then went back to the van for the rest of his kit. But Mitch and Wayne entered the environment a little unsure of where they should be and the hawk-eyed Donnewitz immediately seized upon their uncertainty.

'Lead guitarist... help them set up!' came the command.

Chas stared at the small man sitting on the other side of the control room window.

'*Jawol, Herr Commandant!*' he replied, using the nazi salute before snapping his heels together and goose-stepping towards Mitch and Wayne. '*Raus, Raus*! Rhythm guitarist vill plug in *zere* and bass guitarist vill plug in *heah!*' he ordered with an aggressive pointing of a finger.

Chas's performance brought nervous smiles from his fellow musicians but behind the glass screen Donnewitz just glared. 'You can fuck around all you like but it won't get the record made!' his voice barked through the speaker.

Chas defiantly goose-stepped back to his stool and then sat down to tune his guitar.

Twenty minutes later, singer and musicians were set up and ready for recording *Spirit Rising*. The decision had been made to first complete the six songs that wouldn't need any exotic instrumentation and then lay down the tracks that would form the backbone of the others, ready for the other musicians that would arrive in a week's time.

Jamie, the spare body that had been helping out with moving instruments and furniture, now walked a little nervously into the control room and sat on a stool right in the back corner behind Donnewitz, as daunted by the sound man's abrupt manner as the others. Although he had messed around with the basic soundboard that the band used for gigs, he was fascinated by the size and sophistication of the equipment in the room and dying to ask about all its functions. But he kept quiet as he studied the small man's lightning fast hands playing over the mixing board, adjusting sound levels and balance. Then, without turning around, Donnewitz spoke to him.

'You can come and sit next to me, Jamie.'

Jamie quickly took his stool over to the console.

'I've been told you played a big part in arrangin' these songs.' Donnewitz said.

'Yes sir, I helped out some,' Jamie softly replied.

'Marty to you. Well, you've done a fine job and I'm gonna help you make 'em even better. I want you to watch what I do and learn. Later on you can do some mixing yourself. I'll guide you. Ask me anythin' at any time. Don't be afraid.'

Jamie nodded with enthusiasm.

Fittingly, they started with the first song that had been written, the drums, rhythm guitar and bass for *Song Catcher* laid down before Wayne took his flute to the 'bright' area, a tiled cubicle set up for the recording of any instrument that needed an increase in natural reverberation rather than adding it electronically. Chas's lead work then followed.

'It's a relief that he can play as well as he plays around,' Donnewitz said to Jamie. After Grace's contribution there came another approving comment from the engineer. 'Your Mom's got a mighty fine voice.'

'The best,' Jamie replied.

The early afternoon was spent adjusting and tweaking the instrumental contribution before Donnewitz began the major part of the mixing. He worked quickly but answered Jamie's questions with none of the impatience he had regularly shown to the others that day. By the end of the afternoon, he had *Song Catcher* mixed and on the master tape and his apprentice endowed with the basics of the process.

Everyone was ecstatic when they heard the final version. Donnewitz had done exactly what he had told Jamie he would do. His expertise had given Song Catcher even more power than it had previously delivered but 'Good song' was the only comment made by him as he left the studio, giving only Jamie a brief nod as he went.

EIGHTEEN

A week of studio sessions flew by for Warrior and, at the end of it, most of the songs were completed to their required extent and the others were ready for mixing with their exotic content. By then, the group was obediently obeying every command from the man that had turned their great songs into brilliant ones. During the next couple of days, the studio would look like a musicians' convention as the extra players and singers trooped in and out. They all did their parts efficiently but the one musician Jamie most wanted to hear turned up a day late, holding up the completion of two songs, one of them he now held most dear.

The band were taking a break in the studio when the Aussie sauntered in through the open doorway, barefoot, all Rasta hair and instant karma clothes, half-bearded, ear-ringed and with a four-and-a-half foot didgeridoo strapped over his shoulder.

'G'day,' he said.

No one was particularly happy with the late arrival but Donnewitz reacted to the laconic entrance like a junkyard dog that hadn't been fed for days.

'Where the *hell* have you been? Dontcha realize the whole studio has been waitin' on ya? These places don't come for fuckin' free, man!'

'Don't get yer balls in a knot, mate. I'm here now. Whaddya want me to do... besides give ya an enema with a hollow tree branch?'

The comment brought loud laughter from the others but Donnewitz stormed out of the control room and approached the latecomer as if he were about to hit him. The smiling Aussie backed off, whipped the didgeridoo from his shoulder and held it out like a Samurai sword. The laughter grew louder as Donnewitz came angrily on, halting before the weapon then grasping it firmly and pushing it aside. His face looked like he was about to explode but, when he spoke to the didgeridoo player, his words came in a calm and controlled way. 'The village idiot's part has already been filled by the lead guitarist. Now, if you're able to use that thing for its real purpose, there're two songs we want you on. I'll play what we already have then Jamie will explain what he wants done,' he said, before wheeling around and heading back to the control room.

Jamie stared - a little puzzled - as the engineer departed. Donnewitz had had his back to everyone but him as he was talking to the didgeridoo player. Despite the angry words, he had seen a genuine smile briefly cross the man's face. It gave the impression of someone sharing a joke with a person he knew. He was still thinking about that secret look when the Aussie stared straight at him, ignoring all the other males in the room who could possibly have been 'Jamie'. He held out his hand and Jamie took it tentatively.

'Owyergoin', mate? I'm Pete Halfpenny, or Six Pack to me friends,' he said with a broad smile.

Jamie smiled at the nickname. 'I'm fine... thanks,' he replied and then introduced him to the others, before a prompt came from the control room and they both sat down to listen to *The Mountains I* and *The Water Talks*.

Donnewitz played the two songs twice over and then Jamie led the Aussie into the 'bright' cubicle where he explained what he wanted to hear from the didgeridoo. On *The Mountains I* it was to be a constant backbeat, like the muted call of a bullfrog, never to vary throughout the entire song, its trance-inducing sound representing the earth, with the light playing of a sitar representing running water. Occasionally, there was a drum roll of thunder and a crack of lightning from Chas's guitar sizzling above the pre-recorded track of the throat singers, their yodel-like rendition of the melody undulating, like rolling hills, lifting, falling and then lifting again as they approached the center of the song. At that point, Grace's powerful voice rose out of the soundscape like mountains out of the plains, singing the Lakota words, 'singing' the land, before fading away into it again.

On *The Water Talks*, the low-pitched tone of the didgeridoo, allied with the mournful sound of Wayne's harmonica, were used to introduce the Lakota lyrics when Chas's guitar and Grace's voice sang their muted but powerful opening duet. In the main body of the song, the didgeridoo's high-pitched tones would represent the crying of the Mother; its middle range the roaring sound of machinery; its low burbling qualities the sound of the water talking. This was all tracked by Chas's bluesy guitar work and Boss's rhythmic beat of a tambourine, re-producing the sound of the hawk bells Jamie had heard on Kili radio. Grace's impassioned voice sang out the double-edged pain of the song's contemporary lyrics.

It took nearly three hours to get the sounds Jamie wanted for both songs but, at the end of the session, Six Pack was as calm and cool as when they started. He casually shouldered the didgeridoo and was about to leave when Jamie asked him to hang around until after the mixing was done, eager now to learn something about the strange but simple instrument.

'No worries,' the Aussie replied with a smile.

Jamie then went to the control room and sat down at the mixing desk, just as eager to put into practice what he had learned from the man next to him. For a few seconds he watched as his teacher fiddled with the controls and then asked in a hesitant way, 'Can I do these two songs, Marty?'

'Yeah... I reckon you can.'

Jamie tentatively introduced the didgeridoo track on *The Mountains I*, playing around a bit with its tone and volume before adding the sitar and the throat singers, constantly adjusting until the point where his mother's voice was to come in. This he took the most care over, his mentor helping him, hawk eyes watching the needles on the tone and volume meters and doing some subtle adjustment as the student sought to bring the perfect introduction to the chorus. After an hour, Jamie was finally happy with his work but played the track to himself through his headphones first. Before the song had finished, he jumped up out of his seat and switched on the mike to the studio.

'Getta load o' thisth, you guysth!'

He played the song through again and, by the time it was finished, everyone in the studio was grinning and holding their fists up in triumph. He followed up with *The Water Talks* another hour later, his efforts bringing an even greater response from the band. Contrary to his original opposition, Chas was ecstatic about the final version. Grace smiled, her eyes shining proudly.

All the songs on the album were completed now, the mastering of them the only thing left to be done. This final mix, to make the highs and lows more cohesive from song to song, was only for Donnewitz's experienced ears and hands.

Jamie went outside where he sat down in the alleyway with Six Pack to receive his first lesson with the didgeridoo. Normally, someone so young wouldn't have the breathing capacity in his diaphragm to power the instrument fully but, in its malformed way, the growth in Jamie's upper body had produced the chest cavity and lungs of someone years older. Yet, although his air supply was adequate enough, his thin upper lip would prove to be at first a hindrance in producing anything more than a hollow sound. He couldn't quite get the vibrating action required to make the instrument sing until his coach told him to bring his lower lip right up above the upper then tilt his mouth down a bit into the mouthpiece.

'Now, make a sound with yer lips, ya know, like yer about ta give birth to a politician.'

Jamie frowned at the puzzling instruction, mouth still to the didgeridoo.

'Like this!' Six Pack said, lifting one buttock slightly and farting loudly.

Jamie burst into laughter and, with his lips still inside the mouthpiece and his nose snorting in short breaths and exhaling through his mouth, without any conscious effort, out of the slightly flared end of the instrument came his first successful notes. He kept laughing and playing, hanging onto the circular pattern of breathing Six Pack had been teaching him until he felt he had grasped the idea. Then he stopped and laid the instrument aside, collapsing in loud, honking amusement before making a suggestion to his grinning companion.

'Ya gotta come and spend the night with us, man. I wanna learn more about the didge.'

'Fine with me, mate... I've got nothin' much to do.'

There was no objection when Jamie put his request to Mark to make room for an extra body that night. Six Pack's stay turned into a long jam session, with Jamie rapidly improving on the didgeridoo, even beginning to learn how to use his tongue to change the tone. 'When you get it right it will feel part of you, you'll be able to sing your story,' Six Pack had said and, by the time Jamie was ordered to bed, that's how he had begun to feel, glowing with his success as he lay in his bunk listening to the others kicking on in the lounge. He was ecstatic at being able to control an instrument for once in his life. He thought also of what Six Pack had said in the alleyway earlier that day, about how an old Aborigine had taught him to play but not before the cultural importance of the didgeridoo had been explained to him. The young Australian then gave him an explanation of the Dreamtime, when the world as the Aborigine knows it began, of how the didgeridoo had played its part in sounding their world into being. 'It's got magic and power. When it sings... you have ta listen,' Six Pack finished. And Jamie could feel the power as he nodded off to its haunting tones. He thought he could still hear them when he awoke early the next morning and enthusiastically jumped out of bed and raced into the lounge.

When he entered the room, Jamie had expected to see Six Pack sitting there playing the didgeridoo but the nomad was nowhere to be seen. All that remained of his presence was the instrument lying on the sofa with a small piece of paper laid against it. *For Jamie* was all that was written on it.

Jamie looked sadly at the note then picked up the instrument and walked to his mother's room.

Grace was sitting up on the bed working on the notes for the J card of the album when Jamie came in and sat next to her.

'What's up, Hon... you look a little glum? I thought you'd be out there with Six Pack playing that by now.'

'He's gone. But he left the didge for me.'

'Well, don't be sad about him leaving like that. Some people gotta wander.'

'Yeah,' Jamie said dismissively and then sat in serious-faced contemplation for a while, vacantly watching his mother scribbling on her notebook before he spoke again.

'Mom... when I stayed with Looks Back he told me that I should seek four spirit guides to help me on my way.'

'Mmmm,' Grace hummed again as she turned a page over.

Another brief silence followed then, 'I think Marty and Six Pack are two of 'em.'

Grace looked up and stared into Jamie's eyes.

'If you think so, then they are.'

Jamie nodded in confirmation then got up and left the room, lifting the instrument that was taller than him and balancing it across his shoulder as he went.

Grace watched him go. Two plus two equals four, she thought. Then from the lounge she heard the sound of the instrument that she knew would be dominating most of her waking hours in the immediate future, its unique tone once again nagging at her from someplace else. She thought about it for a moment until a loud undisciplined yelping sound broke her concentration and brought a rueful smile to her face. She continued on with her task of translating the Lakota verses of each song into English before turning her attention to the wording of something just as important.

The eulogy for Eyes That Cut would be placed at the top of the foldout section of the lyrics, like a headstone for the ancestral songwriting partner whose songs had made the album unique. The words flowed easily from Grace's pen: *Eyes That Cut, the catcher of all the Lakota songs within the songs of this album, was my great, great grandfather, an Oglala warrior poet. He could be seen as a kind of rock star of the nineteenth century who, for most of his life, enjoyed the freedom of the Great Plains and sang about it. In fighting to maintain that freedom he died bravely, yet he does not rest in peace. This album sings for him. It is a battle cry against the decimation of nature and of native cultures, wherever it and they still exist – Sings At Dawn (Grace Howard).*

Grace had been working on the album cover too, the front of it to be dominated by a buckskin war shield with two eagle feathers hanging from the bottom and four red, music notes placed around the edge at each point of the compass. At the center of the shield was the image of a compact disk. Upon it would be placed a geometric Native American design in colors of red, white, black and yellow. The background to the shield was aqua and written in black letters around the top of it was *Warrior*, around the bottom, *Spirit Rising*. The back of the cover would be a black and white photograph taken when she had gone to pick up Jamie at Pine Ridge. It was of Looks Back, the proud elder, head held high whilst standing in front of the contradiction of his tumbledown environment.

Grace handed all of her material to Mark in the early afternoon and he raced it off to the printer, where it would be fed into a computer and spat out in hard copy in a week's time, ready to go with the CD that hopefully would be manufactured by the following week. Later that afternoon, he joined the others at the studio to listen to the master tapes that would be used. The band members set up two cassette recorders to tape the music for their own use until the CD was completed. They then sat in stunned silence listening to what they had produced, the pride in their work written across all of their faces, even that of the tetchy sound man who had hounded them for perfection all the way.

Their manager was no less impressed. Over the period of the recording, Mark had only caught snippets of the work in between his constant coming and going but, as he listened to the complete master, he was overcome by excitement. He constantly strode back and forth in the small control room, almost manic in his appreciation of the music, raising his fist at the completion of each song. Occasionally, he cried out with joy and he cast beaming smiles at the others as he packed the tapes in a box, before hurriedly departing to the duplication house where the album would begin its commercial journey with an initial order of ten thousand CD's. It was a big number for a relatively unknown group's first effort but to Mark, the fifty thousand dollars he had outlaid was not an expensive gamble. He considered that it was just the primer of a return cash flow that would enable him to multiply the next order.

After the hearing, Donnewitz simply said, 'It's a good album,' before heading for the door. It was faint praise but the group felt as though royalty had bestowed a knighthood upon them. Jamie watched with disappointment as his mentor of the mixing board swept out of the studio. He had expected more. He couldn't let him go just like that. He raced out into the parking lot, chasing after him like an abandoned dog. He called out, but Donnewitz didn't appear to hear him.

Jamie watched sadly as the loner was about to turn the corner of a building and disappear from his life. 'See ya, Marty,' he whispered and then turned to go back to the studio, only to be halted when he heard Donnewitz call out in reply.

Jamie turned around just in time to see the last glimpse of his friend, one arm raised in farewell, before the street finally swallowed him. He stood puzzled for a few seconds then wandered distractedly back into the studio. The others were dismantling equipment and carrying it out to the van and he stopped his mother as she walked past with part of Boss's drum kit.

'Mom, did you tell Marty about me being a song catcher?'

'No, Hon... unless you hadn't noticed we didn't quite get round to the niceties of a social chat. Why?'

'He used Song Catcher when he called out goodbye to me.'

'Boss calls you by it sometimes... maybe he overheard him.'

'Yeah... but Boss never says it in Lakota.'

*

The group had finished their work a week early so they decided to have a day off before heading home. The following morning, Grace slept in until the late hour of seven and then spent most of the day like everyone else, lying around in different parts of the house and garden, keeping to herself and away from what they had been doing non-stop for nearly two weeks. In the afternoon they were brought back together again in the lounge room where Mark laid out his plans for the release of the CD and the concert that would follow.

'I am going to allow a month out there for the CD before the first show is lined up. I've decided to make it Rapid City, right in the heart of where I'll be concentrating the initial marketing. The set design is going to be kept simple. Just a giant blow-up of the album cover hung like a tapestry behind the band. I'll be hiring a pro outfit to do the sound system and stagecraft but there will be no whiz-bang effects, no fancy dress and just enough lighting so that you can be seen. The music will do it all. As for the CD, as soon as it's ready I'll get a hundred to you to distribute where you think best. After that I expect to be on the road permanently for a few weeks but you'll be kept informed of progress.'

Mark asked for questions but there were none. The band was tired. They had done their part. Like warriors, they were happy now to leave the next battle for their chief to plan and, getting their product before the gatekeepers of the industry, would be the biggest battle of all. Initially, it would be done in the form of a promotion pack, a press kit for the DJs and journalists. For this a photo was needed to go along with the CD and the information sheet about the band. A professional photographer took it in Mark's back garden later in the afternoon, with nothing out of the ordinary in the standard unsmiling study except for the inclusion of a small boy sitting cross-legged below his mother.

The band moved out early the next morning, a two-day journey ahead of them. It was one that would go quickly for all, their thoughts and conversation almost totally consumed by the CD and its imminent release. But in Boss's pickup, Grace was a little quieter than her companions. She knew the album that had come together so easily was going to be a success and, as their vehicle tore along the highway, she constantly reflected upon the connection of people and incidents that had brought the music into being. More specifically, she was thinking of the man who had set it all in motion early on a Sunday morning.

She flushed with the remembrance of what had happened that day in the Black Hills. Ever since writing the Eyes That Cut eulogy for the J card she had been thinking about the conflicting emotions she shared in that moment with the attractive surveyor. In a practical way, she needed his help but she was now beginning to feel pleased that the business she had with him would allow them to make contact again.

NINETEEN

Gary sat in the reception area of Hal Whitman's office, resignation ready to slap on his desk. Although he was feeling uneasy about his impending unemployment, the thought of Grace transcended all. It wasn't just his growing curiosity over her plans about the valley project. Ever since the moment in the hills that morning, the all-too-brief embrace of her angry body had been clinging to him like a second skin.

'Send Schroeder in, Lisa,' Whitman's voice came through his secretary's intercom, interrupting Gary's thoughts.

When he entered Whitman's lavishly decorated office, the project manager was busily playing his role, shuffling through a pile of paperwork and scribbling signatures. Gary closed the door, strolled across the room and sat down in one of the plush chairs opposite a desk that was designed with a large ego in mind.

Whitman looked up from the sweeping expanse of his workplace. 'I'd say sit down but I see you already have.' He fiddled with the paperwork for a few seconds more then put it aside. 'What is it? Why are you in town? You're supposed to be settin' the levels for the condo area today.' His voice was uncharacteristically calm.

Gary leaned over and placed the envelope on the desk.

Whitman opened it and quickly read through the brief note of resignation. He then leaned back in the chair, clasped his hands behind his head and fixed Gary with a level gaze.

'On what grounds?'

'I don't need grounds but, since you asked, I've been uncomfortable about doing the job for some time. Mostly it's the atmosphere created by your pistol-packing guards. I didn't like the way they laid into those protestors a couple of months ago and there was another incident there today with them waving guns at some innocents.'

'What else?' Whitman calmly inquired.

'You could add that I don't like working for you.'

A thin smile formed on Whitman's face. 'No one does. That's the price of getting people to work harder. They like the bonuses at the end of the job, though.'

They sat staring challengingly at each other for a few seconds before Whitman spoke again. 'Okay. If that's how you want it... go. Surveyors are a dime a dozen. I'll have another one on site by tomorrow. Leave your keys with Lisa.' He signaled the end of their meeting by turning back to his paperwork.

Gary was relieved he had finally made the decision but was still puzzled by Whitman's manner. He had expected a barrage of abuse. He walked out deliberately leaving the door open, unclipping his site keys from his key chain and placing them on Lisa's desk.

Whitman raised his head and watched until Gary had passed through the reception area. He then pushed the button to his secretary's intercom.

'Get me head office, Lisa.'

In a Manhattan high-rise, silver-haired Jim Blair, the overseer of all Prestige Development Corporation's projects answered Whitman's call and listened in icy silence to the information about Gary.

'One of our security guards was comin' back from a break in Vegas when he spotted him drivin' out of an access track with a car full of Indians followin'. He rang me straight away and I told him to tail them. Both vehicles came to Rapid City and the Indians went up to his apartment. When they came out one of them was carryin' somethin'. They took off and not long after, Schroeder turned up here with his resignation. I've still got someone keepin' an eye on him. The only thing I can figure is that he found somethin' Indian on site and now he's handed it over. I think he's a bit of a bleedin' heart.'

'Leave it with me,' Blair said. After he rang off, he connected to an internal number.

Three floors down, a heavy-set, bull-necked man in his mid-fifties, hair shaved to near bald and with a gold earring in one ear, picked up the phone.

'John Kilmont,' he answered in a voice that rasped like dry bread being rubbed against a food grater.

'Got a job for you, John. There might be a little trouble again out on the Hidden Valley site.'

Kilmont listened carefully.

'Yes, Mister Blair, I'll get right onto it.'

John Kilmont leaned back in his chair, pulled out his second cigar for the morning, lit it up, took a puff, and then a light smile creased his granite-jawed countenance. Things had been getting a little too quiet around the place lately for the security chief of Prestige Developments, a small and struggling building company his employers had bought about ten years ago. It was a change of ownership that brought a huge influx of funds and a new policy - the very efficient use of bribery and coercion to bring difficult contracts in on time. Along the length and breadth of the Americas and in South East Asia, it had left a trail of wealthier village headmen, police officers, Mayors, councilors, union leaders and executives of rival companies. In the shadows of that payoff trail, there were a steadily growing number of battered or missing persons that had gotten in the way of their progress. Yet the size of their slush fund was huge when compared to the aggressive pricing policy they used to undercut the opposition. So too, was the extremely generous bonus scheme that had made very wealthy men of those at the top. Kilmont was one who had become a millionaire several times over as reward for his efforts in keeping the company operating without interference, externally or internally. Much higher rewards were being reaped because of the company's unblemished record of contract completion and, even the slightest sign that something might challenge that, was jumped upon with all the savagery of a tigress protecting its young.

'Kilmont here,' he said as Whitman answered his call. 'Mister Blair tells me you have an ex-employee who may have gone native. Give me the story again.'

Whitman repeated what he had told Blair, before adding, 'This guy's always been a bit of a wise ass.'

'Well, maybe we can give him a little more wisdom. Keep your guy on him until I get some people down there. It's a shame you didn't have the time to get someone on the injuns' trail but hopefully he can tell us what that's all about.'

After hanging up, Kilmont took a miniature note book out of his top pocket, flipped through it and made another call. After a few rings, a gentle voice answered.

'Hellooo.'

'I've got something for you, Princess. It's out in the mid-west. Interested?'

'I'll do anything for you, darling. When do I leave?'

'In a few days. I'll be in touch soon with the details. There'll probably be another couple of bodies going with you.'

'Mmmm, I hope they will be nice ones. *Byeeee.*'

A slight shiver went through Kilmont as he put the phone down. The former Brooklyn detective had made a career out of intimidating people but hearing the sweet voice of a person he knew got a special kind of enjoyment out of it always made his skin crawl.

*

By the time Gary stepped into the elevator, the small pleasure of his resigning had gone. His relief about not having to work for Prestige was being replaced by concern over his financial position. He had sacrificed two week's wages by not giving any notice and, although he had managed to put some money aside over the last few months, with loan repayments to be made, he figured he could only survive for a few weeks without work. When he got home, he immediately hit the job ad sites on the Internet. He doubted if he could find any surveying work after his walkout from Prestige but decided to try anyway.

Over the following week, Gary sent out preliminary email applications to several potential employers, receiving the standard 'we will contact you' replies. From his experience, the follow up to those could take from weeks to months and he knew he would have to find something in the meantime. He scanned the local papers and found a job ad, placed by the Rapid City Commission, looking for a second string surveyor on a road project just out of town. It was only for two months and for about half the pay he had been getting from Prestige but it was an immediate start and would keep him afloat until he found something more substantial. He applied for the job without mentioning his recent stint at Prestige, explaining he was on a working holiday and needed to top up his traveling capital. His previous work record and quality references won him the contract and he was asked at the final interview to start the next day. Feeling buoyed by the turn of events, he treated himself to a celebratory evening meal at a nearby restaurant but, when he arrived home and slipped his key into the front door, his mood instantly changed. The lock didn't sound right. There was no solid unlocking click.

Gary stared at the handle for a few seconds before gently turning it and pushing the door slightly ajar. He stood very still and listened intently for a moment longer before opening it further and tentatively entering the living area. He could smell the fragrance of perfume in the air. He turned on the entry light and scanned the room.

'Hi honey... you're *hoooome*,' an effeminate voice sang from a shadowy corner of the room.

Gary peered confusedly as the figure seated in a lounge chair stood up. The immaculately groomed person in business suit, shirt and tie walked over in a foxy manner and closed the door gently before turning to him. 'Hello, Gary. My friends call me Princess. Please be a friend.' The words were dressed with a sweet smile and a slender, manicured hand was offered to him.

Gary passed on the handshake and stared back guardedly at the diminutive person before him, dressed like a man but with the soft features of a female, the attractive face contradicted by dead, gray eyes. He nervously demanded an explanation. 'Who the *hell* are you? What are you doing here?'

Princess turned away then sauntered to the front window, stared down at the almost empty street for a few seconds then offered a casual observation. 'Rapid City. It's a funny name for a place so slow.'

'*What* are you doing here?' Gary irritably repeated.

'I've come to talk to you about the little powwow you had with your Indian friends the other day.'

Gary stared at his visitor, speechless.

The still smiling Princess turned and walked slowly back to stand almost touching him. 'Yes, you were seen and followed.'

A breath sweetened by freshener wafted into Gary's face as questions stampeded through his mind. He wondered how and when they had been spotted and just how long they had been watching him. Had they seen him frequenting the tower site? One thing was certain, Whitman must have been aware of his meeting with the three when he resigned. That explained his unusual calmness. Did they know about the bundle? The only way to divert attention from that was to go on the attack.

'There's nothing to talk about! I met them after they were being threatened at the entrance to the site. I felt sorry for them. They live nearby so I invited them up for a coffee. Now *get* out!'

In one swift, smooth action, Princess's right hand went under the suit jacket, pulled out a small revolver and rammed it hard underneath Gary's jaw. He froze as the hammer was clicked back.

'Don't *fuck* with me, Mr Surveyor! One of them was seen carrying something away from your apartment that they didn't take in. What was it?'

Gary thought quickly. 'It was an arrow quiver kicked up during the earthworks. I was going to keep it, until I met those people at the entrance. As I said, I felt sorry for them and decided to hand it over.'

Gary winced at the pain as the gun was rammed up even harder.

"Why were you all on that access road?'

Now Gary knew the answer as to when they had been sighted, he felt slightly relieved. He could mostly tell the truth about that.

'The valley holds importance for these people. They wanted to see the mess that was being made of it. I had already decided to resign that day so I figured nothing could be lost if I took them up for a view.'

The revolver eased back a little. 'Yes, I was told you might be a bleeding heart.'

Princess's other hand suddenly grabbed Gary's crotch, not in a painful way but firmly enough to make the heart follow. 'I dearly hope that nothing more comes of you fraternizing with these people. Believe me... you haven't any idea of what you are dealing with here.' The hand began to massage him. 'Mmmmm... I would like to come back for some more of this. Please don't make me.'

The hand let go and Princess reached up and put it around Gary's neck, pulling his head downwards. Soft lips then tenderly closed on his, lingering for a moment before they broke away from their stunned and unresponsive target. A knee was then slammed up viciously between his legs.

Gary fell to the ground in agony.

Princess walked slowly to the door and without turning called out, 'That was lesson number one. Please don't make me come back for lesson number two. It would be such a shame... a sweet looking man like you. Just be aware we will still be watching and listening. 'Byeeee,' came the gentle farewell as the door opened then softly closed again.

Gary remained on the ground for over a minute trying to catch his breath, moaning and heaving with the deep cramping pain in his groin and stomach. When he had recovered enough to sit up, his hands began to shake and bile lifted to his throat. He got to his feet and moved as quickly as he could to the bathroom and threw up. He then stripped and stepped into the shower, turning the hot water on full blast and soaping and shampooing twice over, trying to cleanse himself of the touch of the person who had just departed. One thought, however, transcended his disgust at the memory. He had to warn Grace. He dressed and walked out onto the landing to make the call, Princess's parting words 'still listening' almost certainly indicated that bugs were planted somewhere in the apartment. He headed to the cleaners' closet, stepped inside, closed the door then took out his wallet. He found the number then punched it into his cell phone.

It was nearly nine pm and Grace had only just arrived back from Seattle a half hour before. She was unpacking when the phone rang and muttered irritably as she pulled it out of her bag.

'Grace ... it's Gary Schroeder. Sorry about calling you at this hour but I need to tell you something.' Without going into details, Gary quickly told her what had transpired. 'Someone saw us together on the access track that morning and followed us here. They also saw your grandfather taking the bundle back to your car. I told them that it was just an old arrow quiver. I don't know whether I was believed but I feel it doesn't matter much to them what it was. There's something else going on here, I'm sure of it. I feel they're protecting something bigger than the progress of that project.' He hesitated for a moment then told her of his suspicion about the drug running, of what he had seen that Sunday. 'I thought about taking it to the DEA but I've got no real evidence. They would probably see it as a trouble making call designed to upset the project and treat it as such.'

Grace didn't respond immediately as she silently digested Gary's startling revelation. That Gary had been threatened with a gun was frightening enough but the talk of a possible drug connection brought another dimension to the fight over the valley's destruction.

It was Gary's turn to get irritable. '*Grace*?'

'Yeah, I'm sorry. I'm just trying to get my head around all this.' Another brief silence followed, 'I will understand if you don't want to go any further with the bundle, Gary. I don't want you to risk your life over it.'

Gary felt strangely offended. Sure, he'd had the hell frightened out of him but, as he stood there in the closet with his nether regions still throbbing with pain and his jaw aching from the imprint of a gun barrel, his fear had begun to turn into anger.

'No. I'll still back you up but I'm worried about them getting you on their radar.'

'It's a concern but the fact they are worried is important.'

The same purposeful manner Grace had displayed at Gary's apartment came through in her tone of voice. The question that had been nagging him since that day suddenly popped out. 'Just how do you intend to sink the development? The discovery of the bundle on site won't be enough to do it. I understand how important it is to you and your people but the archaeological laws are on their side.'

'Oh, I know all about the archo laws. Many of my people could gain a degree in them from what's been learnt over the years. The key is *how* I intend to use the bundle's discovery.'

'And how is that?'

'With music.'

'Aaaah... yeah?' came Gary's tentative reply.

Only the members of the band, Jamie and Looks Back had an idea of what Grace was planning. Not even Mark had been told but she figured the threat to Gary's life gave him the right to know. She quickly gave him a background of the band's rapid progress and told him of the impending release of the CD.

Grace's confidence about her music and belief in its power to change things momentarily silenced Gary. But he knew about the fickleness of the music industry, the many good bands that had never made it to recording and the others that had been sunk by poor marketing when they had.

'Well, I hope you are right. I was in the music industry in a past life and I've got some idea of how hard it is to break into the big time.'

Grace surfed over his negativity. 'What will you do now?' she asked.

'Well, I was supposed to be starting a temporary job tomorrow just outside Rapid City but I won't be hanging around here any longer. I might head back to California.'

There was a few seconds silence as Grace contemplated something.

'Okay, I'll keep in touch, Grace,' Gary finally said, but just as he was about to say goodbye, Grace interrupted.

'Do you want a job as a roadie for a while? We've always had trouble keeping them and we've just lost the last one to a one month prison sentence for dodged parking fines. It doesn't pay much but at least you'll be able to eat.'

Gary thought about it for only a few seconds. It just felt like the right fit at the moment, not least of all because he would be meeting up with Grace again. 'Yeah, I could do that for a while but I'm concerned I might bring attention to you.'

'If all goes to plan we're gonna be exposed in the not too distant future anyway and big enough, I hope, to provide some insurance against attack. For now, all they'll see is a band going about their business trying to make a buck. If you are aware of anyone tailing you just do your best to shake 'em... if it doesn't work, too bad.'

After getting Grace's address, Gary hung up, again impressed by her confident manner but still questioning what her music could do to change things. For a moment he wondered if he was getting tied up with the kind of a dreamer he had once been, before his dreams turned into a theodolite.

*

As Gary was making his way back to his apartment, Kilmont was putting a call through to a man sitting in the rear seat of a silver BMW parked a hundred yards away from the apartment building.

'Yeah,' the man answered and, after listening for a while, said, 'Well, he said a prayer into the john straight after Princess left, so I guess you could say he's suitably intimidated. But I gotta tell ya, Boss, I'm almost sorry that we put an ear in the bathroom.' Another listening silence followed and then he said, 'Yeah... okay,' before hanging up.

An older man in the front seat looked into the rear vision mirror, his mouth filled with part of a hamburger. He jerked his head upwards and gave a questioning grunt.

'He wants you to fly back to New York. Somethin' about the Quebec project. I have to stay here for a while to remind our friend of his obligations,' the younger one replied.

TWENTY

The next morning, after informing an annoyed head surveyor at the City Commission that he had to head back to California because of family problems, Gary hit the road to Deloraine, North Dakota - with a silver BMW on his tail. He had been aware of his shadow for the past twelve hours, spotting the intimidating-looking man when he looked out his front window soon after Princess had left his apartment. There was no clandestine attempt at surveillance. The BMW had been parked directly across the road, the man leaning against it, smoking. He gave a casual wave when he first saw Gary at the window and over the next few hours made a show of his presence by keeping the interior light of the car on as he ate or read a newspaper. Gary jammed a kitchen chair under the front door knob then pulled the sofa over to where he could watch the vehicle without being seen. There he spent a mostly sleepless night, worrying about another break-in. The man's presence had brought another worry. No matter how unconcerned Grace seemed to be about them finding out her location, he was determined not to allow it to happen, even if it meant aborting his trip up there.

Gary had unsuccessfully tried to shake off his pursuer in a speeding back street exit from Rapid City but the driver of the BMW easily accounted for his every move. By the time the traffic thinned out on highway 90, approaching the border of the Badlands National Park, it was keeping a constant hundred-yard gap from him. He kept trying to shake him off, picking up the pace on the run through the Badlands but every time he came out of a bend and put the foot down, the BMW closed the gap. He grew more worried as each mile passed. He thought about leaving the highway. His Chevy was built for rough terrain. Maybe the BMW could be shaken on a dirt track. If he could do that closer to where he had to take a left on Interstate 83 and head north, his tail wouldn't know whether he had turned or continued on. After that, the confusion for his shadow would only grow, with any number of routes crisscrossing or leading off both highways. He thought again. Leaving the highway and its traffic would expose him. He didn't know for sure whether this guy was an intimidator or an eliminator. Maybe it was exactly what he wanted him to do, so he could pull up next to him and poke a shotgun barrel out of the window and make all his plans instantly obsolete.

Tired from lack of sleep and the constant pressure of his traveling companion, he decided to stop for a coffee. He pulled off the highway and drove into the town of Murdo, about twenty miles short of his turnoff, where he pulled up at a diner. Soon after going into the building, the BMW pulled in and parked right next to his car. The driver got out and entered the diner, sitting a few seats along from Gary and watching him in the wall mirror behind the counter.

Gary remained as calm as he could, slowly drinking his coffee. When he had finished he got up and headed to the washroom. He paused as he put his hand on the swing door with the angry steer's head painted on it. Just to the right was a door marked 'Fire Exit' and he stepped over to check if it was locked. For the first time since leaving Rapid City he saw a real chance of ridding himself of his shadow. If he could get around to the front without him noticing, he could let the air out of one of his tires. That would be enough to give him the time needed. He turned the handle and the door opened. He hurried around the blind side of the building but, when he got to the front, he saw that the BMW was gone. He looked up and down the road. There was no sign of it anywhere. At first he was confused and then came a glimmer of hope. He got into his vehicle and headed out, his eyes scanning yards, buildings and his rear-vision mirror. As he approached the outskirts of Murdo, he burst into a few lines of Canned Heat's *On The Road Again*, smiling with relief at his escape, before his smile suddenly dropped away.

The BMW was parked in a layoff on a bend in the road just outside Murdo, camouflaged by the shade of trees. From there the driver had a clear view of the diner and he was doing the smiling now as he casually watched Gary go past.

Ten seconds later Gary's tail had grown again but, as he accelerated along the highway, anger now replaced nervousness. A few miles short of the turnoff to 83, after rounding the sweeping bend of a small hill, he pulled into a rest area. He got out and went behind a stunted tree to relieve himself, looking up sourly as the BMW pulled in at the other end of the parking area. Ignoring his tormentor, he continued emptying his bladder then zipped up and walked twenty paces to the vehicle barrier bordering the layoff where he pretended to be enjoying the view of the rolling, dry grass landscape stretching unbroken to the horizon.

The driver of the BMW got out, lit up a cigarette, and then he too stepped over to casually look out on the view.

Gary stood there for a couple of minutes before finally losing it.

'Asshole!' he yelled out, and then raised the universal signal of discontent.

His target turned and stared blankly, responding to the single digit semaphore with a casual puff of cigarette smoke.

Gary got angrier and braver. He stepped back into his car, started it up, swung wildly around on the gravel surface and accelerated straight at him, closing rapidly before swinging away five yards short, then driving onto the highway and disappearing around a bend.

The driver of the BMW didn't even blink at the intimidation. He stood steadfastly before the car's approach, one hand in a pocket, the other holding his cigarette to his mouth, as the gravel sprayed across his trousers. He then casually flicked his cigarette away, took the car keys from his pocket and started to walk back towards his vehicle but, after a couple of paces, something caused him to stop and look upwards. He took off his shades and searched the sun-bleached sky for the thin, faraway sound he had heard.

'Screeeeeee... screeeeeeee!' the cry came, louder this time, closing fast. 'Screeeeeee... screeeeeee...shuuuuuuwhooooooo!' He ducked as he felt the strong rush of wind across his head, his casual manner dragged away in the slipstream of the phantom's passing. He looked up again, still unable to see anything as the cry swept up into the sky and faded away. He sprinted to his car in fright but, just as he was about to open the door, he heard the squawk of the auto lock. He pressed the unlock button repeatedly but nothing happened. The presence in the sky was approaching again, its cry coming much swifter and louder than before. His fear exploded into blind panic and sent him running onto the road, his hands held over his ears, screaming out from the assault to his hearing. He stopped in the middle of the highway and dropped to his knees, eyes clamped shut from the pain as the sound speared through him, and then it suddenly ceased. From around the bend in the road, there came a new sound, like the rumbling of thunder, quickly followed by a deafening '*Maaaaaaaaaaaaaaaarp!*'

The transfixed figure on the road opened his eyes just in time to make out the words *MEAT EATER* artistically written in red paint on a plastic strip above the chromed letters that spelt out, MACK. The front bumper of the giant rig made its road-kill a second later, its eighteen squealing, screeching tires bouncing the carcass from sidewall to sidewall down the entire length of the chassis.

*

It didn't take long for John Kilmont to find out what had happened to his man in South Dakota. The last update he had received from him had been at Murdo and, after the hour for the agreed next call had passed without contact, he rang his employee's cell-phone number several times only to have it finally answered by someone else. One of the road patrol officers attending the accident, had just moments before, smashed a window in the BMW to gain access when the cell-phone played a silly little tune from the coat laid across the passenger seat. After a minute or so of mutually hesitant, identification-seeking conversation, the officer explained what had happened.

'Apparently your guy was just kneelin' on the highway with his hands over his ears. The truck driver said that when he sounded the horn he made no attempt to get out of the way, he just looked at the truck as though he was waitin' for it. It was a dual trailer unit with forty tons of canned goods on board and it didn't leave much to identify after it hit your boy. The coroner will tell us if he was under the influence of anythin' but, if that wasn't the case, then only the Almighty can tell us what the hell he was doin'.'

After half-truthfully explaining that the dead man was on his way back to New York from a company project in South Dakota, Kilmont told the officer that someone would be in touch about arrangements for the body when it was released, thanked him for the information and then hung up. After putting the phone down, he leaned back in his chair, genuinely perplexed by the strange circumstances, although not particularly troubled by the loss. As far as he was concerned, all of his foot soldiers were expendable. As his mind focused on the bigger picture, Kilmont recalled what the deceased one had last told him. The target was running scared. That would have to be enough for now. He would wait and deal with anything else on the Hidden Valley project when and if it arose. He picked up the phone.

'We've gone as far as we can go with that matter relating to Hidden Valley, Mister Blair. The employee has taken his severance pay and headed east.'

'Okay,' came the calm reply.

TWENTY-ONE

Gary was heading north, not east, traveling up the spine of the Great Plains and no longer running scared. He couldn't quite believe that he had lost his tail but, since leaving him covered in dust at the layoff, there had been no sign of the BMW. Five minutes later, he had turned left at Vivien on 83 heading for the wide Missouri, almost laughing out loud at his good fortune and wanting no answer to the mystery. Virtually overnight, his business had become music again and, although he still had no idea about how good Grace's was and serious doubts about how she intended to use it, he felt reinvigorated by the unexpected change in direction.

He arrived in Deloraine later that night and booked into a motel. The next morning, he rang Grace and she gave him directions to Chas's place where, a couple of hours later, he met the other members of the band. Grace had already given them the background on him and he was immediately accepted into the group, the description of his intimidation greeted with a declaration from Chas. 'Should make for interestin' stage choreography... dodgin' fuckin' bullets while we play!'

It brought some nervous laughter and a strong demand from Grace that nothing of what had happened to Gary should be mentioned to Jamie, who was at that moment in the stables helping Chas's wife, Kelly feed her two horses.

Immediately following the brief meeting, Gary began work as the group's road manager, a title that he and everyone else knew translated into general gofer. He started by helping load up the group's van for a two-day road trip, the first date to be that night in a Grand Forks nightclub two hundred miles to the east, followed by a country club performance the next night in Minot, a further two hundred and twenty miles back west. After the loading job was finished, Boss then handed over the keys to what in the coming weeks would become almost a second home to Gary.

Gary drove out onto the highway with Boss in the passenger's seat and Jamie in the back of the van. Normally Jamie would stay behind with Chas's wife during the school semester but, since the beginning of the summer vacation, he had been going along on all the overnight trips. Mostly it was for the fun of it. This time, however, there were a couple of practical reasons for his inclusion. As well as losing their former roadie, their regular sound engineer had just been called up for military service and, courtesy of what Jamie had learned in the Seattle recording sessions, he was given the temporary job on the relatively simple sound desk. He was looking forward to that and the extra pocket money but the other reason for his inclusion brought him more excitement. Since being given the didgeridoo, he had been practicing day and night in an attempt to copy Six Pack's work on *The Water Talks* and had become competent enough for Grace to ask him to play the part in the song when they tried it out on an audience for the first time.

Learning the job on the run shifted up to highway speed for Gary, with Boss outlining the tasks he would be required to carry out although, for much of the time, they had to work their conversation around the small person in the back, avidly rehearsing for his big moment. Boss would still remain the treasurer for now, until Mark Hammond took total control of bookings and finances but everything else involved in moving the group from one place to another on time was to be Gary's responsibility. The pay for the job dropped him down another level in earning capacity but he had been given free accommodation in a self-contained bunkhouse in Chas's barn and not long into the drive, Boss offered him the chance to earn a few more bucks.

'Ya say ya bin in a band before... well, if ya know anythin' about a mixin' desk maybe y'all c'n man ours fer awhaal. Jamie ain't gonna be able to do it much longer, he's gotta go back to *school* soon.'

A deep flatulent note of disapproval came from the didgeridoo after Boss turned and aimed his loud emphasis on the 's' word at its player. The sound of the instrument drew a brief chuckle from Boss but Gary remained straight faced, deep in thought. He had occasionally heard the didgeridoo on records before but, as soon as the boy had started playing he had a sense of hearing it recently in some other way. He put the thought on hold to answer Boss.

'It's been a long time since I fiddled with a board but that one doesn't look too complicated. I think I could handle it.'

'I'll help ya,' came the cry from the back, followed immediately by a yelping run of notes on the didgeridoo.

The two men smiled again and listened to Jamie's playing for a while, before Boss turned around and called out to the performer. 'I think ya got it down to a tee, mah man.' He then took a cassette from a large case behind him and slipped it into the deck, running it fast forward until he finally found the track he wanted. 'Listen to this,' he said to Gary, as he turned up the volume on the four-speaker customized system, instantly filling the van with the decibel levels of a nightclub.

For Gary, the next three minutes and twenty-seven seconds smashed any doubt or apprehension he might have held about the quality of the group's music. He listened to *The Water Talks* in a state of amazement but the song that followed affected him more.

'Wind it back a little, will ya?' he blurted out. 'I want to hear that again!'

Boss re-wound the tape and as Gary listened to *Song Catcher* once more, a shiver went down his spine. It wasn't just the power of the song and Grace's voice; it was hearing the melody line he had been picking out on his guitar ever since his dream of weeks before.

'That's only two numbers, man. Listen to the rest of it,' Boss said. He quickly rewound the tape back to the beginning.

By then, Jamie had laid down his instrument and moved right up next to Gary's ear. As the album played through, he gave him a running commentary on each song's construction, pre-empting the introduction of instruments and explaining the reasons for each subtle change in tone and melody.

Gary couldn't quite believe what he was hearing both from the tape and from the boy talking hoarsely in his ear. Already surprised to hear that Jamie would be running the sound desk for the two gigs and that he was also going to play the didgeridoo, now he was stunned by his expert commentary. He looked quizzically at Boss and received a knowing smile and raised eyebrows. By the time the tape had played through, they were pulling into a roadhouse behind the lead car.

Jamie jumped out immediately to bother his mother for food and drink but Gary remained where he was, stunned, watching the singer he had been listening to for over an hour and a half being a mother now, studiously ignoring Jamie's requests for whatever wasn't good for him.

'I suggest ya get somethin' ta eat, man. Ya won't get a chance agin 'til late tonight,' Boss said as he climbed out.

Gary stopped him with a question. 'What exactly *is* Jamie's part in the music?'

'The biggest, man. Without him we'd still be playin' fer li'l ol' beer money. He's got a genius gift fer arrangin' and he's a damn faan lyricist too. I thought Grace woulda tol' y'all that.'

Gary shook his head slowly then got out of the car and followed Boss into the roadhouse, his eyes only for the woman at the counter who was gathering coffee and food to go. Apart from brief conversations on the phone that morning and later at Chas's place, they had hardly spoken to each other and, as he headed towards the counter, he suddenly felt nervous about speaking to her now.

Grace saved him. 'Ears talked off yet?' she casually asked, turning around as Gary stopped next to her, her face carrying a smile that conveyed a certain degree of warmth.

With the smile came a flash of something in her eyes that Gary had seen before and it brought the compulsion to hold her again, the music he had just been listening to accelerating his desire. He wanted to flood her with compliments about it, shout them out to the other people in the place. But he controlled himself.

'Yeah... some,' he limply replied.

'Well, see ya in Grand Forks,' Grace said, as she made her way to the entrance.

'Yeah,' came a limper reply, before he absent-mindedly ordered a coffee to go then took it back to the van.

Several minutes later, Boss climbed into the van looking like a Viking with looted goods cradled in his arms. Jamie hopped in carrying the trophies of his nagging, a can of Coke in one hand and a half-empty pack of potato chips in the other. He offered some to Gary, who declined, and then to Boss but swiftly pulled the packet away before the beefy hand could enter it.

'Just *jokin'*, man... you've got enough there to feed the whole band.'

'A Drummer needs his vittles. It takes a whole heapa them there calories to keep the sticks a'movin'. Take this, man,' he said, and handed Gary one of his four cheeseburgers. 'I meant what I said about not eatin' til late. Gig don't finish til ten and the packin' up two hours after that. Y'all gonna burn a lotta energy bah then.'

Gary took it with thanks, the enticing smell of the burger reminding him he hadn't eaten since breakfast and he ate it hurriedly with one hand as he drove off behind the other vehicle.

*

The initial effect of the tape on Gary was instantly accentuated when the band began playing at eight o'clock that night. As a group they were tight and professional, their music distinctly different but it was the lead singer that raised their performance to another level. From the first number he stood almost mesmerized by the way Grace took ownership of the stage when she sang, oozing passion, projecting the effect of her voice with her sensuous image, all the vocal qualities in the tape even more pronounced. She had a sweetness of voice that could imperceptibly drop away, like a silken veil, exposing a raunchy, earthy quality beneath and then just as seamlessly be lifted again. It was a unique instrument and right now, it was electrifying both himself and the other couple of hundred that had jammed the small venue, another fifty or so waiting outside in the vain hope that someone would leave. It was the audience's response that confirmed to Gary just where this quality outfit was headed, as they jived with abandon to the hard rocking numbers and stared shiny-eyed and quiet when the ballads were sung. It was amazing stuff and not least because most of the songs they played were not from the album he had heard earlier that day.

It had been planned that Mitch, unneeded on *The Water Talks*, would watch the mixing desk during Jamie's performance in it but Gary had been getting lessons for most of the session and when the budding performer's turn came to go on stage he was suddenly thrust into the job.

Grace finished her song, looked at her son, who gave her a nod and a wide smile. She then began to introduce the next number. 'This one is off our upcoming album. It's called *The Water Talks* and it's pretty special because most of the lyrics were written by my son, Jamie.' She turned again to acknowledge the small figure seated on a stool, still smiling widely, with the didgeridoo now raised off the floor and balanced on another stool.

Grace allowed a brief moment of scattered applause and whistling, before she went on. 'He's going to play the didgeridoo, an instrument of the earth that holds a special place in the culture of the Australian Aborigine. We use it with respect for them, just as our music aims to bring respect for the Lakota.'

The last words brought some loud vocal support from the ever-growing number of Native Americans that were appearing in the group's audiences and Grace nodded to them before raising her hand for Wayne to begin the song.

As the notes of Wayne's harmonica began to drift through the room, Jamie came in almost perfectly with the low-pitched tone of the didgeridoo. The sound of it sent an appreciative murmur through those listening but, when Grace's voice and Chas's guitar took up the first Lakota verse in unison, the crowd was temporarily stunned into silence.

Even with the distraction of having to manage the board, Gary would be floored once more by *The Water Talks*, to the words and the melodic quality of the blues ballad. He understood that part of it was about the valley but there was something else there in Grace's voice. It was what had affected him most when he first heard it on the tape – a restrained cry of anguish.

The song finished to an even more rapturous response than those before, with Jamie clapped all the way back to the desk, beaming with delight even though he had made the occasional mistake. He had tasted the sweet nectar of applause. The stars were in his eyes now and his concentration at the desk dropped away so much that Gary had to prompt him when members of the band sent unhappy signals with hand and head.

Jamie got a lecture at the end of the night about his deteriorating performance on the desk. He nodded contritely but the words didn't really reach him. He was preparing himself for the next night's gig, sitting in a corner with the didgeridoo as the others dismantled the equipment, trying to perfect the parts he felt he had messed up in the song.

Jamie's distraction continued the next night in Minot and Gary had to take over the desk just a couple of songs into the performance. His efforts that night were greeted by the occasional glare from an unhappy musician but, from that point on he improved rapidly, getting endless practice as the band rehearsed in the barn every afternoon that they weren't playing and often on days that they were.

A week passed with it hardly registering on Gary, the pace relentlessly picking up. He had, by then, driven many hundreds of miles delivering *Warrior* to its audiences, in between sorting out the tangle of cables and leads that had to be connected to the equipment he constantly carted in and out of the van. His sleep was snatched any time he could find a gap, his meals taken mostly on the run, his home a storeroom with a van annex and he had no future to speak of beyond what he knew would be a temporary job - but he didn't care. Like the band, he was running on adrenalin, his world filled with the excitement their music generated and he was happy to be playing a small part in helping deliver it to their ever-growing number of fans. He was even happier to find out that, apart from Jamie, there was no other male in Grace's life.

The excitement jumped another notch during the second week of Gary's employment, when the CD arrived, delivered in person by Mark Hammond. He had brought forward the schedule for his distribution tour and decided to begin it in the band's hometown, although he had already rushed out many copies in the promo packs sent to DJs and music publications all over the northern parts of the country.

Like the band, Mark had been on the run since the recording; the website was designed and on the Net; his three-car garage had been turned into a mailroom with a bank of telephones and computers attended by two young female assistants he had hired to handle the orders he expected to turn into a flood. He was negotiating hard for the concert planned in Rapid City in about six weeks time And he was gathering the personnel they had used in the studio to perform in the show. Two of those, the Aussie didgeridoo player and the sound engineer had both declined his offer to take part when asked at the recording session but it was Donnewitz who was a major reason for accelerating plans to get the CD onto the market. Two weeks had passed and the sound engineer hadn't contacted him about the five thousand dollars he was to be paid for his work in the studio. This was mystifying to Mark but also irritating, seeing the money burning a hole in his personal bank account while his expenses climbed to the point of having to take out a second mortgage on his home. When the suppliers of his office equipment sent a second demand for payment, he decided to use Donnewitz's money to pay their bill. The thought of the rabid sound engineer chasing him for his fee was the motivation for hitting the road earlier than planned.

After only a brief meeting with the band at Chas's place, Mark was on his way again, his response to hearing about the threats made to Gary, 'Well, the sooner I get this album out there and the quicker you get into the big time, the less room they are going to have to make trouble. And if they try, that'll just generate more sales.' His first customers were the two small record stores in Deloraine. Both storeowners happily took a hundred copies, without any doubt they would soon be sold.

Elated with the first sale, Mark then took off on a circular pattern to the east and north of Deloraine before zigzagging south, hitting the main towns and cities in all the Midwest states. He did a u-turn at Denver and headed north again across the Rockies and back to Seattle, before heading over the border to Vancouver.

As Mark traveled, he monitored the airwaves for the music he most wanted to hear. He had contacted every radio station DJ personally to convince them to play the record. Most didn't need persuading. Those that had attended the group's live performances were actually waiting for the release. Mark was filling up at a service station when *Song Catcher* was first introduced by an enthusiastic DJ. He cranked the volume up full blast, called Grace on his cellphone and held it at the car window.

'Listen to this, Gracie! It's coming out of Triple One in Bismarck. You're on the way, kid!' he yelled over her recorded voice. 'So are the sales. I've sold nearly two thousand so far and the two stores in Deloraine have re-ordered!'

'Yeah... it's great, Mark,' came the subdued reply.

The voice that answered Mark was like a mouse's compared to the one that was firing out across the concourse of the fuel station, the volume of the radio causing an elderly patron to glare while a young mechanic started banging away keeping time with a spanner on a metal bench.

'Both of the store owners in Deloraine asked if you could do a signing session for them. I managed to bump up the size of the orders on the promise that you would do it.'

There was a brief pause before Grace answered, 'Yeah... okay.'

Mark was concerned at the tone of reluctance in Grace's voice. He knew that at some stage he was going to have to do some coaching of her but didn't think he would have to apply the pep talk so soon. 'Think of it as practice, Grace. There's going be a lot more of it coming up in the very near future!'

'Yeah, I know, Mark. I'll be okay,' Grace said, with little conviction.

'We'll all be okay!' Mark declared before ringing off.

By the time Mark returned to Seattle six days later, he had heard several of the songs off the album being played on a dozen or more Midwest stations. Some of the DJ's gave them as much airplay as those of established international artists and expected their promotion of the band to be repaid with an interview. Over the next few days, requests started to pour in from local newspapers, radio and television stations and record stores. His cell-phone was rapidly heading towards meltdown and by the end of that first week, sales of the album had reached six thousand. But the slowdown Mark had anticipated eventually came. The songs were being played less frequently on the radio the closer he got to his home base and the size of new orders reducing in direct relation to how far the stores were from the epicenter in North Dakota. But it was a good start, the sales giving him the cash flow to order twenty thousand more copies. He then dived into the task of getting exposure in a big city, where the real sales would be made but where he knew he wouldn't have the easy task of selling to the already converted.

He hit the Seattle region for two days solid and then headed across the border to Vancouver, delivering copies already ordered by his former clients and making small sales to other stores. Once again he targeted the radio stations, vigorously following up the promo packs he had sent the program managers. By midway through the second week, he began to understand just how difficult it was going to be to get airplay in a big city. But he was more frustrated than worried. He knew that, as soon as someone in the right place listened to the CD, the twenty thousand just delivered to him would quickly move out again. Proof of that was constantly filtering in. Even though the orders from the Midwest area were tapering off, sales had gradually risen to near ten thousand through the promotional playing of the album in some of the small stores around Seattle and Vancouver. The owners were becoming almost as keen as Mark to see it get some wider attention and increase their sales, and eventually it would be their repeated queries that gave him the idea of how to gain some radio attention. He would run his own private poll of the stores that had re-ordered the CD, asking them to fax him a list of all album sales over the last seven days and add their comments about *Spirit Rising* at the bottom. He would then deliver the result to the radio stations. Most of the stores readily complied and he quickly went to work on an information sheet but the next day something occurred to make him halt all proceedings.

Mark was seated at one of the computers in his garage office, putting the finishing touches to his sales sheet when he suddenly heard one of his girls call out to him.

'Wow, Mark! Take a look at this!'

He read the fax message and shouted out in delight. It was an entirely unexpected order from a chain of stores in the Chicago area - the five hundred discs requested, by far the biggest single order yet. He rang the purchaser straightaway to ask where they had heard the album. He was told people were asking for it after hearing songs from the CD being played on 6 RR Chicago but when he checked the list of stations to which he had sent promos he could find nothing under that name.

*

The week of the record's release was a blossoming one for most connected with *Warrior* but no more so than for Jamie. At the end of it, he would attain the longed-for-status of teenager and, while his mother was beginning to shrink from all the attention that came with the mushrooming popularity of *Spirit Rising*, his confidence and personality were uncurling like the petals of a flower warming to its moment in the sun. He breezed through the signing sessions, radio interviews and several TV appearances like a pro, his eagerness to speak about and his ability to interpret the music often leaving members of the record-buying public and interviewers without questions to ask. The unlikelihood of a boy being an integral part of the exciting new sound was already lifting the profile of the popular group higher but it was something else he did that provided the catalyst for their ultimate propulsion into the big time. Within a few days of Mark delivering the group's copies of the CD, Jamie sent out the one he had promised to Bright Face at Pine Ridge and another to Ray Cicconi at Radical Radio, politely asking the DJ if he might be able to play a number on air sometime.

'Sometime' started the day Cicconi received his copy of *Spirit Rising*. His young listener had told him a while ago that his mother was a singer with a small-town band and, at the time he had responded with friendly but mild interest. What he heard after vacantly putting on the CD for a quick listen had him instantly typing an email.

Jamie
Tune in tonight little buddy. I'll be playing something extra special.
Ray the Dee Jay

That night, Jamie and Grace sat by the radio as Cicconi introduced *The Mountains I* with, 'If ya think we play great music here, then getta load o' this!' Two more numbers followed without a break, the instrumental, *Sweet Grass* and then the steamy, *Come To Me*.

For once, the fadeout of a song came uninterrupted by Ray's DJ speak and, when the sensual ballad had finished he whispered in a low, gravelly and suggestive tone. 'Well, helloooooo, Grace.'

'What're ya blushin' for, Mom?' Jamie asked, slyly.

'Shhhh... listen to what he's got to say.'

Ray carried on, speaking quietly and almost seriously to his late night audience. 'Some of you have probably heard me occasionally speak to a young friend of mine by the name of Jamie. Well I'm here to tell ya that that was his mom you just heard singin'. She's a member of a group called *Warrior* and the name of the album those three songs come from is called *Spirit Rising*. And guess whose name is right there in the cover as a songwriter? You got it. It's none other than young Jamie Howard! *Right on*, Jamie! Now, all you guys out there who've just felt the need to go and have a cold shower, do it quick, caus' after the break there'll be more of *Spirit Rising*!'

'What's he mean by a cold shower, Mom?' Jamie slyly agitated again.

Grace turned the radio down, looked at the deadpan face, blushed slightly again and then smiled back. 'It means he likes my singing.'

'You're blushin' again, Mom.'

'No I'm not.'

'Yes you are.'

'No I'm not.'

'Yes...'

'Quit it, Jamie. Get onto the computer and thank Ray for both of us. He's just done the album a very big favor.'

Jamie brought his face right up close to his mother's and then spoke in his deepest, huskiest voice, 'Okay, but maybe I should go and have a cold shower too, oh sexy one.' He ducked his mother's attempt to swat him, honking his way to his room where he sat down before his computer and opened up the email. Underneath Ray's message he typed.

Thanks for the plug, man. Mom says so too... and you made her blush!

Jamie

The reply came straight back.

It's a pleasure, my man. Tell your Mom that blushing is going to be the least of her problems when the word spreads about your record. It rocked my socks off, rolled my soul and spun my head faster than a CD.

Ray the dizzy Dee Jay

'You little shit... you *told* him!' Grace cried, after Jamie called her in to read the reply.

Jamie had vacated the seat before the computer and was standing by the door ready to make his getaway when his mother read the message but, instead of chasing him, Grace sat down and stared at the DJ's words for a while, focusing on the well-meaning 'least of her problems' bit. The words flashed at her like an amber light but she knew there would be no stopping now.

Jamie crept up behind Grace and put his arms around her neck. 'What's up, Mom?'

Grace shifted her gaze slightly to the portable CD and tape player standing on a shelf above Jamie's record collection. 'Oh, nothing, Hon. Just noticed how old and grubby that player looks,' she replied.

'Well, when we're rich and famous I can get another one.'

'Yeah,' Grace replied.

*

The qualifications Jamie had set for acquiring a new sound system would begin to be met very soon after Mark received his surprise request from Chicago. Over the next few days several large orders began to flow in from stores scattered around Illinois. Alerted to Radical Radio's broadcasting of the album, employees of other stations had slush piles searched for vaguely remembered promo packs and then rapidly caught up on airplay. Very soon the album was getting played

Graham McDonald

on stations in bordering states too, the flow of orders from there rapidly climbing and within a week, Mark was worrying more about keeping up with demand than how to get the CD moving. He hired two more girls to handle the packing and delivery, his order of twenty thousand followed by one of forty and then sixty, and all the while the sales figures were feeding into the system that supplied ratings on the Billboard top two hundred album chart. A mere two weeks after *Spirit Rising* was released it crept into one hundred and ninety eight on the chart and soon it would take another big leap in its rapid climb towards popularity.

TWENTY-TWO

It was early Monday morning when cub reporter Roma Chavez of the New York- based music magazine *Sounds* went to the Billboard site on her computer to check the latest chart movements. It was a routine task for her, trying to find something of interest for others higher up to write about. She was also in charge of filtering the promo packs that endlessly poured into her back-room office from all over the States; many never listened to because of lack of time, particularly those with unknown record labels. Most disappeared into a storeroom and were instantly forgotten but when she saw the name *Spirit Rising* as a new entry at the bottom of the general Billboard chart, it jogged her memory.

Roma went to the small storeroom where thousands of discs were filed wherever there was enough space to put them but, after an hour of searching lucklessly, she gave up and went back to browsing through the day's newspapers and industry periodicals for snippets of information that could be regurgitated in *Sounds*.

Gradually gaining countrywide readership over the five years since an ex-Rolling Stone journalist had launched it, *Sounds* wrote only about music and it was Roma's wide appreciation and knowledge that landed her the job she hoped would kick-start her journalist's career. But it had turned out to be more like a rope-start on a flooded lawnmower. After a year, she hadn't yet been given an assignment that went beyond the occasional three or four paragraph gossip article about the social habits and behavior of those who made the music. Boredom had set in months ago and the only thing stopping her throwing in her job was the oversupply of journalists in a city she didn't want to leave. Spotting *Spirit Rising* on the Billboard charts proved to be an ignition point for her flagging career.

It was there again the following morning, fifteen places higher. This time Roma checked the category lists but found nothing on any of them. That was strange. If it had shown up on the open chart it would nearly always emerge in a category and, because of the narrower range of competition, at a higher listing. Now she *had* to find the promo pack. For the whole of that day she did a work-interrupted but meticulous search of the storeroom from the doorway back, all the while cursing her careless filing methods. Very late in the day, she finally came across it.

Roma put the CD on the player in the small living room of her cramped Greenwich Village apartment that night and sat down to the Thai takeaway she had picked up on the way there. Three-quarters of an hour later, the food was still standing uneaten on the coffee table. She understood now just why the album hadn't appeared on a category chart. It had elements of everything in it, from Rock to Folk and Jazz to Classical but it also had a distinctly different sound that defied being labeled by any of the slick titles used to describe crossover music. She listened to the album twice more. It had an organic quality. With each replay she found something new in the songs, the natural richness of voice and instrument unhindered by the overuse of electronic variation, with each song connecting to make the whole. The combined effect was stunningly effective, drawing her in to make her feel as if she too were part of the music.

Roma read through the J card and the letter that had come with the promo pack. She had initially discarded the CD without listening to it because she thought it to be just another Tribal Rock effort, a small flicker on the music scene in the mid to late nineties that had died away quickly. But it was much more than that. As well as spiritual, cultural, environmental and political themes, there was mystery, too. She saw it in the eulogy written for Eyes That Cut and found more of it in the words of *The Water Talks* and *Song Catcher*.

After Roma closed the J card her eyes lingered on the cover. '*Warrior Spirit Rising,*' she said out aloud, with no hesitation between the band's name and the record title. It perfectly expressed the songwriting collaboration of a nineteenth century Lakota warrior-poet with two of his modern day descendants, one of them just twelve-years old. And there was the distinctive and powerful voice of the mother. Where had she come from? Roma knew that the CD hadn't yet broken on the east coast but it would only be matter of time before others who also perused Billboard trumpeted it to the industry. She picked up the phone and rang the owner of Aktrix Records in Seattle, suitably exaggerating her position at *Sounds* and quickly organized an interview of the mother and son. The next morning she applied for two days leave, using the grounds that her father in Detroit was very ill and then she flew right over him, heading for a town in North Dakota she'd never heard of before.

*

Immediately after getting off the line from Roma Chavez, Mark rang Grace.

'It's time to kill some of the gigs,' he said the moment she answered. 'The record's taking off... sales are over seventy thousand and rapidly climbing, and the supercharger is about to kick in. I've just had a call from a journalist with *Sounds* magazine in New York. She wants to do an article on *Warrior* in this month's issue but specifically wants to speak to you and Jamie. As you know, these people can be the enemy if they're not handled right so I'll be flying down to make sure we get what we want from her. I guess I don't need to tell you what this means, Gracie. New York and LA are the bull's eyes and it looks like we've just hit one. It's going to happen big time from here, so get prepared!'

Grace quietly agreed to the interview that had already been arranged, said goodbye and then remained seated by the phone, contemplating what was ahead. In all the interviews so far, when answering questions on the political content of some of the songs, she had spoken of the social problems facing the Lakota only in a general sense, restraining herself from mentioning the valley project as she bided her time for a moment of maximum impact. Now, like the next link in a chain, the moment she had been waiting for appeared to have come. Her challenge to Prestige would be broadcast throughout the music world and hopefully beyond. She picked up the phone again and rang another person she needed to be at the interview.

TWENTY-THREE

Two weeks ago, Gary felt as though he had been hired at the beginning of a stampede and he watched over *Warrior's* headlong rush towards popularity with amazement. Yet, although he was pleased in playing a part in maintaining the group's momentum, he was concerned at how it seemed to have changed the demeanor of the lead singer. As the attention grew, she withdrew into herself. Although still forceful on stage, away from it she was strangely nervous, the confidence she had displayed earlier replaced by a growing defensiveness. He dearly wanted to get closer to find out what was wrong but their relationship didn't go beyond work and when the gigs or practice sessions were done with she quickly went her way, always, it seemed, with other pressing things to do. But then came the night of Jamie's birthday party.

*

'You like my Mom, huh?'

Gary had been sitting in Jamie's bedroom listening to some of his record collection on the sound system Grace had given him for his birthday. The house and backyard were full of people but Jamie had shut the door on the noise and was giving Gary an enthusiastic description of what the four-speaker sound system could do when the totally unexpected question came.

Gary hesitated for a moment, caught by the suddenness and frankness, before he finally responded. 'What's there not to like?'

Jamie smiled. 'Apart from havin' a big problem with crumbs on the sofa and clothes lyin' around the joint, not a whole lot. Why dontcha ask her for a date?'

Gary smiled ruefully. 'Oh, I don't think your Mom is that interested in me. Besides, she's got a career heating up and I don't think she'll be able to find time for anything except her work from here on in. Anyway, soon enough I'll have to be moving on and looking for another career of my own.'

Jamie suddenly went very quiet. He stared fixedly at the wall behind the stereo until his guest felt uncomfortable enough to get up and leave but just as Gary reached the doorway, a voice spoke out.

'Yer can't go givin' up on 'er now, man.'

Gary stopped and turned to look at the back of the boy. He had grown accustomed to the occasional Lennon-speak but this time it sounded as if the whole room had delivered the words.

'Huh?' came his startled response.

Jamie turned around and looked at Gary in puzzlement. 'Where ya goin', man? Ya said you would sing me *Red Rooster.*'

Gary walked back, sat down and looked suspiciously into Jamie's eyes, before picking up the guitar that had been gathering dust in a corner of the room ever since the didgeridoo had moved in. He quickly tuned it then began to sing the Willie Dixon blues number. Halfway through it, Jamie picked up the didgeridoo and joined in, adding an unobtrusive bass tone to the lazy theme of the song. It worked and Jamie insisted they do it again. At the end of the second run through, the door opened.

'Sounds good,' said Grace, who had stopped on her way past after delivering some food out to the guests.

Jamie saw his chance. He flipped through the swing section of his record collection, found a 'Best Of' tape and slipped it into the player, before fleeing the room. 'Gotta go and eat,' he called out, smiling mischievously at his mother as he raced past.

I'll kill him later, Grace thought, as alone she struggled to find something to say to the man before her.

'What was the name of your group?' she finally asked.

'Blues Train... but we never quite got onto the rails.'

Grace smiled in a sardonic way. 'Maybe you were lucky.'

'Maybe,' Gary said, as he put the guitar back in the corner.

'If you're hungry, Cal's burning some steaks out back,' Grace said emptily, still leaning on the doorway, staring fixedly at the floor, allowing the melodic strains of Glenn Miller's *Moonlight Serenade* to wash over her.

'What is it, Grace?' Gary asked after a few seconds.

Grace looked up slowly and gazed at the blue eyes, seeing again the look of genuine compassion that had pulled her up short that day in the Black Hills. She wandered into the room and sat down on the edge of Jamie's bed. Now that the all-consuming task of completing the CD was over, the pressure building since its release made her feel like a hunted animal. A large part of the problem was not being able to speak to anyone about it. There were times over the last couple of weeks that she had wanted to reach out to the man before her, the relative stranger who might listen to her without judging but fear of showing him weakness held her back. Now, the distance she had kept between them fell away.

'I'm afraid of what's ahead,' she said, her head tilted and eyes fixed imploringly on his but with her arms crossed.

Gary was momentarily struck speechless by the deep vulnerability he saw in her eyes. He was afraid too. Although it had happened weeks ago, he could still feel the cold imprint of the gun barrel on his jaw but she had always appeared more angry than afraid of what Prestige might do. There was something else that was deeply troubling her and, at the moment, he doubted that any words of his could help her. He stood up just as Les Brown's orchestra moved into their version of *Blue Moon*. Smiling warmly, he held out his hand.

Grace looked up with doleful eyes and, after a slight hesitation, rose to the invitation. She took his hand and they danced, slow, gentle and close, unmindful of the door softly closing behind them.

The power of music flowed through *Blue Moon* and into Artie Shaw's rendition of *Moonglow*, with not a word spoken, just silent tears shed on a sympathetic shoulder. Then, as the classic dance number faded, Grace lifted her head from Gary's shoulder, put her hand around the back of his neck and pulled his head towards hers.

What Gary felt in the embrace was much more than sexual. The tender, yearning pressure of her soft lips and her clinging body were a cry for help and he measured his response to it. As much as he wanted her physically he now felt an overwhelming desire to protect her.

They eased away from their embrace and stared unbrokenly into each other's eyes for a few seconds.

'Tell me about it.'

Grace sat down on the bed again and Gary pulled the chair over, reached out and held both of her hands. Grace looked down as she spoke but she held onto those hands like a lifeline.

'I ran from what is coming once before and nearly killed myself in the process. It turned me into a doper and I'm terrified of what the pressure will do this time. I don't know if I can cope with the crowds that we'll have to perform before... all the people that want a piece of me. I can't explain it, it's more than stage fright... it's stage terror. I don't see the audience as all these different people having a good time. I see it as one thing, a monster intent on consuming my soul only, this time, I know I can't run... there's too many people besides me to consider, and that terrifies me most of all.'

Gary was shocked. Until now, all he had seen of her was a quiet sort of strength and he had always admired her non-smoking, non-drinking control. Now he knew why she never joined in the winding down sessions after practicing and performing. He looked at the bowed figure, put a hand under her chin and gently lifted her head.

'I said I would hang around as a witness to finding the bundle and I'll hang around as long as you need me for anything else. I'll be there when you go on stage and I'll be there when you come off, or any other place you want me to be,' he added, hopefully.

A warm, amused smile formed on Grace's face. She leaned forward, held both her hands gently to Gary's cheeks. 'I get the picture, Itan´- ćan,' she said softly.

Gary stared into her embracing eyes, his brow creasing with concentration. Then he remembered. The words were Lakota for Spirit Keeper.

A flush of pride spread through Gary. He now felt truly responsible for the spirit of the person before him and, no matter what was up ahead, he would not allow her to become lost. He put his hands up to her face.

'You're a knockout, Grace... on and off stage. The music's fantastic and *you* own it. All you're gonna get from those big crowds is love, believe me. And, as for those who might want a piece of you, all I can see around you at the moment are those who care for you. Feed on that.'

Grace nodded but, as she leaned away, the smile slowly faded from her face.

*

Grace's call about the *Sounds* interview came to Gary just as he retired to his bunk after doing some late night equipment maintenance.

'Hi, just ringing to tell you it looks like the thing we spoke about the other day is gonna happen tomorrow morning,' Grace said, with excitement in her voice. 'A journalist from *Sounds* magazine out of New York wants to do an interview with Jamie and me. If I feel she's the right one, I'm gonna push the red button. Can you be at my place by eight o'clock?' Grace asked.

'I'm at your place all the time,' Gary replied, as he lay in the bed where they had consummated their relationship a day after Jamie's birthday. It happened when they had been left alone during a break from practice, when the rest of the band had gone into town for a meal. Five minutes after the others departed they were in his bed, the beautiful, savage, stolen hour bringing more than either had hoped for.

Grace chuckled lightly. 'Okay, I'll see you soon,' she said then hung up, all trace of amusement gone from her face as she contemplated her next move, the sounds of the battle growing louder.

TWENTY-FOUR

It had only taken a few minutes for Grace to make up her mind about the very young reporter that turned up for the interview. Soon after she was in the door, Roma Chavez had revealed her true position at *Sounds* and, while it had annoyed Mark to find out she hadn't written anything major for the magazine, Grace admired her initiative and enthusiasm. When Roma asked her insightful questions about the connections she saw in the album, all was sealed. For twenty minutes non-stop, Grace talked into Roma's tape recorder about the Hidden Valley matter, with Gary corroborating her information. Another half-hour of questions about the music followed, punctuated by impressive answers from the small boy present. A beaming reporter hurried out to her hire car and drove quickly to Bismarck Airport.

*

Darcy Farrell lifted his eyes from the J card of the *Warrior* CD and stared blank-faced at his fired-up young reporter.

He had been listening to the tape of Roma's interview with Grace and was now listening to her excited commentary on how the album had gone from 198 to 92 on the Billboard in three days, and how she would write the article if he would give her the chance. She had broken several rules in seeking out the story but her boiling enthusiasm had kept Darcy listening. He finally held up a hand to halt Roma's relentless entreating.

'There are names here that I know. Grace Howard was around in the eighties, heading up the slippery slope until she suddenly disappeared. And this producer, Marty Donnewitz... he was one of the best back then but I vaguely remember someone telling me he died years ago down in Mexico. Drugs or somethin'. There's a couple of well-respected session people here from those days too.'

He took the CD out, swung around on his chair and slipped it into the player behind him. He listened to *Song Catcher* right through and to brief sections of all the other numbers before turning it off.

His face remained expressionless as he studied the J card again, before he looked up at Roma, a rare smile spreading across his face.

Roma's widened into a broad grin.

'Have you spoken to this Prestige Developments yet?' He asked.

'Yeah, I spoke with their PR department. They handed me the standard response, denying all knowledge of what was dug up there before adding the threat of legal action if we went ahead with the article. But as you just heard, all can be proved.'

Darcy nodded his head slowly. He wasn't averse to a challenge. It was his gambling nature that had inspired him to start up *Sounds* against the advice of everyone and it was pleasing to see a junior employee exhibiting something of the same courage.

'Write it, and fast. Look up the files on Grace Howard and add something about what she was doin' in the eighties. Get it to me first thing in the mornin'.'

Roma didn't leave the building that night and was waiting for her boss outside his office when he came in the next morning. She was a mess but the article wasn't. It started with a short section on Grace's promising career in the eighties and built into a glowing description of her current outfit's unique sound before throwing down the gauntlet to Prestige towards the end.

Darcy read the three pages of text and then handed it back to Roma.

'It's good work. Get it to Moony straight away.' He picked up the phone as Roma hurried out of the room. 'Moony... Roma's bringin' over an article that I want as the headliner, you'll have to shift that Eminem one further in.'

There was a moaning response from the other end of the line.

Darcy didn't listen very long to his chief editor's complaint. 'I know it'll be difficult. What isn't in this business? Just do it. It's gonna be a big item and we've got first run at it. Find a photo of the singer for the front page.'

The presses rolled a day later with Grace's 'before and now' images on the cover, with the title 'A Spirit Rises Again' underneath and Roma's article covering the first two pages of the magazine. It was moving out onto the highways and runways soon after and, by the time it was being read by the record-buying public, the album had reached 43 with over one hundred and fifty thousand copies sold. Everyone involved in the CD and its promotion was beginning to glow with its success but, even before *Sounds* had hit the streets, those who saw the record's popularity as poison were working on an antidote.

*

The afternoon he was contacted by his PR department about the upcoming article in *Sounds*, Jim Blair made one of his rare visits to the lower environs of Prestige Developments. He strolled into his security head's office without being announced. In his hand he had a copy of *Spirit Rising*. He placed it on John Kilmont's desk.

'I'm disappointed, John. That surveyor from the Hidden Valley project you said you had silenced has raised his head again. He has teamed up with a Sioux woman singer and it looks like they intend to use their music to broadcast an anti-Prestige message over most of the country.'

Blair opened the CD cover and took out the booklet. Pointing to the lyrics of *The Water Talks*, he said, 'Just read this and you'll get the idea. A journalist from a music magazine already has. She contacted us about something the surveyor found dug up out there, a sacred artifact of some description. The story's going to be in their next edition, due out tomorrow. We can't do anything about the article and it's pointless now to argue about our rights under Archaeological laws but we can stop the momentum of all this. The popularity of the music is what's doing the damage so we've got to silence the singer and it *has* to look like an accident. The surveyor can wait till later and I expect you to do a better job on this one than you did with your first try. You understand me, John?'

Kilmont nodded almost shamefacedly as his superior wheeled around and walked out of his office, leaving him to think about the consequences if he failed to get the job done this time. He knew he was as expendable as his foot soldiers and that their eradicating abilities could just as easily be turned on him.

He pondered on the best way to solve the problem but it wasn't until the next day, after reading the article in *Sounds* that he finally decided on a plan. It was the part trumpeting the Rapid City concert that was of most interest to him. He pulled out his tiny notebook and flipped through it until he found the number he wanted.

A few seconds later, amidst the mess of disemboweled appliances in the back room of a small Brooklyn electrical repair shop, a man with greasy long hair and large black-framed glasses picked up a grubby phone and grunted hello. He listened to Kilmont's job offer, inquired about the salary package then grunted his acceptance.

TWENTY-FIVE

Within a few days of *Sounds* reaching its market, the sales of *Spirit Rising* trebled. A video clip was made of the group performing *Song Catcher* and *North Wind* and Mark submitted it to all the major TV music programs. MTV began playing it, giving both songs daily exposure on international television and, after a few days, the album sales went past the gold-plated mark of half a million. It had become one of the fastest moving albums of all time, the attention that the general press was giving to the story behind it keeping its momentum going. Soon, the first trickle of music loving, environmentally conscious young protestors joined a band of Native Americans setting up camp outside the Hidden Valley site. They pointedly erected a couple of large tipis and defied the demands of increasing numbers of security guards and police to move on, reveling in their relative protection from TV and newspaper coverage.

While the pressure began to slowly build at the project site, a reporter and photographer from the New York Times went to Pine Ridge to interview Looks Back. He allowed them to photograph the bundle on the spirit post then gave them

263

a brief explanation of its importance and the ritual attached to it, adding that it would be opened at the appropriate time. Afterwards, he insisted they take some photos of him with a crow's feather stuck in his hair and his firewood-chopping axe cradled like a weapon in the crook of his arm. The picture and article made George a bit of a cult figure, with every part of the media seeking him out. Like a flock of chickens, they came to feed on the words of this eccentric personality and George tossed them what he figured they wanted. But, scattered amongst the earthy one-liners thrown from a 'quaint old Indian', were his carefully crafted comments about the Black Hills and the Hidden Valley development, adding more fuel to the fire that *Spirit Rising* had begun.

All the while, the band that had ignited the fire rolled on towards their first big show at Rapid City, with Gary the roadie now Grace's very personal assistant, press agent and bodyguard, vetting every request for interviews and the questions that went with them. Ever since the interview with *Sounds* and his subsequent contact with the DEA, he had been with her nearly every hour of the day, waking or sleeping, keeping a constant eye on the activity around her.

As he and Grace had discussed prior to the interview, Gary had rung the drug authorities' regional office. He was put through to a female officer who listened quietly to his information before politely responding. 'Send us a hard copy of your information and I will pass it on to the appropriate people for consideration. You must be aware however that, although we endeavor to follow through on as many calls as we can, we receive thousands a year on drug related allegations and can only respond according to the availability of resources.' The officer thanked him for calling then said goodbye.

Although at first deflated by what he figured was a kiss off, once he had sat down and put it all on paper he could see where they might get the impression that it was the work of an overstretched imagination. It just seemed unbelievable. He sent it anyway but with little hope that anything would come of it. Meanwhile, he turned all his energy to his new job.

Gary's efforts at shielding Grace from the worst of the attention allowed her to relax a little. Other burdens were also being lifted. A lot of money was now pouring into her bank account and the years of frugality and respect for the hard-earned dollar meant she knew how to handle it. She was looking for a house to buy and investments were being made that would set her and Jamie up for life, with other funds directed to foundations on Pine Ridge that were aspiring to improve the health and education of its residents. Because of Gary's management she also had more time to concentrate on her art, rehearsing constantly for the Rapid City showdown and working on songs for another album. Everything seemed to be going well - until the night the rider came again.

The dream hadn't entered Grace's sleep for weeks and she had almost forgotten about it but, one night, just days before they were to head off to Rapid City, the faintly familiar tones began to rumble through her sleeping mind once more.

Closer and closer the horse and rider had come and, with the image, the sense of indefinable sadness flooded through her once more. The warrior dismounted. He was still faceless and still carrying the object that looked like a large arrow quiver but there was something else not visible in the previous dreams, something lying across the neck of the pony. The warrior put down the quiver and lifted the buckskin-wrapped bundle from his horse, laid it gently on the ground, kneeled down and untied its thong binding before unrolling it. As he did so the indistinct soundtrack suddenly became recognizable; the quiver became a didgeridoo and, as its tones grew louder, the bundle began to grow, unrolling itself now as the warrior regained his feet and stepped away. Soon, *Spirit Rising's* cover design was being revealed and, as the buckskin continued to unroll, something took shape in its hidden folds. The form of a body tumbled over and over inside it and the tones of the didgeridoo became louder and wilder, then the beads of her necklace spilled out of the bundle. She looked up at the warrior. The blurred image of his face suddenly sharpened and, through the blood-red slash that crossed it, there spread a familiar sad, defiant smile. She reached out for him but something began dragging her down towards the bundle. She struggled frantically against the invisible force but it just grew stronger. The sound of the didgeridoo continued to increase and gradually the image of the warrior began to recede until, like a switch being thrown, all sound and vision suddenly ceased.

Grace gave out a great heaving moan as her body jerked upright in bed, tears now streaming down her face.

Before her stood a startled boy, the instrument he had been playing as he walked from his bedroom, silent now but still aimed at his sleeping mother. He looked with concern at the response to his wakeup call. 'Sorry, Mom... I didn't mean to frighten ya.'

Grace put her hands to her face, took some deep breaths and slowly wiped the tears away. She looked up again and then sputtered a weak laugh at the sight of her son and the didgeridoo.

'Just a bad dream, Hon. Probably the second helping of those chili beans last night.'

Grace turned away and stared out of the window into the gray gloom of dawn then spoke with feigned enthusiasm. 'It's breakfast time. Let's do the lot this morning. Flapjacks, eggs, bacon, hash brown, fried tomatoes and toast. You can get all the makin's out while I get dressed.'

'Okay.'

Grace watched Jamie as he walked from the room then crossed her arms on her raised knees and rested her forehead on them. 'It was only a dream' she kept saying to herself but, as the gray light turned to gold and the kitchen rattled to the touch of its young chef, she sent a silent prayer in Lakota to the rider.

TWENTY-SIX

The group arrived in Rapid City three days before the concert date and, although Grace coped with most of the lead-up preparation, on the final day of rehearsal and sound checks, the first tremor set in. Several times she had to be urged to project a voice that had never needed effort before and, after a fourth failure to satisfy the sound engineers, Chas let fly.

'Jesus Gracie, sing like that tomorrow night and we'll soon be back duckin' beer bottles!'

The comment finally ignited her.

'Fuck you, Chas... and fuck all of them! Do they have to be here while I do this?' she yelled, waving her hand around the stadium at the small army of security men and the workers setting up seating and lighting, before her eyes settled on one particular guard standing off to one side of the stage. The man had been getting on her nerves over the previous two days, appearing to pay more attention to their rehearsal than working at his job. She focused all her fear and frustration on him.

'If ya wanna see the show buddy, buy a fucking ticket like everyone else!' she shrieked.

The man wearing large black-framed glasses stared back impassively.

The kind of 'Indian' drumbeat that marked a thousand bad Westerns started up behind Grace and she turned with fire still in her eyes.

'Easy, momma, they gotta job to do just like y'all,' Boss called out.

The drummer's smiling face and calm words took the edge from Grace's anger. She took a few deep breaths and tried again. The thumbs up eventually came from the sound engineers and Grace hurried off the stage, the ever-vigilant Gary quickly catching up and putting an arm around her as she strode to the dressing room.

'I can't do it! I just can't do it! My voice is shrinking. It feels like there's a fucking car parked on my chest!' Grace cried out as they headed towards the temporary sanctuary of the dressing room, where the trembling she had fought against on stage turned into a violent shaking. Since the dream a week ago she had been treading water in a sea of nervousness and fear. Now she felt as though she was slipping beneath its surface.

Gary stared non-plussed at Grace's wretched form, her head bowed in defeat, her arms hugging herself to try and stop the shaking. Many times since joining forces, they had lain together discussing her fears of performing and he thought his constant reassurance had managed to calm her. But it was clear that the gentle path he had taken had not done the job. Maybe nothing could. There seemed to be another level to her fear now and he felt unable to ease it but, recalling the fire and anger she had leveled at him in the Black Hills, he decided to take one last shot.

'I've had it with all this, Grace! For weeks I've been stroking and pampering that ego of yours to get you here in one piece and now you're gonna make a mess of everything. Everyone else is going okay. Take some spirit from your son.

If you can get up before two hundred people, you can do it before thousands. Get some spine. I've laid it on the line for you. Now you do it for all of us!'

Grace raised her head and stared open-mouthed as Gary got up and headed for the door. She jumped to her feet.

'Typical fucking male, you've got what you want and now you're deserting me! Well fuck off then! You're fired! I don't ever wanna see you again! And just for the record, I faked it every time!'

Grace burst into tears as the door slammed on her lie. The moment she said those last words she wanted to cry out for him to come back. But pride became her war shield and instead she continued the attack. She wrenched open the door.

'And you're not a Spirit Keeper, you're a fucking Spirit *cheater*! You said you'd be here...'

Grace's tirade suddenly halted at the sight of Gary standing arms crossed a few steps from the door with his eyebrows raised and face creased with a crooked smile.

'What's Lakota for fucking Spirit cheater?' he asked.

Grace's head dropped as Gary stepped forward and closed his arms around her. Then she looked up suddenly and stared intensely, pleadingly, into his eyes. 'I want you to promise that if anything happens to me, you'll look after Jamie.'

Gary was startled by the words and the look in her eyes. Retaliation from Prestige had been constantly on his mind ever since the experience in his apartment but, in the time that he had been with Grace, all she had ever displayed towards them was defiance. She was obviously desperately afraid of how all this would affect her son, even though she had never spoken to him of her fears before now. He pulled her head down onto his shoulder and spoke comfortingly. 'You know I will... but nothing's gonna happen to you. It's all out in the open now. It's too late for them to do anything.'

TWENTY-SEVEN

The following night came too quickly for Grace but not quickly enough for *Warrior's* fans. The stadium had filled early and the capacity crowd of over thirty thousand people was growing restless after an hour of listening to the support group, a good, but not too good, country rock outfit called Tequila. The impatient catcalls and whistling began for the group that had just hit number one on the Billboard 200 and the crowd's impatience to hear them performing live closed the support act down a couple of numbers short.

As the headline act waited for their moment a unified chant of '*War-ri-or, War-ri-or*' rolled around the stadium and echoed down the tunnel to their dressing room.

'Jesus, man, will ya listen to that? We've got 'em by the short and curlies! Let's get out there!' Chas shouted.

'Control yourself! Give the support some time to get off!' Mark snapped, eyeing Grace critically as he spoke. After weeks of twenty-hour days, his nerves felt like the strings on a piano that had been wound up to snapping point and he was just waiting for the critical and unfeeling hands of the music world to bang down on the keys. He could see others were struggling too. He had run into Wayne in the washroom, puffing more energetically than usual on his medicinal herb and Boss and Mitch had started on the Scotch much earlier than usual. Jamie, however, seemed quite relaxed, calmly going over his parts on the didgeridoo. It was the lead singer that Mark was most worried about. His and the group's future hung on her performance and, after the blowup the day before, she seemed now to have withdrawn almost totally, that necklace of hers getting constant attention from the moment she entered the dressing room. He walked over to her.

'You okay, Grace?'

Grace looked up with unsure eyes and gave a weak nod of the head.

Mark looked at Gary seated on the arm of Grace's chair and raised his eyebrows. Gary gave a slow, hopeful nod back.

In the dressing room next door, the sound of the other musicians and singers checking their instruments increased as the bemused members of Tequila moved down the tunnel. One of the stage crew followed, calling out that there were five minutes before the backing members were to take their places. As part of Mark's production planning, Jamie would then follow half a minute after they were set up and Grace soon after that.

Grace's heartbeat burst into overdrive the moment she heard the stagehand. Her grip suddenly tightened on Gary's. She began to tremble and sweat; the desire to throw up almost irresistible. She wanted to run out of the dressing room and out of her life. 'Leave me,' she said weakly to Gary.

Gary got up as the band members headed out of the room, a brief holding of her head against his thigh his last act of assurance before he left.

Now that they were alone, Jamie put down the didgeridoo. In recent weeks he had been engrossed in the music, leaving

Gary to focus on his mother's needs but he had always kept a weather eye on her. He walked around to the back of her chair and put his arms around her neck.

'Sing it for us, Mom,' he whispered in her ear.

Grace tried hard to find the words but her throat had begun to tighten hours before. She looked longingly at the bottles of liquor lined up in Boss and Mitch's corner and then her desperate eyes flashed towards Wayne's guitar case where she knew he hid his stash. She wondered how much liquor she could drink and how much dope she could smoke in the next couple of minutes before her appearance on stage. Anxiety overwhelmed her. She didn't know who she was anymore. All she wanted to be was that other person, struggling along with Jamie in their ordinary lives. She didn't want to be Joan of Arc. She didn't want to be famous or wealthy. She didn't want to sing – she couldn't sing and not even Jamie's remedy would work for her now.

'I... I can't,' came her thin, choking reply.

A roar came from the stadium as the group arrived on stage and Grace wrapped her hands around herself and began to sob. Then she heard a familiar singsong accent whisper in her ear, *'Don't worry, Mother, yer'll get by with a little help from yer friends'.*

The arms around Grace's neck hugged her briefly then slipped away but, at that precise moment, another roar came from the stadium, immediately followed by a small voice sounding out on the PA system. 'Hi, I'm Jamie Howard,' it said. A louder roar came and Grace raised her head and looked around the empty dressing room in astonishment.

Jamie's voice continued. 'My mom will be out soon but I'd like to sing the first song. It's called, *The Water Talks.*'

The stadium erupted again but the musicians looked at each other in confusion. The number wasn't due to be sung until midway through the performance and certainly not by the boy who normally couldn't sing to save anyone's life.

Chas quickly stepped over to Jamie.

'Hey, man. You know we were gonna start with *Buffalo Run*! And where the hell is Grace?'

'Just stick with me, Chas.'

For a moment, Chas was startled by the look of intensity in Jamie's eyes but then turned to the rest of the group and nodded for them to proceed.

The other band members continued to look on, puzzled and concerned as Jamie moved to his place and clipped a mike in the bracket that had been fixed to the end of the didgeridoo. He appeared totally confident but they knew he couldn't sing the song properly and that he would have to break away from his playing to do it.

A disconcerted Wayne stepped up to a mike, harmonica in hand and, when he and Jamie started the intro, the crowd erupted then, just as their combination began to approach the first line of the Lakota lyrics, there came a greater explosion from the crowd.

Grace appeared on the stage and grabbed one of the mikes. She smiled at Chas then raised her hand and, as guitar and voice became one, she looked down at the front of the crowd where Looks Back and the other hundred free ticket-holders from Pine Ridge were seated. They were a mixture of young and old; the elderly sitting quietly, eyes shining; the youths joining in with the raucousness of the rest of the audience. As the song continued, their pride flowed like a river into Grace, hers bursting out in a supremely powerful and passionate version of *The Water Talks*. When it ended the audience roared, the band members beamed and, standing in the wings, two men clasped each other's shoulder with gleeful relief. The singer, however, just calmly smiled and bowed her head, appreciating the crowd and secretly glowing over what had happened in the darkness of the dressing room.

It was just after Grace had heard Jamie's voice over the PA that it came. The cheers of the crowd changed into the rushing sound of wings, accompanied by the high pitched cry of freedom that rolled down the tunnel and over her like a wave, before turning into the melodic strains of a flute. That faded into the whispering voice of a man speaking in Lakota. 'Sings At Dawn... your voice flies like an eagle. Make the people fly with you.' Within seconds, Sings At Dawn had raced down the tunnel and out into the Black Hills to sing to the sky.

Diamonds would spill from the next ninety minutes as singer and band built a bridge to the universe, song by unique song, before ending with the one that had started it all.

There was a special moment planned for the execution of *Song Catcher*. After the first set of lyrics, the lights would dim on Grace and she would step back from the mike and disappear in the shadows, allowing Chas to shine with a lead break before she suddenly came forward again. The spotlight would then explode on her, arms at her side, head held high as she sang the powerful native chorus. She would then grab the mike and go into a supercharged rendition of the next English verse. It was to be the highlight of the night, a choreographed moment that was to provide the detonation to a blast of tight, powerful sound, all designed to lay waste to an audience already whipped up into a frenzy. But, just as Grace began to move forward from the darkness to sing the Lakota chorus, Jamie, who had been standing behind the other musicians after performing on the previous song, suddenly appeared at the mike next to hers.

Grace stopped in her tracks, at first confused then shocked when Jamie began to sing, not with the defective instrument she knew but with a man's fine vibrato, and it wasn't the chorus of *Song Catcher* but the Lakota words of a song she had never heard before.

In the darkness
I see you
Your light shines as the sun

As Jamie sang those words, he stared intensely into the audience, his eyes fixed on a point just behind the row of Lakota onlookers. Grace followed his gaze and, for one fleeting moment, a spotlight swept across the image of a calm, smiling old woman in a bright yellow floral scarf. She turned back to see Jamie staring at her now in that strange sharp-eyed way with his 'It's okay, Mom' kind of smile on his face.

The overwhelming sadness of Grace's dream suddenly flooded through her once more. She opened her mouth to cry out just as Jamie, eyes still firmly fixed on hers, grabbed the microphone tightly with one hand and then the stand with the other.

Jamie's body began to shake violently as the leads to his and the two other mikes began to smolder. A shower of sparks, smoke and arcing electricity exploded out of the bank of amplifiers behind him and he was hurled backwards to land just below Boss's drum stand. The stage was plunged into darkness; the deathly silence that fell on the crowd was ripped apart by Grace's anguished scream as she rushed to Jamie, fell to her knees and held him to her. As Boss roughly pulled her away to apply mouth to mouth, she felt a tug on her neck and looked down to see Jamie's hand holding her snapped necklace, the beads spilling to the floor.

Below in the audience, Looks Back watched without expression. After a few moments he turned around and made his way out of the stadium.

TWENTY-EIGHT

As he had done on many thousands of afternoons before, Looks Back sat at the front of his trailer and gazed towards the setting sun. Hanging around his neck was a CD player sent to him weeks ago by Jamie and he hummed and sang softly in tune with the music coming through the earphones clasped to his ears. On his lap, there was a brown paper parcel and on top of it there rested a round object wrapped in clean beaded doeskin. He stood up as Bright Face's pickup topped the rise and rumbled down towards him, then walked over and stepped into the vehicle. Neither men spoke until they were well down the road leading to the valley, when Jesse questioned the stern old man.

'You sure you still wanna do this?'

Looks Back stared solemnly ahead. After a while, he lifted his hand to straighten something underneath his shirt then touched the package next to him before finally speaking. 'Will you get this to Grace?' he asked.

A glum Jesse nodded.

'And don't forget to look after Skinnybones. All he needs is a feed once a day and a few jelly beans.'

Jesse nodded again.

For two weeks prior to the Rapid City concert, Looks Back had been taking driving lessons, learning how to operate a front-end loader similar to those being used to tear up the valley. Jesse had taken him every day to a site that was being cleared for new housing near the Pine Ridge village, paying one of the machinery drivers a six-pack of beer for an hour's lessons after his work was finished for the day. Now the old man had the basics of how to use the machine and the only thing that remained was to get into the compound at the development and choose his weapon.

It was late afternoon when they turned off the highway several miles to the south of the valley. They were heading for the western side of the development, a rugged approach that would mean a long laborious climb for the old man but the only place they felt confident the security people wouldn't consider an access point. No one would expect an attempt to come in through the wall of sheer-faced hills on that side, where there was a pass once used by their ancestors but now known to very few. It was wide enough for only a horse and rider and it led into a natural tunnel before emerging again a hundred yards further on, where it wound down towards the valley floor. The trail there was camouflaged by boulders and the tree-lined skirt of the ancient hills would enable Looks Back to get to the security fence that ran just beyond without being seen. He would wait until dark before cutting his way through the chain mesh. He figured that, once inside, security would be too busy with what was going on at the front entrance to respond immediately. There, the trickle of protesters had gradually grown into a flood, flowing in from all parts of the country. Their numbers had blocked entry to the site and caused police re-enforcements to be brought from as far away as Pierre and Mitchell.

Looks Back told Jesse to leave him when they were halfway down the slope to the tree line. The young man shook his hand and gave him a swift, solid hug then walked back into the hills behind. Looks Back then scrambled off the track and over a small ridge to a narrow gully. On a shelf of dirt and rocks halfway up the steep face of the gully he knelt on his knees, took a garden trowel out of his belt and dug a hole. When he had gone down about a foot, he placed the heart of Eyes That Cut in the hole and covered it over, placing a number of rocks as naturally as possible on top of the disturbed ground. He then got to his feet, looked to the sky and softly chanted a song, before clambering back down to the trail and moving purposefully on.

When he finally reached the cover of the tree line, Looks Back sat down. He was about twenty yards from where the security fence cut through the trees and could see clearly down into the valley. He began to study and memorize the path he would take to the machinery compound located on the other side. There were light posts dotted around the golf course and he figured he would have to skirt its perimeter to remain unseen but their glow would help him find his way on the moonless night. One problem however, was the security booth at the entrance to the compound.

Looks Back put his hand into his inside coat pocket and pulled out a weighty foot-long club he had fashioned out of hardwood. He tapped it in the palm of his other hand for a moment as he stared fixedly at the security guard sitting inside the booth. He then took his coat and shirt off and straightened the bone breastplate strapped to his chest, his fingers running lightly, almost affectionately over the fractures in it. Dressed in the breechclouts and moccasins he once wore to ceremonial dances, he now felt the part. To apply the finishing touch, he reached into his coat pocket and took out a small round tin, opened it and smeared a thick layer of the bright red makeup diagonally across his face.

As the shadow of the hills brought their early dusk to the valley, Looks Back switched the CD player on again and placed the earphones over his head. He rubbed the arthritic pain in his knees that had been seriously stirred up by the tough trek in before the music began to slowly edge the aching from his mind. He rolled up his coat to make a pillow and lay back with his bare flesh touching the Grandmother's, his arms stretched out, his hands holding hers, his mind drifting back to the last thing he had heard and seen at the concert the night before. There, as the stage exploded in showering light, the rider of his vision had appeared again, the fine voice filling his mind, the singer's image briefly forming in the smoke and sparks and, just as before, the boy lay at his feet.

As darkness fell, Looks Back emptied his mind of all but what was ahead. He stood up, took a pair of wire cutters from his coat and walked to the fence, quickly snipping through the mesh before squeezing through. He moved like a young man now, as if hunting deer; light on his feet and keenly observant as he skirted below the man-made lake and up the other side of the project to where the machinery compound stood. When he got close enough, he took the CD player off and crept along under the window of the small booth. He turned it up to full volume and placed it on the ground then slipped back around the corner of the booth.

It took a little while but finally the thin, high-pitched sound interrupted the guard's view of the action at the entrance coming through one of the CCTV screens on his security panel. He got up to investigate the sound and peered confusedly when he spotted the CD player on the ground. He picked it up and put one earpiece to an ear. *Warrior's* powerful music, a strong aroma of aniseed and a painful blow to the back of the head were the last things his senses recorded before he descended into blackness.

Looks Back dropped the club, picked up the CD player then took a bundle of keys from the guard's belt. He quickly tried several before finding the one that unlocked the gate. He then made his way to a front-end loader conveniently parked in a corner away from the others - the one that had been delivered from San Francisco a couple of days before. It had a vehicle number ending with forty-four, a good sign, Looks Back thought as he clambered quickly into its cabin. He put his glasses on, took a penlight from a pocket then took the wire cutters and quickly stripped the insulation off two wires. He touched them together and the machine started with a roar.

The half opened gates of the compound were first to go, followed by two legs of a water tower, the tank barely missing Looks Back's machine as it brought its five thousand gallons of water slamming to the ground. The crushing of three pickups parked nearby followed before he lined up and demolished a twelve-foot high, sixty-foot long brick wall, complete with doors and window frames. He was far from expert at using the front-end loader but his clumsiness only helped him as he gouged towards a transportable office and mess hall complex, their flimsy construction collapsing like cardboard before the heavy steel blade.

Looks Back then bounced the machine away towards the man-made lake at the bottom. He had placed the CD earphones on again and, with the *Warrior* album cranked up to full volume, he ploughed into one of the side walls. As he shifted a large bucket-load of soil, he sang out loudly with his granddaughter, chanting the Lakota chorus to *Song Catcher*, oblivious to the headlights of several rapidly approaching vehicles. He reversed the machine wildly, sending the vehicles swerving out of the way before they skidded to a halt and disgorged their occupants.

Guns were being waved at Looks Back from every direction as he sent the vehicle crashing into the wall. A large stream of water broke through the base and quickly became a flood, wiping out one corner of the lake's wall. He kept attacking the spot until all the water was freely running away then drove into the middle of the lake and gouged into the center of the front wall. By the time he saw the two creeks finally running into one again, he was loudly wailing the chorus to *Buffalo Run* and, as the song began to fade away, he turned the machine and ran it at two police cars parked in a feeble attempt to stop his rampaging progress. He brushed them aside before a volley of shots rang out and the loader bounced away uncontrollably to slam against a light pole.

TWENTY-NINE

Like the water tower Looks Back had brought down in the valley, the entire structure of Prestige Developments would similarly follow. Its walls had begun to shake within minutes of the premature end of the Rapid City concert, when security guards at the venue found one of their peers writhing in pain in a dark backstage corner. The man had two badly broken legs, the result of dropping nearly fifty feet from a lighting access walkway above the back of the sound stage, a position he had taken up just before the concert began. It was the perfect place to wait for him to carry out his work, when the number he had seen choreographed in rehearsal would bring the woman to the mike alone.

At first, those who found the moaning form at the back of the stage thought he had been blown off the walkway by the explosion but, when later questioned about the remote control device found lying next to him, he quickly gave forth, his confession punctuated by the raving recollections of something else.

*

283

With the aid of John Kilmont's contacts, electronics genius Albert Beros had become an employee of the New York-based firm that had won the security contract for the *Warrior* event. Like many such outfits, Greater Security's personnel list was sprinkled with ex-policemen and there was one in its upper level of management that Kilmont knew well, a former bagman partner during his policing days. With habitual stealth, he used a go-between who also knew the man, another ex-detective who was now a self-employed contractor for anything that turned a buck. Supplied with a 'no questions asked' contract and a generous bribe, his contact approached their former colleague with a paid request to give a job to a friend of his living in Rapid City, an unemployed security guard who had heard that Greater Security were seeking extra men for the concert. True to Kilmont's expectation, the man took the cash, with the only proviso that the 'friend' came with appropriate papers.

Equipped with a false identity and security clearance supplied by another Kilmont contact, Beros slipped easily into the organization and into the much tighter-than-usual security milling around *Warrior's* first concert. Claiming a need for extra dollars, he volunteered for the better-paid but undesirable two-man early morning shifts, doing his real work during his partner's meal breaks. He booby trapped the mike stands so that, at any given time, a remote control device could open customized in-line resistors in the amplifiers and allow the full flow of mains power to travel through the leads. Upon any investigation of the mess that would be made of the mixer-amplifier box during the uninhibited power surge, the melted-down resistors would appear to be part of a failed standard transforming system.

Beros had wired all three mikes just in case his target used a different part of the stage than she had during rehearsal when singing the number he had chosen. When she grabbed any of those mikes and stand, she would be instantly earthed. In the end his system had worked perfectly, except that it had delivered the massive shock to the wrong person and, very soon after, one of a quite different kind to him.

It was the sound that had first caught Beros' attention, a faint tone that had begun the moment he pressed the button of the remote control and the shower of sparks lit up the stage. There came a rush of air along the walkway. He peered into the darkness at the far end and saw a shadow detach from it and start moving swiftly towards him. The shape stretched out either side of the walkway, pulsing in time with the waves of air that now rushed over him, the tone suddenly becoming a high-pitched cry.

Beros backed away in terror from the indefinable thing closing on him, his hands held over his ears as the sound intensified, his stumbling flight coming to a sudden halt when his back touched the end rail of the walkway. The blackness moved closer and he began to shake uncontrollably, whimpering like a child as he climbed over the rail. As the thing closed on him, he dropped down to hang swinging and screaming from the bottom of the walkway. Something very sharp and powerful curled into the top of his hands. He screamed from the pain of the vice-like grip lifting him from the walkway and into air that had suddenly become very much colder. As he looked down, the darkness below began turning into a distant landscape of sun-bleached badlands. Around and around in a wide upward spiral he went, screaming louder and louder, until he was finally released from his clawed manacles. He wailed madly as he fell into darkness again, his arms and legs frantically grasping at the air until he hit the concrete concourse.

Beros' feet were about one foot closer to his face after the fall and it took six-hours on the operating table to put him back together again. But the police didn't wait for the anesthetic to fully wear off before the questioning began. Their terrified suspect was more intent on telling them about what had confronted him on the walkway but, in between bouts of incoherent raving, he confessed all, uncaring of what the police or Kilmont could do to him. Kilmont in turn would waste little time cashing in his insurance policy of having total knowledge of Prestige's drug running activities. They had figured it was their insurance policy, tying him in to culpability so he would more strongly defend their interests. But, when it came to his survival, the ruthlessness he displayed in shielding the black heart of the company was just as vigorously applied to the matter of his future welfare. He did a deal with the police, gaining a place on the witness protection program.

Kilmont's information would reveal all about the stream of heroin and cocaine flowing from overseas through the East Bay port of San Francisco; the machine drug mules with customized hollow compartments added to their ballast sections; the unhindered passage guaranteed by highly rewarded people in crucial areas of the port's customs control; the projects in the US used as distribution points and the company's creative financial structure, set up by in-house accountants to supply the final rinse in a money laundering scheme that washed mind-staggering amounts of money from the enterprise.

Prestige was instantly halted from trading after Kilmont's testimony. The DEA was brought in and, unlike with their approach to Gary's unsubstantiated allegation, they moved swiftly. A systematic investigation of Prestige's books and shipping papers tallied with the information Kilmont had given to the police. They found the material evidence needed in the front-end loader impounded by the police after Looks Back's rampage, its chassis cut open to reveal the cargo recently shipped back from the project in Ecuador. The score sheet filled up quickly. All the top executives of the company were arrested to be eventually convicted and jailed but, unlike the man who had sent them to prison, they would refuse to talk about things they knew would kill them.

The DEA continued to aggressively investigate the case they hoped would lead to even bigger scalps but, like so many times before, the expertly constructed maze of legitimacy that covered the tracks of organized crime would again frustrate all attempts to find the Medusa head. That would remain hissing from the shadows but, for one particular victim of its venomous influence, the trimming job would ultimately bring some sense of satisfaction.

THIRTY

Grace looked up from the letter she had been reading and stared out through the living room window onto the fields of her Wyoming ranch. The spring thaw had begun and patches of green were now spreading through the snow like the light that had been gradually illuminating her darkness. As she gazed at the mottled landscape, the man who had waited patiently during the period she had gone away to lacerate herself, walked to the front of the house leading two saddled horses. She smiled as he threw the reins over a fence rail and began a conversation with the animals, affectionately rubbing their heads as he spoke. She knew how they felt.

Seven months had passed since the Rapid City concert and for much of it Gary had been carefully nursing Grace. At first, shock had imprisoned her grief, rendering her unable to shed tears and he had kept a mute vigil through this period, before stoically bearing the explosion of great anger which mushroomed out of it. He listened, cooked and cleaned as she ranted against everything she believed had led to the loss of her son and her grandfather, going beyond her hatred of Prestige to blame herself, her people, him and the music. She even spurned her spirituality, believing it had delivered only cruelty, lifting her up then slamming her down just as she had come to embrace it totally. He left her alone when she closed the door on everything and surrendered to the self-destructive part of her nature by going on a drinking binge then, almost a week into it, there came the day of the turning. It had started as usual, with Grace dragging herself from bed mid-afternoon and heading for her ritual throw-up before a gargle from the bourbon bottle. She had taken a rare shower and, after toweling herself down, she looked up to see something written in the condensation on the mirror. She stared stunned at the words until the droplets of condensation erased them then she dropped to her knees and, for the first time since Jamie's death, began to sob.

For several minutes, Grace's body shook and heaved with the purging, before she finally dragged herself to her feet. She went to her bedside cabinet and took a small jewelry box out of a drawer, opening it to reveal the item that had been providing constant, nightmarish flashbacks since the concert. She took the loose stones of the necklace from the box, strung them back on their cord then placed it around her neck. She would wear it constantly over the following weeks as her grief and the guilt that had driven her to the edge began to recede. Stillness came and out of it grew understanding and acceptance. Jamie was the arrow, let fly the moment he had been born and her part had been to clear the way for his trajectory. With renewed strength, she would set about the final stage of doing so. The consortium that had hired Prestige for the valley project saw the impossibility of continuing with it and put the land back on the market, a market that consisted only of her.

Although it was painful having to buy back part of what had always been her people's, Grace's consolation came in knowing that the money to do so would be provided by the system that had taken the land away in the first place. And there was plenty of it. Although *Warrior* had effectively disbanded the night of the Rapid City concert, the album sales had almost quadrupled since, surging on the emotions unleashed immediately following Jamie's and then Looks Back's deaths. *Spirit Rising* was destined to remain on the constantly selling list along with all the classic albums of the past, guaranteeing a never-ending source of income for those directly connected with the making of it.

Thanks to Mark's initial allocation of song rights, Jamie's estate would be a major benefactor of the album's sales and Grace intended to serve her son's memory by using his large financial legacy to help restore the valley. When the purchase of the land was completed, she intended to erase all signs of the development's existence. Native trees would be replanted and the earth seeded with the grass and wildflowers of the Great Plains region. Jamie and Looks Back would be shifted from their graves in Pine Ridge and re-buried on a slope of the valley. With them would go the items Jesse Bright Face had delivered to Grace a day after Looks Back's death. The lock of hair, the feathers, the braided grass and the flute were now in Jamie's coffin, along with his didgeridoo, while the breastplate remained with her grandfather, fastened to his chest as it had been in his dying moment. The pictograph, however, she had decided to keep and it now hung in its protective glass-covered frame on the wall of the ranch house's living room.

At the sound of Gary's familiar two-tone whistle, Grace put the letter aside. It was one of the thousands piled up in a storage room in their barn. Most were for Jamie, fan mail sent before his death but many had come afterwards, carrying messages of condolence to her. They were not easy to read, their repetitive theme of sorrow, anger and sympathy constantly challenging her restored emotional strength but she had set herself the task to answer as many of them as possible.

Gary was sitting on his mount now and holding the reins of hers. She took them and climbed up onto the saddle of the striking chestnut gelding. Therapy, she had called him and he had lived up to his name but the man seated on the other horse was the doctor. His idea to buy the small ranch in sight of the Black Hills had been a lifesaver. The long rides she took through the valleys and foothills nearby eventually brought back the desire to work again. Soon, she would be going back into the recording studio with Chas and Boss to do an album of Jamie's favorite songs, and one in particular would be taking pride of place on it. It had haunted her mind ever since the turning and prompted her again to visit somewhere special.

'I'd like to spend a little while at the grove, Hon.'

'Sure,' Gary replied as they both drew their horses around and set off slowly.

A mile away from the ranch, Gary continued at an ambling pace along the trail as Grace rode down to a gully where the thawing spring sunshine had sent the water of a creek talking its way through a grove of silver birch. She dismounted and sat down near the water's edge. She closed her eyes and began to meditate, gradually melding into the natural world around her. Soon, she felt a thin pair of arms slide around her neck and heard a small voice whisper the words scrawled across the mirror of her mind.

Sing it for us, Mom

Made in the USA
Charleston, SC
19 November 2012